A SEVERED HEAD

A
SEVERED HEAD

Iris Murdoch

1969
CHATTO & WINDUS
LONDON

Published by
Chatto & Windus Ltd
42 William IV Street
London WC 2
★
Clarke, Irwin & Co. Ltd
Toronto

First published 1961
Second Impression 1961
Third Impression 1961
Fourth Impression 1961
Fifth Impression 1969

SBN 7011 0980 7

Printed in Great Britain by
William Lewis (Printers) Ltd
Cardiff

❋ *Chapter One* ❋

"YOU'RE sure she doesn't know?" said Georgie.
"Antonia? About us? Certain."

Georgie was silent for a moment and then said, "Good."
That curt 'Good' was characteristic of her, typical of a toughness which had, to my mind, more to do with honesty than
with ruthlessness. I liked the dry way in which she accepted
our relationship. Only with a person so eminently sensible
could I have deceived my wife.

We lay half embraced in front of Georgie's gas fire. She
reclined against my shoulder while I examined a tress of her
dark hair, surprised again to find in it so many threads of a
pure reddish gold. Her hair was as straight as a horse's tail,
almost as coarse, and very long. Georgie's room was obscure
now except for the light of the fire and a trio of red candles
burning upon the mantelpiece. The candles, together with a
few scraggy bits of holly dotted about at random, were as
near as Georgie, whose 'effects' were always a little ram-
shackle, could get to Christmas decorations, yet the room had
a glitter all the same as of some half-descried treasure cavern.
In front of the candles, as at an altar, stood one of my presents
to her, a pair of Chinese incense holders in the form of little
bronze warriors, who held aloft as spears the glowing sticks
of incense. Their grey fumes drifted hazily to and fro until
sent by the warmth of the candle flames to circle suddenly
dervish-like upward to the darkness above. The room was
heavy with a stifling smell of Kashmir poppy and sandalwood.
Bright wrapping-paper from our exchange of presents lay all
about, and pushed into a corner was the table which still bore

the remains of our meal and the empty bottle of Château Sancy de Parabère 1955. I had been with Georgie since lunchtime. Outside the window and curtained away was the end of the cold raw misty London afternoon now turned to an evening which still contained in a kind of faintly luminous haze what had never, even at midday, really been daylight.

Georgie sighed and rolled over with her head in my lap. She was dressed now except for her shoes and stockings. "When must you go?"

"About five."

"Don't let me catch you being mean with time."

Such remarks were as near as I ever got to feeling the sharper edge of her love. I could not have wished for a more tactful mistress.

"Antonia's session ends at five," I said. "I should be back at Hereford Square soon after that. She always wants to discuss it. And we have a dinner engagement." I lifted Georgie's head a little and drew her hair forward, spreading it over her breasts. Rodin would have liked that.

"How is Antonia's analysis going?"

"Fizzingly. She enjoys it disgracefully. Of course, it's all for fun anyhow. She's got a tremendous transference."

"Palmer Anderson," said Georgie, naming Antonia's psycho-analyst, who was also a close friend of Antonia and myself. "Yes, I can imagine becoming addicted to him. He has a clever face. I imagine he's good at his trade."

"I don't know," I said. "I dislike what you call his trade. But he's certainly good at something. Perhaps he's just good. He's not simply sweet and polite and gentle as only Americans can be sweet and polite and gentle, though he *is* that. He has real power in him."

"You sound rather carried away by him yourself!" said

8

Georgie. She edged into a more comfortable position, her head in the crook of my knee.

"Perhaps I am," I said. "Knowing him has made a lot of difference to me."

"In what way?"

"I can't say exactly. Perhaps he has made me worry less about the rules!"

"The rules!" Georgie laughed. "Darling, surely you became indifferent to the rules long ago."

"Good heavens, no!" I said. "I'm not indifferent to them now. I'm not a Child of Nature like you. No, it's not exactly that. But Palmer is good at setting people free."

"If you think I don't worry—but never mind. As for setting people free, I don't trust these professional liberators. Anyone who is good at setting people free is also good at enslaving them, if we are to believe Plato. The trouble with you, Martin, is that you are always looking for a master."

I laughed. "Now that I have a mistress I don't want a master! But how did you come across Palmer? Oh, of course, through the sister."

"The sister," said Georgie. "Yes, the curious Honor Klein. I saw him at a party she gave for her pupils once. But she didn't introduce him."

"Is *she* any good?"

"Honor? You mean as an anthropologist? She's quite well thought of in Cambridge. She never actually taught me, of course. Anyway, she was usually away visiting one of her savage tribes. She was supposed to organise my work and help me with my moral problems. God!"

"She's Palmer's half-sister, isn't she? How does it work? They seem to be several nationalities between them."

"I think this is it," said Georgie. "They share a Scottish

mother who married Anderson first and then Klein when Anderson died."

"I know about Anderson. He was Danish-American, an architect or something. But what about the other father?"

"Emmanuel Klein. You ought to know about him. He was not a bad classical scholar. A German Jew, of course."

"I knew he was a learned something-or-other," I said. "Palmer spoke of him once or twice. Interesting. He said he still had nightmares about his step-father. I suspect he's a bit frightened of his sister too, though he never actually says so."

"She could inspire awe," said Georgie. "There's something primitive about her. Perhaps it's all those tribes. But you've met her, haven't you?"

"I have just met her," I said, "though I can't recall much about her. She just seemed the Female Don in person. Why do those women have to look like that?"

"Those women!" Georgie laughed. "I'm one of them now, darling! Anyway, *she* certainly has power in her."

"*You* have power without looking like a haystack!"

"Me?" said Georgie. "I'm not in that class. I don't carry half so many guns."

"You said I was carried away by the brother. You seem to be carried away by the sister."

"Oh, I don't *like* her," said Georgie. "That's another matter."

She sat up abruptly and retrieved her hair and began very rapidly to plait it. She tossed the heavy plait back over her shoulder. Then she hitched up her skirt and some layers of stiff white petticoat and began to draw on a pair of peacock-blue stockings which I had given her. I loved to give Georgie outrageous things, absurd garments and gewgaws which I could not possibly have given Antonia, barbarous necklaces and velvet pants and purple underwear and black openwork tights which drove me mad. I rose now and wandered about the room, watching her possessively as with a tense demure consciousness of my gaze she adjusted the lurid stockings.

Georgie's room, a large untidy bed-sittingroom which looked out on to what was virtually an alley-way in the proximity of Covent Garden, was full of things which I had given her. I had for long, and vainly, waged a battle with Georgie's relentless lack of taste. The numerous Italian prints, French paper-weights, pieces of Derby, Worcester, Coleport, Spode, Copeland, and other bric-à-brac—for I hardly ever arrived without bringing something—lay about, for all my efforts, in a dusty hurly-burly more reminiscent of a junk shop than a civilised room. Georgie was, somehow, not de-signed by nature to possess things. Whereas when Antonia or I bought anything, which we constantly did, it found its place at once in the rich and highly integrated mosaic of our surroundings, Georgie seemed to have no such carapace. There was no one of her possessions which she would not, at the drop of a hat, have given away and not missed; and mean-while her things lay about in a sort of impermanent jumble on which my continually renewed sortings and orderings seemed to have little effect. This characteristic of my beloved ex-asperated me, but since it was also a part, after all, of Georgie's remarkable detachment and lack of worldly pretention, I admired it and loved it as well. It was, moreover, as I some-times reflected, the very image and symbol of my relation to Georgie, my mode of possessing her, or more precisely the way in which I, as it were, failed to possess her. I possessed Antonia in a way not totally unlike the way in which I possessed the magnificent set of original prints by Audubon which adorned our staircase at home. I did not possess Georgie. Georgie was simply there.

When Georgie had finished with her stockings, she leaned back against the armchair and looked up at me. She had, with her dark heavy hair, rather light clear greyish-blue eyes. Her face was broad, strong rather than delicate, but her remarkably pale complexion had a finish of ivory. Her large somewhat upturned nose, her despair and my joy, which she was always contracting and stroking in a vain attempt to make it aquiline, now forgotten in repose, gave to her expression a certain attentive animal quality which softened the edge of her cleverness. Now in the incense-laden half-light, her face was full of curves and shadows. For some time we held each other's gaze. This sort of quiet gazing, which was like a feeding of the heart, was something which I had not experienced with any other woman. Antonia and I never looked at each other like that. Antonia would not have sustained such a steady gaze for so long: warm, possessive, and coquettish, she would not so have exposed herself.

"River goddess," I said at last.

"Merchant prince."

"Do you love me?"

"Yes, to distraction. Do you love me?"

"Yes, infinitely."

"Not infinitely," said Georgie. "Let us be exact. Your love is a great but finite quantity."

We both knew what she referred to, but there were some topics which it was profitless to discuss, and this we both knew also. There was no question of my leaving my wife.

"Do you want me to put my hand in the fire?" I said.

Georgie still kept my gaze. At such moments her intelligence and her lucidity made her beauty ring like a silver coin.

Then with a quick movement she turned about and laid her head upon my feet, prostrating herself before me. As I briefly contemplated her homage I reflected that there was no one in the world at whose feet I would myself have lain in such an attitude of abandonment. Then I knelt down and gathered her into my arms.

A little later when we had finished for the moment with kissing each other and had lit cigarettes, Georgie said, "She knows your brother."

"Who knows my brother?"

"Honor Klein."

"Are you still on about her? Yes, I believe so. They met on some committee at the time of the Mexican Art Exhibition."

"When am I going to meet your brother?" said Georgie.

"Never, as far as I'm concerned!"

"You said you always used to pass your girls on to him, because he couldn't get any of his own!"

"Maybe," I said, "but I'm certainly not going to pass you on!" Ever since I had made that injudicious remark my brother Alexander had become an object of romantic fantasy to my mistress.

"I want to meet him," said Georgie, "just because he's your brother. I adore siblings, having none of my own. Does he resemble you?"

"Yes, a bit," I said. "All Lynch-Gibbons resemble each other. Only he's round-shouldered and not so handsome. I'll introduce you to my sister Rosemary if you like."

"I don't want to meet your sister Rosemary," said Georgie, "I want to meet Alexander, and I shall go on and on at you about it, just as I shall go on and on at you about that trip to New York."

Georgie had an obsession about seeing New York, and I

had in fact very rashly promised to take her with me on a business trip which I had made to that city last autumn. At the last moment, however, some qualm of conscience, or more likely some failure of nerve, at the prospect of having to lie on quite such a scale to Antonia made me change my mind. I have never seen anyone so bitterly and so childishly disappointed; and I had since then renewed my promise to take her with me on the next occasion.

"There's no need to nag me about *that*," I said. "One of these days we'll go to New York together, on condition I hear no more nonsense about your paying your own fare. Think how much you disapprove of unearned income! You might at least let me spend mine on a sensible project!"

"Of course it's ludicrous your being a business man," said Georgie. "You're far too clever. You ought to have been a don."

"You imagine that being a don is the only proper way of being clever. Perhaps you are turning into a blue stocking after all." I caressed one of her legs.

"You got the best History first of your year, didn't you?" said Georgie. "What did Alexander get, by the way?"

"He got a second. So you see how unworthy of your attention he is."

"At least he had the sense not to go into business," said Georgie. My brother is a talented and quite well-known sculptor.

I was in fact half of Georgie's opinion that I should have been a don, and the subject was a painful one. My father had been a prosperous wine merchant, founder of the firm of Lynch-Gibbon and McCabe. On his death the firm had split into two parts, a larger part which remained with the McCabe family, and a smaller part which comprised the original claret connection in which my grandfather had been interested, which I now managed myself. I knew too, although she never said so, that Georgie believed that my having stayed in business had something to do with Antonia. Her belief was not totally erroneous.

As I had no taste for this particular discussion and also wanted to get off the subject of my dear brother, I said, "What will you be doing on Christmas Day? I shall want to think about you."

Georgie frowned. "Oh, I shall be out with some of the chaps from the School. There'll be a big party." She added, "I won't want to think about you. It's odd how it hurts at these times not to be part of your proper family."

I had no answer to that. I said, "I shall be having a quiet day with Antonia. We're staying in London this time. Rosemary will be at Rembers with Alexander."

"I don't want to know," said Georgie. "I don't want to know what you do when you're not with me. It's better not to feed the imagination. I prefer to think that when you aren't here you don't exist."

In fact, I thought along these lines myself. I was lying beside her now and holding her feet, her beautiful Acropolis feet as I called them, which were partly visible through the fine blue stocking. I kissed them, and returned to gazing at her. The heavy rope of hair descended between her breasts and she had swept a few escaping tresses severely back behind her ears. She had a beautifully shaped head: yes, positively Alexander must never meet her. I said, "I'm bloody lucky."

"You mean you're bloody safe," said Georgie. "Oh yes, you're safe, damn you!"

"*Liaison dangereuse*," I said. "And yet we lie, somehow, out of danger."

"*You* do," said Georgie. "If Antonia ever found out about this, you'd drop me like a hot potato."

"Nonsense!" I said. Yet I wondered if she wasn't right. "She won't find out," I said, "and if she did, I'd manage. You are essential to me."

"No one is *essential* to anyone," said Georgie. "There you go looking at your watch again. All right, go if you must. What about one for the road? Shall I open that bottle of Nuits de Young?"

"How many times must I tell you never to drink claret unless it has been open at least three hours?"

"Don't be so holy about it," said Georgie. "As far as I'm concerned the stuff is just booze."

"Little barbarian!" I said affectionately. "You can give me some gin and French. Then I really must go."

Georgie brought me the glass and we sat enlaced like a beautiful netsuke in front of the warm murmuring fire. Her room seemed a subterranean place, remote, enclosed, hidden. It was for me a moment of great peace. I did not know then that it was the last, the very last moment of peace, the end of the old innocent world, the final moment before I was plunged into the nightmare of which these ensuing pages tell the story.

I pushed up the sleeve of her jersey and stroked her arm. "Wonderful stuff, flesh."

"When'll I see you?" said Georgie.

"Not till after Christmas." I said. "I'll come if I can about the twenty-eighth or twenty-ninth. But I'll ring up anyway before that."

"I wonder if we'll ever be able to be more open about this?" said Georgie. "I do rather hate the lies. Well, I suppose not."

"Not," I said. I didn't like the hard words she used, but I

16

had to give it her back as sharply. "We're stuck with the lies, I'm afraid. Yet, you know, this may sound perverse, but part of the nature, almost of the charm, of this relation is its being so utterly private."

"You mean its being clandestine is of its essence," said Georgie, "and if it were exposed to the daylight it would crumble to pieces? I don't think I like that idea."

"I didn't quite say that," I said. "But knowledge, other people's knowledge, does inevitably modify what it touches. Remember the legend of Psyche, whose child, if she told about her pregnancy, would be mortal, whereas if she kept silent it would be a god."

It was an unfortunate speech on which to part from Georgie, for it brought our minds back to something which I at least preferred never now to think about. Last spring my beloved had become pregnant. There was nothing to be done but to get rid of the child. Georgie had gone through with the hideous business in the manner that I would have expected of her, calm, laconic, matter-of-fact, even cheering me along with her surly wit. We had found it exceedingly difficult to discuss the matter even at the time, and we had not spoken of it since. What vast wound that catastrophe had perhaps made in Georgie's proud and upright spirit I did not know. For myself, I got off with an extraordinary ease. Because of Georgie's character, her toughness and the stoical nature of her devotion to me, I had not had to pay. It had all been quite uncannily painless. I was left with a sense of not having suffered enough. Only sometimes in dreams did I experience certain horrors, glimpses of a punishment which would perhaps yet find its hour.

✳ *Chapter Two* ✳

IN almost every marriage there is a selfish and an unselfish partner. A pattern is set up and soon becomes inflexible, of one person always making the demands and one person always giving way. In my own marriage I early established myself as the one who took rather than gave. Like Dr Johnson, I started promptly upon the way in which I intended to go on. I was the more zealous in doing so in that I was counted by the world, and counted myself, very lucky to have got Antonia.

I had, of course, misled Georgie about the success of my marriage. What married man who keeps a mistress does not so mislead her? My marriage with Antonia, apart from the fact, which was a continuing grief to me, that it was childless, was perfectly happy and successful. It was just that I wanted Georgie as well and did not see why I should not have her. Although, as I had remarked, I was not indifferent to the 'rules', I was certainly capable of being cool and rational about adultery. I had married Antonia in a church, but that was largely for social reasons; and I did not think that the marriage bond, though solemn, was uniquely sacred. It may be relevant here to add that I hold no religious beliefs whatever. Roughly, I cannot imagine any omnipotent sentient being sufficiently cruel to create the world we inhabit.

I seem to have started here upon some general explanation of myself, and it may be as well to continue this before I plunge into a narrative of events which may, once under way, offer few opportunities for meditation. My name, as you will have gathered, is Martin Lynch-Gibbon, and I come on my father's side of an Anglo-Irish family. My clever artistic mother was Welsh. I have never lived in Ireland, though I retain a sentimental sense of connection with that poor bitch of a country. My brother Alexander is forty-five, and my sister Rosemary is thirty-seven: my age is forty-one, and I feel myself at times, after a manner which is not without its curious melancholy charms, to be an old man.

To describe one's character is difficult and not necessarily illuminating. The story which follows will reveal, whether I will or no, what sort of person I am. Let me offer here only a few elementary facts. I grew up into the war, during which I spent on the whole a safe and inactive time. I suffer intermittently from a complex of disorders of which asthma and hay fever are the best known, though not the most disagreeable, and I never succeeded in passing as completely fit. I went on to Oxford when the war was over, and so began my life as an ordinary citizen at a comparatively advanced age. I am a very tall, reasonably good-looking man. I used to be a good boxer, and passed when I was younger as a raffish quarrelsome violent fellow. This reputation was precious to me: equally precious is the reputation which I have more lately gained of having become morose, something of a recluse, something indeed of a philosopher and cynic, one who expects little and watches the world go by. Antonia accuses me of being flippant; but Georgie once pleased me more by saying that I had the face of someone laughing at something tragic. My face, I might add, is the long pale rather heavy old-fashioned face that all the Lynch-Gibbons have, which is a cross between the philosopher Hume and the actor Garrick, and my hair is the brown floppy hair which fades with age to the colour of white pepper. Our family, thank God, never becomes bald.

I took a decisive step when I married Antonia. I was then thirty, and she was thirty-five. She looks now, for all her beauty, a little older than her years, and has more than once been taken for my mother. My real mother, who among other things was a painter, died when I was sixteen, but at the time of my marriage my father was still alive and I had hitherto been but casually involved in the wine trade. I was more concerned, though that also in a dilettante fashion, with being a military historian, a type of study in which, if I could have brought myself to abandon my amateur status, I might have excelled. When I married Antonia, however, everything came, for some time, to a standstill. As I say, I was fortunate to get her. Antonia had been, and indeed still was, a somewhat eccentric society beauty. Her father was a distinguished regular soldier, and her mother, who came out of the Bloomsbury world, was something of a minor poet and a remote relation of Virginia Woolf. For some reason Antonia never got a sensible education, though she lived abroad a great deal and speaks three languages fluently; and also, for some reason, and although much courted, she did not marry young. She moved in a fashionable society, more fashionable than that which I frequented, and became, through her protracted refusal to marry, one of its scandals. Her marriage to me, when it came, was a sensation.

I was not sure at the time, and am still not sure, whether I was precisely what Antonia wanted, or whether she didn't take me simply because she felt it was time to take somebody. However that may be, we were formidably happy; and for quite a long time, handsome clever couple that we were, we were everyone's darlings. So for a while everything was for me at a standstill and I was absorbed completely into the delightful task of being Antonia's husband. When I as it were came round, emerged, that is, from the warm golden haze of those honeymoon years, I found that certain roads were closed to me. My father had died meanwhile, and I settled down to being a wine merchant, still and even here feeling myself something of an amateur and none the worse for that; and although my conception of myself had somewhat altered, I did not stop feeling happy. After all, as Antonia's husband I could not be other than happy.

Let me now attempt to describe Antonia. She is a woman long accustomed to admiration, long accustomed to think of herself as beautiful. She has long goldenish hair—I prefer women with long hair—which she wears usually in an old-fashioned knot or bun, and indeed 'golden' is the best general epithet for her appearance. She is like some rich gilded object over which time has cast the moonlit pallor of a gentle veneer; or in a more effective simile one might compare her to the water-haunted sunlight on an old pavement in Venice, for there is always something a little fluid and shivering, a little mobile and tremulous about Antonia. She has, especially of late, aged, her face taking on that look which is sometimes described as 'ravaged' and which I notice is usually applied when, as in this case, there is a slight drooping and discomposing of essentially fine features. To my mind such a look can be, and is in the case of Antonia, exceedingly moving and attractive, composing a dignity which was not to be found in the same face when younger. Antonia has great tawny-coloured intelligent searching eyes and a mobile expressive mouth which is usually twisted into some pout of amusement or tender interest. She is a tall woman, and although always a little inclined to plumpness has been called 'willowy', which I take as a reference to her characteristic twisted and unsymmetrical poses. Her face and body are never to be discovered quite in repose.

Antonia has a sharp appetite for personal relations. She is an intense and passionate woman and has passed for this reason for being humourless, though this latter charge in fact is false. Antonia, like me, has no religion; but she achieves what might be called religiosity in relation to certain beliefs. She holds that all human beings should aspire towards, and are within working distance of, a perfect communion of souls. This creed, which borrows as little from popular Oriental cults as it does from Antonia's vestigial Christianity, may best be described as a metaphysic of the drawing-room. In the form in which Antonia holds it, it is original to her, although I can discern its statelier predecessor in Antonia's now frail but resolutely exquisite mother with whom I have maintained a tenuous but gallant relationship. Antonia's undogmatic apprehension of an imminent spiritual interlocking where nothing is withheld and nothing hidden certainly makes up in zeal for what it lacks in clarity. The mere presence of such a belief in a woman, particularly in a beautiful woman, tends of course to create a rich centripetal eddy of emotion round about her, thereby providing itself with an immediate pragmatic verification; and in the early days particularly people were always falling in love with Antonia and wanting to tell her all their troubles. I had no objection to this, as it eased some of my anxieties about her welfare by making her happier than if she had had no soul to commune with but my own.

Of late she had been much taken up with Palmer Anderson, 'Anderson' as she always called him, since she had a mystique about persons whose names, like her own, began with A. This mystique had been active also in relation to my brother Alexander, between whom and my wife there existed a very considerable, almost sentimental, tenderness, though this had been less evident of late since Anderson had become all the rage. I cannot think of anyone less in need of psycho-analysis than Antonia, and I think she went into analysis with Palmer at least partly with the idea of operating on him. I once said sarcastically that I didn't see why I should pay out so many guineas per week so that Antonia should question Palmer about his childhood, and she laughed merrily and did not deny the insinuation. Also, of course, psycho-analysis was for her a 'craze' like earlier ones that she had had for learning contract bridge, learning Russian, learning to sculpt (with Alexander), doing social work (with Rosemary) and studying Italian Renaissance history (with me). I should add that whatever Antonia took up she proved surprisingly good at, and I had no doubt that she and Palmer were getting on famously.

A word about Palmer is necessary; and this I find difficult. The pages that follow will show how and why my feelings on the subject of Palmer are mixed ones. I shall only try now to describe him as I saw him at the start, before I knew certain crucial facts about him, and when I was still more than a little 'carried away'. Palmer strikes one immediately as an American, though he is in fact only half American and grew up in Europe. He has that tall lanky 'rangy' loose-jointed graceful close-cropped formidably clean American look. He has silver-grey hair which grows soft, furry and inch-long all over his very round rather smallish head, and a smooth face which looks uncannily younger than his years. It is hard to believe he is over fifty. He dresses in the American style with belts instead of braces and so on, and affects many foppish and casual rig-outs, involving bright silk handkerchiefs instead of ties. I can never indeed see a gay clean silk handkerchief without thinking of Palmer; there is something about this object which is singularly reminiscent of him. Palmer conveys an immediate impression of gentleness and sweetness and almost, so far have good manners here assumed the air of a major virtue, of goodness. He is also a beautifully cultivated person. It was I, not Antonia, who 'discovered' Palmer, and for a long time, before she took him over, I saw a good deal of him. We used to read Dante together; and his relaxed gaiety, his unshadowed enjoyment of his pleasures, eased and complemented, though without dispelling, my affectation of a resigned melancholy. Palmer appeared, in my generously admiring vision of him, as a complete and successful human being. He had come to analysis fairly late, after practising for some time, both in America and in Japan, as an ordinary doctor, and he had achieved a considerable reputation as that fashionable kind of modern magician. He spent half the week in Cambridge, where he lodged with his sister and lent his ear to neurotic undergraduates, and the other half in London, where he seemed to have a formidable number of well-known patients. He worked hard; and as I saw him, he was and deserved to be a being of an exceptional felicity.

I had known Palmer, when this story starts, for nearly four years. I had known Georgie Hands for three years, and she had been my mistress for over eighteen months. Georgie, who is now twenty-six, had been an undergraduate at Cambridge, where she had taken a degree in economics. She had then become a graduate student, and more lately a junior lecturer, at the London School of Economics. I had met her, in her early days in London, when I had visited the School once to give a lecture on Machiavelli's account of the campaigns of Cesare Borgia to a student society, and we had met subsequently a few times, had lunch together, and even exchanged some friendly consoling kisses, without anything remarkable occurring in the heart of either. I had never hitherto deceived my wife, and imagined that I had no possible intention of doing so; and it was pure accident that I never introduced Georgie to Antonia in those early and innocent days. Georgie was living then in a hostel for women students, a dreary place which I never attempted to visit. Then she moved into her little flat; and I promptly fell in love with her. It may sound ludicrous, but I think I fell in love with her as soon as I saw her bed.

I did not fall desperately in love with Georgie; I considered myself by then too old for the desperation and extremity which attends a youthful love. But I loved her with a sort of gaiety and *insouciance* which was more spring-like than the real spring, a miraculous April without its pangs of trans-formation and birth. I loved her with a wild undignified joy, and also with a certain cheerful brutality, both of which were absent from my always more decorous, my essentially sweeter relationship with Antonia. I adored Georgie too for her dry-ness, her toughness, her independence, her lack of intensity, her wit, and altogether for her being such a contrast, such a complement, to the softer and more moist attractions, the more dewy radiance of my lovely wife. I needed both of them, and having both I possessed the world.

If the extent to which Antonia was inside society was im-portant to me, the extent also mattered to which Georgie was outside it. That I could love such a person was a revelation and education to me and something of a triumph: it involved a rediscovery of myself. Georgie's lack of pretention was good for me. Whereas in different ways both Rosemary and Antonia were perpetually playing the rôle of being a woman, Georgie played no rôle: and this was new to me. She was herself, which just happened to involve, and nature had decreed superbly, being a woman. She was concerned neither with rôle nor with status, and it was with exhilaration that at times I positively apprehended her as an outcast.

This sense of being, with Georgie, 'on the run' had suffered a certain change after Georgie's pregnancy. Whereas our lawless existence before that had seemed gay and even innocent, it was after that connected with a certain pain which remained identifiable among all others, not extreme but persistent. We had lost our innocence, and some remaking of our relationship which was then due was continually deferred, as a result partly of my pusillanimity and partly of Georgie's taciturn endurance. I had at the time of the child made a number of extravagant remarks about wishing to join my lot more completely with hers. These remarks had had no sequel, but they remained between us as a text which must some day be revised, ratified, or at least explained. Meanwhile, it was important to me, even very important, that Antonia should think me virtuous; and, with that degree of self-deception which is essential to a prolonged and successful masquerade, I even felt virtuous.

✳ *Chapter Three* ✳

I WAS lying on the big sofa at Hereford Square reading Napier's *History of the Peninsular War* and wondering whether Georgie's incense was going to give me asthma. A bright fire of coal and wood was glowing and murmuring in the grate, and intermittent lamps lit with a soft gold the long room which, even in winter, by some magic of Antonia's, contrived to smell of roses. A large number of expensive Christmas cards were arrayed on the piano; while upon the walls dark evergreens, tied into various clever sprays and joined together by long dropping swags of red and silver ribbon, further proclaimed the season. Antonia's decorations combined a traditional gaiety with the restrained felicity which marked all her domestic arrangements.

I had just come back from Georgie's and was still alone. I had lied to Georgie about the time of Antonia's return—her session with Palmer was not due to end until six—so as to have an interval of quiet before the storm of excited chatter which would undoubtedly follow. Antonia always arrived back from Palmer's house in a state of restless elation. I had supposed, and one is often rather complacently led to believe by persons undergoing such treatment, that a psycho-analysis is a grim and humiliating affair; but in the case of my wife, analysis seemed to produce euphoria and even self-satisfaction. At peace with the world and with myself I breathed the quiet air, lying relaxed and warm in the bright multi-coloured shell which Antonia and I had created, where silk and silver and rosewood, dark mahogany and muted gilt blended sweetly together against a background of Bellini green. I

27

sipped the frosted fragrant Martini which I had just prepared for both of us and thought myself, I dare say, the luckiest of men. Indeed at that moment I was happy with an idle thoughtless happiness which was never to come, with that particular quality of a degenerate innocence, ever in my life again.

I was just looking at my watch, wondering whether she was late, when Antonia appeared in the doorway. Usually when she entered she took possession of a room, gliding immediately to the centre of it, and even, with people she knew well, turning about as if to fill all the crannies and corners with her presence. But tonight, already so marked as unusual, she stayed at the door, as if afraid to enter, or as if conscious of her entrance as dramatic. There she stood wide-eyed, her hand upon the door handle, staring at me in a disconcerting way. I noticed too that she had not changed her clothes, but was still wearing the striped silk blouse and cinnamon-coloured skirt which she had had on in the morning. Normally Antonia put on different clothes three or four times in a day.

"You haven't changed, my love," I said, sitting up. I was still in the slow old world. "What is it? You look a bit bothered. Come and have your drink and tell me all about it." I laid Napier aside.

Antonia came in now, moving in a slow deliberate heavy-footed way and keeping her eyes fixed on me. I wondered if she had seen something which I had missed in the evening papers, some account of a distant cataclysm, or of some accident to an acquaintance, either of which might be announced to me with a certain portentous interest. She sat down at the far end of the sofa, still watching me with a tense unsmiling look. I tinkled the long glass rod in the cocktail jug and poured her out a Martini. "What is it, darling? Has there been an earthquake in China or have you been arrested for speeding?"

"Wait a minute," said Antonia. Her voice sounded thick, almost as if she were drunk. She was taking slow deep breaths, like someone collecting his powers.

I said sharply, "What's the matter, Antonia? Has something bad happened?"

"Yes," said Antonia. "Wait a minute. Sorry."

She sipped her drink and then poured the rest of it into my glass. I realised that she was inarticulate with emotion.

"For God's sake, Antonia," I said, beginning to be thoroughly alarmed. "Whatever is it?"

"Sorry, Martin," said Antonia. "Sorry. Wait a minute. Sorry." She lit a cigarette. Then she said, "Look, Martin, it's this. I've got to tell you now. And there's no way of breaking it gently. It's about me and Anderson." She was looking away from me now and I could see the hand holding the cigarette trembling.

I was still slow. I said, "You and Anderson what, angel?"

"Well, just that," said Antonia, "just that." She threw the cigarette into the fire.

I stared at her and began to think and to read her face. Her manner more than her words frightened me a lot. I was so used to repose in the peace of her simple confident spirit. I had hardly ever seen my golden Antonia so shaken, and this in itself was dreadful. I said gently, "Do I understand you? If you mean you're a bit in love with Palmer, I'm not surprised. I'm a bit in love with him myself."

"Don't be flippant, Martin," said Antonia. "This is serious, it's *fatal*." She turned towards me, but without taking my gaze.

I pushed back the shorter strands of golden hair from her big pale lined brow and drew my hand down her cheek to her mouth. She closed her eyes for a moment, remaining rigid. "Well, do stop looking like that, dearest. You look as if you were going to be shot. Calm down and have your drink. Here, I'll pour you out another one. Now talk to me rationally, and don't frighten me out of my wits."

"You see, it's not a matter of being a bit in love," said Antonia, looking at me now with a glazed troubled stare. She spoke monotonously as if in her sleep, with an air of comatose desperation. "It's matter of being very desperately and deeply in love. Perhaps we ought to have told you sooner, only it was so improbable, such an extreme love. But now we're certain."

"Aren't you both a bit old for this game?" I said. "Come, now!"

Antonia looked at me, her eyes hardened a little, and she became suddenly more present and conscious. Then she smiled sadly and gave a slight shake of the head.

This impressed me. But I said, "Look, darling, need we be quite so serious about this?"

"Yes," said Antonia. "You see, I want a divorce."

She had found the word difficult to utter. At the shock of it I stared at her, and bracing her body stiffly she stared back at me, trying to control her face. She lacked expressions for a scene of this austerity. I said, "Don't be ridiculous, Antonia. Don't say wild things that you don't mean."

"Martin," said Antonia, "please help me. I do mean it, and it will save us a lot of pain if you will understand me *now*, and see what things are like *now*. I know this must be a ghastly shock. But please try. It makes me utterly wretched to hurt you like this. Please help me by understanding. I am quite certain and quite determined. I would not have spoken to you if I were not."

I looked at her. She would soon be in tears, her face stripped, strained like something exposed to a great wind; but there was, in her retention of control, a certain touching dignity. I could not yet believe her or believe that there was anything here which the customary pressure of my will could not sweep aside. I said quietly, "You're in an over-excited state, my sweet. Has that wretch Palmer been giving you drugs, I wonder? You say you're in love with him. All right. That often happens in analysis. But let's not have any more nonsense about divorce. And now can we just abandon this topic for the present? I suggest you finish your drink and then go and dress for dinner."

I tried to rise, but Antonia grasped my arm, lifting a pitiful yet violent face. "*No, no, no,*" she said. "I must say it all now. I can't tell you what this costs me. I want a divorce, Martin. I'm deeply in love. Just believe me, and then let me go away. I know it's absurd and I know it's dreadful, but I'm in love and I'm absolutely relentless. I'm sorry to surprise you and I'm sorry to speak like this, but I've got to make you understand what I mean."

I sat down again. There was a desperate fierceness in her manner, but there was also fear, fear of my reactions. It was the fear which began to convince me and I felt the first light touch of a nightmarish terror. Yet this strange half-savage, half-terrified being was still my Antonia, my dear wife. I said, "Well, well, if you're so much in love with your analyst perhaps you'd better go to bed with him! Only don't talk to me about divorce, for I simply won't hear of it!"

"Martin!" said Antonia in a shocked tone. Then she said,

and her voice became monotonous again, "I've already been to bed with him."

My cheeks became hot with a sudden rush of blood as if I had been struck. My knee was against Antonia's. I captured Antonia's two hands, which were still clawing at my sleeve. in a strong grip in my left hand. "Since when? And how many times?"

She looked back at me, frightened but still firm. Antonia had her own soft frantic evasive way of getting what she wanted. I could feel her will upon me like a leech. She said, "That doesn't matter. If you really want the details, I'll tell you later. Now I just want to tell you the main truth, to tell you that you've got to set me free. This thing has overwhelmed me, Martin. I've simply had to give in to it. Honestly, it's all or nothing."

I crushed her wrists in my left hand. It may seem strange, but I was conscious of wondering and of deciding now how I ought to react, I was very conscious of her fear of a blow. I let go of her hands and said, "Well, let me recommend nothing."

Antonia relaxed and we drew a little apart. She gave a deep sigh and said, "Oh, darling, darling—"

I said, "If I broke your neck now I'd probably get off with three years." I got up and leaned against the mantelpiece looking down at her. "What have I done to deserve this?" I said.

Antonia smiled nervously. She patted her hair, her long fingers straying over the bun, pushing in hair-pins. She adjusted the neck of her blouse. She had a little the air of feeling that the worst was over. She said, "I hate this, Martin. And I've been in torment. You've been so perfect. But I'm beyond thoughts about justification. I'm just desperate."

"Yes, I have been perfect, haven't I?" I said. "But still I don't accept what you say. We've been happy. I want to go on being happy."

"Happy, yes," said Antonia. "But happiness is not the point. We aren't getting anywhere. You know that as well as I do."

"One doesn't have to get anywhere in a marriage. It's not a public conveyance."

"You must face the fact," said Antonia, "that you're a disappointed man."

"I'm damned if I'm a disappointed man," I said, "and if I were it certainly wouldn't be your fault. What you mean is that you're a disappointed woman."

"A marriage is an adventure in development," said Antonia, "and ours is simply at a standstill. I was conscious of that even before I fell in love with Anderson. It's partly my being so much older and being a sort of mother to you. I've kept you from growing up. All this has got to be faced sooner or later." She sipped her drink. She had stopped looking frightened.

"Spare me the clinical stuff, for Christ's sake," I said, "it makes me feel sick. Leave me because you want someone else, let's have honest lust, not pseudo-science. But in any case you aren't going. You can't make changes like this at your age. You're my wife and I love you and I want to go on being married to you, so you'd better resign yourself to having a husband and a lover."

"No," said Antonia. "I've got to go, Martin, I've got to. C'est plus fort que moi." She got up and stood there opposite to me, her stomach thrust out, tall, twisted into a pillar of determination. She added, "I'm extremely grateful to you for being so rational about it."

I stared at her beautiful haggard face, concentrated now in

a look of boldness mixed with a sort of cringing pity. Her big mobile mouth was working as if she were masticating inwardly the tender things she might have said. I had a sense of miserable confusion and of things having utterly escaped my control. "I'm not being rational," I said. "I can hear what you say, Antonia. But your words make no more sense to me than if your were a mad woman. I think I'd better go and talk to Palmer. And if he says we must behave like civilised men I shall kick his teeth in."

"He expects you, darling," said Antonia.

"Antonia," I said, "let me out of this bad dream. Pull yourself together. *This* is what is real, our marriage."

She simply went on shaking her head.

"Anyway, my darling, my Antonia, what would I ever do without you?"

The painful concentration of her face increased and then dissolved as she gave a cry and began suddenly to weep. She looked infinitely pathetic when she was in tears. I went to her and she bowed her head slowly on to my shoulder, not raising her hands to her face. The tears fell between us.

"I knew you'd be good about it," she said in a moment. "I'm so relieved to have told you. I've hated lying about it. And you know, you need never do without me." And she repeated, "Thank you, thank you," as if I had already set her free.

I said, "Well, I haven't broken your neck, have I?"

She said, "My child, my dear child."

❋ *Chapter Four* ❋

"SO you don't hate me, do you, Martin?" said Palmer.
I was lying on the divan in Palmer's study where his patients usually reclined. Indeed I was to all intents and purposes his patient. I was being coaxed along to accept an unpleasant truth in a civilised and rational way.

"No, I don't hate you," I said.

"We are civilised people," said Palmer. "We must try to be very lucid and very honest. We are civilised and intelligent people."

"Yes," I said. I lay still and sipped the large cut-glass tumbler of whisky and water which Palmer had just replenished for me. He himself was not drinking. As he talked he paced to and fro, tall and lean, with his hands behind his back, the purple dressing-gown which he wore loosely over his shirt and trousers making a gentle silky swish. He paced to and fro in front of the line of Japanese prints which decorated the far wall, and bandit faces leered from behind him. His small cropped head moved against the blurred soft blues and charcoal blacks of the prints. The air was warm and dry, agitated by a mysterious breeze from some invisible fan. I was sweating.

"Antonia and I have been happy," I said. "I hope she has not misled you here. I still cannot take this in or accept it. Our marriage is an extremely solid structure."

"Antonia could not mislead me if she tried," said Palmer. "Happiness, my dear Martin, is neither here nor there. Some people, and Antonia is one, conceive of their lives as a progress. Hers has been standing still for too long. She is due to

35

move on." He glanced at me occasionally as he paced, his slightly American voice soft and slow.

"Marriage is an adventure in development," I said.

"Exactly."

"And it is time for Antonia to take a more advanced course."

Palmer smiled. "You are charming to put it so!" he said.

"So the thing has a sort of inevitability."

"I admire your capacity for facing the facts," he said. "Yes, perhaps it has a sort of inevitability. I do not imply this in order to avoid my own responsibility or to help Antonia to shirk hers. There is little point in talking of guilt, and it was not to talk of that that I saw you this evening. You know as well as I do that any such talk would be insincere, whether in your accusations or my confessions. But we are causing hurt and damage. For instance to Antonia's mother, who is fond of you. And there are others. Never mind. We do not close our eyes to this or to anything."

"What about me?" I said. "Damn Antonia's mother!"

"You will not be damaged," said Palmer. He paused in front of me, looking down with a tender concentration. "This is a big thing, Martin, something bigger than ourselves. If it were not so, Antonia and I might have played things differently. It would *then* have been possible to deceive you, though whether we would have done so I don't know. But this is too important and it is something that holds all three of us. You will see. I would not say this unless I were pretty sure. I know Antonia very well, Martin. Better in some ways than you do. That's not your fault but my profession. I know *you* better in some ways than you do."

"I doubt that," I said. "I've never subscribed to your religion. So according to you we're all going to be better off."

"Yes," said Palmer. "I don't say happier, though that might be so too. But we shall grow. You have been a child to Antonia and she a mother to you, and that has kept you both spiritually speaking at a standstill. But you *will* grow up, you *will* change, more than may now seem to you possible. Haven't you sometimes realised the extent to which you now regard yourself both as a child and as an old man?"

This was very acute. "Nonsense," I said. "I reject your explanations. Things were very well between me and Antonia before you turned up."

"Hardly, my dear Martin," said Palmer. "There was your failure to give her a child."

"Her failure to give me a child."

"There you are, Martin," said Palmer. "Each naturally thinks of it as the fault of the other. And the biological evidence is indecisive, as you know."

The warmth and Palmer's almost noiseless movements and his repetition of my name had produced in me a sort of stupor, so that I hardly knew what to say to him. I said, "You aren't hypnotising me, are you?"

"Of course not," said Palmer. "What would that profit me? Relax, Martin. Take your jacket off. You're streaming with perspiration."

I pulled it off and undid my waistcoat and rolled up my shirt sleeves. I had trouble with the cuff links. I tried to sit up a little, but the divan was not made for sitting up, so I lay back again. I stared up at Palmer, who had paused once more in front of me, his smooth clever American face all gentleness and concern, his fur of silver hair shining in the lamplight. There was something abstract in his face. It was impossible to pin wickedness or corruption on to such an image.

"It is an important fact," said Palmer, "that you and I

began it. We began it, did we not, by becoming exceptionally attached to one another. Attachments of that degree are rare in my life. You are certain you are not angry with me?"

"*Cher maître!*" I said. I contemplated Palmer's clear open face with its uncanny youthfulness. "I seem not to know how to be angry with you," I said slowly, "although in a way I want to be. I've drunk too much already this evening and I'm not yet sure what has happened to me. I feel very desolate and hurt and confused, but not angry." It occurred to me then as significant that I had come to see Palmer this evening instead of summoning him to see me. It had not even come into my mind to summon him. It was I who had come running.

"You see, Martin, I am wrapping nothing up," said Palmer.

"Yes, you are," I said, "but very cleverly. It's *all* wrapping. You're too clever for me. No wonder Antonia wants you. She's probably too clever for me too, only I never realised it."

Palmer stood looking at me for a while, serene and detached and tender with only a very little anxiety in his look. He pulled at the top of his dressing-gown where a snowy white shirt emerged, and bared a little more of his long neck. Then he resumed his pacing. He said, as if confidently testing something out, "I knew you'd take it well, I knew you'd take it splendidly."

"I'm not aware that I've yet revealed *how* I'm taking it!" I said. But as I said this I realised with a bitter clarity that I had already fallen into my rôle, my rôle of 'taking it well', which had been prepared for me by Palmer and Antonia. I had put my head straight into the halter which with care and concern and even affection was being held out. It was important to them that I should let them off morally, that I should spare them the necessity of being ruthless. But if I had power, I was already surrendering it. It was already too late for violence. I was indeed facing something big and formidably well organised.

Palmer seemed to ignore my remark. "You see," he said, "it is not at all our idea that you should leave us. In a strange and rather wonderful way we can't do without you. We shall hold on to you, we shall look after you. You'll see."

"I thought I was supposed to grow up."

Palmer laughed. "Oh, don't imagine it will be easy! Nothing here will be easy. It will be a dangerous adventure. But as I say, you're liking me so much is the important thing."

"How do you know I'll go on liking you, Palmer?" I said. I felt my faculties slipping.

"You will," said Palmer.

"Loving one's successful rival?"

"The psyche is a strange thing," he said, "and it has its own mysterious methods of restoring a balance. It automatically seeks its advantage, its consolation. It is almost entirely a matter of mechanics, and mechanical models are the best to understand it with."

"You don't see me then as an angel of compassion?"

Palmer laughed gaily. "Bless you, Martin," he said. "Your irony will be the saving of all three of us."

* Chapter Five *

I ALWAYS think of Rembers as my mother's house, though my grandfather bought it originally and Alexander has had it altered considerably since father died. But somehow the house retains indelibly the mark of my mother's gentle fey rather vague personality, and is in my thought of it perpetually clouded over with a romantic, almost a mediaeval, haze. It ought most probably to be surrounded by a thick forest of twining roses, like the castle of the sleeping beauty. Yet it is not an old house. It was built about 1880 and is half-timbered with its stucco washed a rich Irish pink. It is a solitary place, built on high ground above the river Stour, on the outskirts of a Cotswold hamlet not far from Oxford, and commanding a view of empty hillsides visited only by hares. The yews and the box which my mother planted have grown well, and the garden might look older than the house were it not for the ageless charm of the place, infinitely fresh and infinitely decayed at the same time, like something issued from the imagination of Sir John Millais or Dante Gabriel Rossetti.

It was lunch-time on Christmas eve, and I was in the Oxford train. The sky had been leaden yellow in London and as we passed Reading some snow began to fall in rare large flakes out of a still air. It was very cold. I had decided to spend Christmas with Alexander and Rosemary, and I had telephoned them two days ago to tell them that I was coming, and to tell them briefly that Antonia and I were parting. Antonia and Palmer had pressed me with an astonishing warmth and fervour to spend Christmas with them. It was remarkable how rapidly, after Antonia's revelation, 'they' had come into existence as a sort of institution with its palpable strength, atmosphere and even traditions. Antonia now divided her day between Hereford Square and Palmer's house in Pelham Crescent, doing her best to be in both places at once. I had never seen her so happy; and I realised with mixed feelings that an important part of her happiness consisted in looking after me. I let her. She had insisted on spending the two nights prior to my departure at Hereford Square, where in any case we normally occupied separate rooms. I went to bed each night blind drunk. I had refused their Christmas offer, not through any fear of anger and violence, but through fear of a too great compliance. I needed to withdraw in order to dress myself again in some shreds of dignity and reason. 'They' had whirled me naked. I hoped now to retrieve at least some tawdry semblance of self-respect by playing, before Rosemary and Alexander, the rôle of the deceived husband. More simply, I wanted time to think; more simply still, time to feel.

I was only now beginning really to believe it. The evening of Antonia's revelation, during which I had had a fantastic amount to drink, seemed in retrospect a lurid dream, full of ghoulish configurations and yet somehow mysteriously painless. It was later that the pain came, a pain unutterably obscure and confused like that induced by some deprivation in childhood. The familiar world of ways and objects within which I had lived for so long received me no more; and our lovely house had put on suddenly the air of a superior antique shop. The things in it no longer cohered together. It was odd that the pain worked first and most immediately through *things*, as if they had at once become the sad symbols of a loss which in its entirety I could not yet face. They knew and mourned. The loss of Antonia seemed like the impossible loss forever of all warmth and all security; and it was strange too that although a few days ago I had seemed to divide my being and give to Antonia only a part, it now seemed that with her all was to be dragged away. It was like being flayed. Or more exactly as if the bright figured globe of my existence, which had been so warmly symmetrical to the face of my soul, were twisted harshly off, leaving my naked face against a cold wind and darkness.

Yet I had behaved well. That, at least, had emerged, and was indeed the main thing that had been, almost with a gentle insistence, established. I had taken it well; and a warm radiance of gratitude for this was continually perceptible, in which, deprived of other comforts, I was invited abjectly to bask. It was the inevitability of just such basking which I was now in process of running away from. I had lost the moment of action; this I felt with, at times, a terrible fierceness of regret: although it was by no means clear to me what that lost action might have been. It was evident in a way that was now almost consoling and now scarcely bearable, that Antonia and Palmer were very much in love. The revelation of their love and my compliance with it, indeed as I bitterly reflected virtually my blessing upon it, had released in both of them a frenetic gaiety. I had never seen them so gay, so vital, so absolutely flaunting their colours. They seemed now in spirit to be always waltzing. Against such a force I could hardly, I told myself, have prevailed. Yet, I felt too, if I had only somehow tried, if I had known how to try, in the face of her soft determination and her quick gratitude, to keep Antonia, even if I had failed, one particular nagging misery would now be absent. I had been cheated of some moment of violence, of some special though perhaps fruitless movement of will and power; and for this at least I would never forgive them.

It was ironical, I reflected as I sat in the train, that a week ago I had seemed in secure possession of two women; now I was likely to be in possession of neither. It was not clear to me whether the rupture with Antonia had not in some mysterious way also killed my relation to Georgie, as if these two growths had, so far from competing, strangely nourished each other. I was far from sure of this, however, and my thoughts warily, even shyly, kept returning inconclusively to the image of my mistress. I had not communicated with Georgie since the day of the revelation, and since the thing was not yet common knowledge, she was still presumably ignorant of the change in my situation. I did not look forward to telling her. It was not a time at which I felt well able to have things expected of me; and as I speculated and wondered about what exactly Georgie *would* expect, it occurred to me how little, after all, I knew her. That she would vulgarly press me to marry her was of course out of the question. It was a matter rather of how far and how she would, in her turn, let me off; it was also a matter of whether I wanted to be let off. It was an additional, and when I attended to it a terrible, pain that if in this new situation either Georgie or I 'flagged' we would be betraying and indeed destroying a precious and tender relation which in secrecy and ambiguity had so much flourished. I needed Georgie, I loved her, I felt I could not possibly, especially now, do without her. Yet I did not quite see myself marrying her. Still, it was, I reflected, far too soon to know. I had not yet even begun to fit the pieces together; and there might be some way of fitting them together which would make out a picture of happiness for me and for Georgie. At rare moments, in a quite abstract way, I imagined this happiness, something utterly remote from my present misery and confusion, and yet not totally unconnected with me nor totally impossible.

Rosemary was to meet me at Oxford and drive me to Rembers. I felt in no mood for confronting Rosemary. She had never quite got on with Antonia and would on the one hand be delighted at what had happened, while on the other she would maintain a conventional air of distress: distress such as persons feign at the death of an acquaintance, and which is in fact a glow of excitement and pleasure, perceptible on waking in the morning as a not yet diagnosed sense of all being exceptionally well with the world. Rosemary, I should say, is for her sins a Mrs Michelis, having got married young, and against all our wishes, to a dislikeable stockbroker called Bill Michelis, who subsequently left her; and like most people whose marriages have failed she had a sharp appetite for news of other failed marriages. I had expected Rosemary to marry again, as, quite apart from being a rich girl, she is very attractive to men, but so far she has prudently refrained. Although with her small precise features, refined prim voice and Lynch-Gibbon pedantry in speech, she gives the appearance of a prude, she is in reality far from prudish and is almost undoubtedly at her somewhat mysterious flat in Chelsea, to which she rarely invites me, involved in continual amorous adventures.

It was snowing hard in Oxford, and must have been doing so for some time, as there was a good inch of soft feathery snow on the ground as I stepped out of the train and began to look around for my sister. I soon saw her and noted that she was dressed entirely in black: on instinct, no doubt. She came up to me and leaned back her small pale face, under its little velvet cap, to be kissed. Rosemary has the attractiveness which is sometimes called *petite*. She has the long Lynch-Gibbon face and the powerful nose and mouth, but all scaled down, smoothed over and covered with an exquisite ivory

44

faintly freckled skin. The Lynch-Gibbon face is made for men, I have always felt, and to my eye Rosemary's appearance, for all its sweetness, has always something of an air of caricature.

"Hello, flower," I said, kissing her.

"Hello, Martin," said Rosemary, unsmiling and clearly a little shocked at what she felt as my levity. "This is grave news," she added, as we pushed our way to the exit. I followed her trim black figure out, and we got into Alexander's Sunbeam Rapier.

"It's bloody news," I said. "Never mind. How are you and Alexander?"

"We're as well as can be expected," said Rosemary. She sounded weighed down by my troubles. "Oh, Martin, *I am* sorry!"

"Me too," I said. "I like the cute little hat, Rosemary. Is it new?"

"Dear Martin," said Rosemary, "don't play-act with me."

Now we were driving along St Giles. The snow was falling steadily out of a tawny sky. Its white blanket emphasised the black gauntness of the bare plane trees and made the yellow fronts of the tall Georgian houses glow to a rich terracotta.

"I can hardly believe it," said Rosemary. "You and Antonia parting, after such a long time! Do you know, I was very surprised indeed."

I could hardly bear her relish. I looked down at her small high-heeled black-shod feet on the pedals. "Have you been snowed up at Rembers?"

"Not really," said Rosemary, "though I must say it seems to have snowed more there than here. Isn't it odd how it always seems to snow more in the country? Water Lane was blocked last week, but the other roads are fairly clear. The

Gilliad-Smiths have been using chains on their car. We haven't bothered. Alexander says it's bad for the tyres. Still, Badgett had to help push us out of the gate once or twice. Where will you live now, Martin?"

"I don't know," I said. "Certainly not at Hereford Square. I suppose I'd better find a flat."

"Darling, it's impossible to get a flat," said Rosemary, "at least a flat that's fit to live in, unless you pay the earth."

"Then I shall pay the earth," I said. "How long have you been down here?"

"About a week," said Rosemary. "Don't let Antonia cheat you about the furniture and things. I suppose as she's the guilty party it should all really belong to you."

"Not at all," I said, "there's no such rule! And her money went into the house as well as mine. We shall sort things out amicably."

"I think you're wonderful!" said Rosemary. "You don't seem in the least bitter. I should be mad with rage if I were you. You treated that man as your best friend."

"He's still my best friend."

"You're very philosophical about it," said Rosemary. "But don't overdo it. You must be miserable and bitter somewhere in your soul. A bit of good cursing may be just what you need."

"I'm miserable everywhere in my soul," I said. "Bitterness is another thing. There's no point in it. Can we talk about something else?"

"Well, Alexander and I will stand by you," said Rosemary. "We'll look for a flat for you and we'll help you move in and then if you like I'll come and be your part-time housekeeper. I should like that. I haven't seen half enough of you in these last two or three years. I was just thinking that the other day.

And you'll have to *have* a housekeeper, won't you, and professional ones cost the earth."

"You're very thoughtful," I said. "What's Alexander working on just now?"

"He says he's stuck," said Rosemary. "By the way, Alexander's dreadfully cut up about you and Antonia."

"Naturally," I said. "He adores Antonia."

"I happened to be there when he opened her letter," said Rosemary. "I've never seen him so shaken."

"Her letter?" I said. "So she wrote to him about it, did she?" Somehow this irritated me terribly.

"Well, I gather so," said Rosemary. "Anyhow all I'm saying is, be kind and tactful to Alexander, be specially nice to him."

"To console him for my wife having left me," I said. "All right, flower."

"Martin!" said Rosemary. Some minutes later we turned into the gate of Rembers.

✳ *Chapter Six* ✳

" 'Since I left Plumtree
Down in Tennessee
It's the first time I've been warm!' "

quoted Alexander, as he dangled his long broad-nailed hand
in front of his new fan heater. The sleeve of his white smock
fluttered and rippled in the warm wind.

It was half an hour later and we were sitting in the bay
window annexe of Alexander's studio drinking tea and looking out at the falling snow and the south face of the house
which could still be seen in the failing afternoon light, its
timberings loaded with soft undulating lines of whiteness
against the dulled pink. A holly wreath with a red bow hanging on the hall door was sifted over and almost invisible. The
nearer flakes fell white, but farther off they merged into a
yellowish curtain which prevented our view and made
Rembers enclosed and solitary.

In the creamy white smock, self-consciously old-fashioned,
my brother seemed dressed to represent a miller in an opera.
His big pale face in repose had an eighteenth-century appearance, heavy, intelligent, the slightest bit degenerate, speaking
of a past of generals and gentlemen adventurers, profoundly
English in the way in which only Anglo-Irish faces can now
be. One might have called him 'noble' in the sense of the
word which is usually reserved for animals.

It was an odd thing about Alexander, and one which I
noted ever anew, especially when I saw him at Rembers, that
although the form of his face perfectly recalled my father, its
spirit and animation perfectly recalled my mother. More than

in Rosemary or me, here she lived on, as indeed we both profoundly apprehended in our relation to Alexander. We passed as being, and I suppose we were, a very united family; and though I ruled our financial fortunes and largely played my father's rôle, Alexander in playing my mother's was the real head of the family. Here in the house and here in the studio, whose white-washed walls were still dotted with her water-colours and pastel-shaded lithographs, I recalled her clearly, with a sad shudder of memory, and with that particular painful guilty thrilling sense of being both stifled and protected with which a return to my old home always afflicted me; and now it was as if my pain for Antonia had become the same pain, so closely was it now blended in quality, though more intense, with the obscure *malaise* of my homecomings. Perhaps indeed it had always been the same pain, a mingled shadow cast forward and backward across my destiny.

We had not yet put the lights on, and we sat together in the window-seat, not looking at each other but turned toward the silent movement of the snow and the now invisible 'view' to enjoy which Alexander had a few years ago had the big bay window built. Beyond the curtain which divided it from the annexe, the studio was almost in darkness. In summer it would be scented with smells of wood, and flower smells from outside and the fresh wet clean smell of clay; but now it smelt only of paraffin from the four big oil-heaters whose equally familiar odour brought me recollections of ill-lit childhood winters.

"And so?"

"Well, there it is."

"And Palmer didn't tell you anything else?"

"I didn't ask him anything else."

"And you say you were charming to him?"

"Charming."

"I don't say," said Alexander, "that I would have sprung upon him like a wild animal. But I would have interrogated him. I should have wanted to understand."

"Oh, I *understand*," I said. "You must remember that I am very close to Palmer; which makes it impossible to ask, but also makes it unnecessary."

"And Antonia seems happy?"

"It's the beatific vision."

Alexander sighed. He said, "I'm tempted to say now that I never liked Palmer. He's an imitation human being: beautifully finished, exquisitely coloured, but imitation."

"He's a magician," I said, "and that can inspire dislike. But he's warm-blooded. He needs love as much as anyone else does. I can't help being touched by the way he has tried to *hold* me, as well as Antonia, in this situation."

"I say pish, Sir, I say bah!" said Alexander.

"Antonia wrote to you?" I turned to watch him, his big slow face illumined by the sallow light of the snow.

"Yes," he said. "Yes. I wonder if I might have guessed. But no, any such thing would have seemed to me impossible. When it came to it I was stunned by her letter."

"Surely you didn't get her letter before I telephoned? She would hardly have written to you before she told me!"

"Oh, well, of course not," said Alexander. "But I didn't take it in properly when you rang. She didn't *say* anything in the letter, you know, not anything informative. Tell me though, where will you live now?"

"I don't know. I suppose I'll get a flat. Rosemary has appointed herself as my housekeeper."

Alexander laughed. He said, "Why not come and live here? You don't *have* to run the business, do you?"

"What would I do here?"

"Nothing."

"Come!"

"Why not?" said Alexander. "You could fleet the time idyllically. This place is the earthly paradise, as we all saw with perfect clarity in childhood before we were corrupted by the world. If you insisted on occupation I would teach you how to model in clay or how to carve snakes and weasels out of tree roots. The trouble with people nowadays is they don't know how to do nothing. I've had quite a job teaching Rosemary to do it, and she's certainly more gifted in that direction than you are."

"You're an artist," I said, "and for you doing nothing is doing something. No. I shall get back to Wallenstein and Gustavus Adolphus and *What Is a Good General*." I had for some time been quietly engaged on a monograph on the Thirty Years War in which the competence of these two commanders was compared. This was to be a chapter in a projected larger work on what constituted efficiency in a military leader.

"There are no good generals," said Alexander.

"You are the dupe of Tolstoy who thought all generals were incompetent because all Russian generals were incompetent. Anyway, I shall try to work more seriously in future. Antonia, it must be admitted, was time-consuming."

"Beautifully," said Alexander. He sighed again and we were silent for a minute.

"Show me some of the results of your inactivity," I said.

He rose and pulled back the curtain. He turned the switch in the studio and a number of strips flickered to life overhead, producing the illumination of an overcast afternoon in spring. The great room, which was a Cotswold barn converted by my mother, retained its high roof and rough-hewn wooden rafters from whose scored crevices the warm oily air, gently circulating, seemed to sift down an ancient dust. The long work table, with its scrubbed surface and neat groups of meticulously cleaned tools, spanned the farther wall. Other things, though with an air of having their own places, were dotted about: pieces of uncut stone, enormous tree roots stacked like a tent, wooden blocks of various sizes, like overgrown nursery bricks, tall objects covered with damp grey cloths, a box full of ornamental gourds, a pillar of ebony shaped by nature or art, it was hard to tell which. A row of clay bins flanked the wall by the window, and at the far end was a population of plaster casts, torsos, swinging headless bodies, and heads mounted on rough wooden stands. The floor of blue imitation Dutch encaustic tiles was covered, according to a fantasy of Alexander's, with dry rushes and straw.

Alexander crossed the room and began carefully to undo the cloths which draped one of the tall objects. A revolving pedestal began to appear with something mounted upon it. As he removed the last cloth he switched off the centre lights and turned on a single anglepoise lamp on the work table which he swung round towards the pedestal. There was a clay head in the first stages of composition, the early stages when the wire framework has been roughly filled out and then the clay laid over it in various directions in long strips until the semblance of a head appears. This particular moment has always seemed to me uncanny, when the faceless image acquires a quasi-human personality, and one is put in mind of the making of monsters.

"Who is it?"

"I don't know!" said Alexander. "It's not a portrait. Yet I feel odd about it, as if I were looking for the person it was of. I've never worked quite like this and it may be useless. I did some quite non-realistic heads, you remember, ages ago."

"Your perspex phase."

"Yes, then. But I've never wanted to do an imaginary realistic head before." He moved the lamp slowly and the oblique light made dark lines between the strips of clay.

"Why don't modern sculptors do them?" I asked.

"I don't know," said Alexander. "We don't believe in human nature in the old Greek way any more. There is nothing between schematised symbols and caricature. What I want here is some sort of impossible liberation. Never mind. I shall go on playing with it and interrogating it and perhaps it will tell me something."

"I envy you," I said. "You have a *technique* for discovering more about what is real."

"So have you," said Alexander. "It is called morality."

I laughed. "Rusted through lack of practice, brother. Show me something else."

"Who is this?" said Alexander. He turned the angle-poise directly upward and revealed a bronze head which was mounted on a bracket above the work table.

I felt a shock of surprise even before I recognised it. "I haven't seen that in years." It was Antonia.

Alexander had done the head in the early days of our marriage and then professed dissatisfaction with it and refused to part with it. It was in a light golden bronze and showed a youthful forward-darting Antonia that was not quite familiar to me: a champagne-toasted dancing-on-the-table Antonia that seemed to belong to another age. The shape of the head was excellent, however, and the great flowing pile of hair at the back, wildly tressed and somewhat Grecian: and the big rapacious slightly parted lips, these I knew. But it was a younger, gayer, more keenly directed Antonia than my own. Perhaps she had existed and I had forgotten. There was nothing there of the warm muddle of my wife. I shivered.

"It can't be her without the body," I said. Antonia's swaying body was an essential part of her presence.

"Yes, some people *are* more their body than others," said Alexander, as he played the beam over the head, unshadowing a cheek. "All the same, heads are us most of all, the apex of our incarnation. The best thing about being God would be making the heads."

"I don't think I like a sculpted head alone," I said. "It seems to represent an unfair advantage, an illicit and incomplete relationship."

"An illicit and incomplete relationship," said Alexander. "Yes. Perhaps an obsession. Freud on Medusa. The head can represent the female genitals, feared not desired."

"I didn't mean anything so fancy," I said. "Any savage likes to collect heads."

"You wouldn't let me collect yours!" said Alexander. I had never let Alexander sculpt me, though he had often begged.

"To carry on your pike? No!" As we laughed he drew his hand down over the back of my head, feeling the shape under the hair. A sculptor thinks from the skull outwards.

We stood for a little longer looking up at the head of Antonia until I felt the misery rising in my heart. I said, "I could face a stiff drink soon. By the way, I sent off a case of Vierge de Clèry and some brandy."

"They came this morning," said Alexander. "But no port! 'All claret would be port if it could.' "

"Not if I could catch it in time!" I said. We had this argument every Christmas.

"I'm afraid we've got the usual mob coming tomorrow,"

said Alexander. "I wasn't able to put them off. Rosemary says they look forward to it! But with luck we may be snowed up."

We wandered across to the door and opened it, pausing on the threshold to look at the scene outside. The cold air touched us sharply. It was darker now, but the last light of day lingered with a living glow which seemed to emerge from the snow itself. The white untrodden sheet stretched away to where the two great acacia trees, loaded now and half sketched in in black, marked the end of the lawn and framed the now hidden vista of hills wherein were folded the lost ironstone villages of Sibford Gower and Sibford Ferris. The snow fell silent and straight down out of a windless sky, and through the open door we apprehended its positive silence. We were shuttered as in a tomb. Then darkly blurred as in a Chinese picture, a blackbird on its way to roost moved suddenly in the lee of a bush, turned its head towards us and then sped away noiselessly low over the snow. In the last twilight of the afternoon we saw its eye and its orange beak.

> " 'The ousel-cock, so black of hue,
>   With orange-tawny bill,' "

Alexander murmured.

"You quote too aptly, brother."

"*Too* aptly?"

"You don't recall the rest?"

"No."

> " 'The throstle with his note so true,
>   The wren with little quill,
>   The finch, the sparrow, and the lark,
>   The plain-song cuckoo gray,
>   Whose note full many a man doth mark,
>   And dare not answer nay.' "

Alexander was silent for a moment. Then he said, "Have you been faithful to Antonia?"

The question took me by surprise. However I replied at once, "Yes, of course."

Alexander sighed. The light came on in the drawing-room and cast into the darkening air a cone of gold into which the snowflakes, grey now and scarcely visible above, filtered to become, before they came to rest, tinsel for a moment. The evergreen kissing bough which Rosemary laboriously plaited every Christmas, as my mother had taught her to do, was to be seen hanging in the window, decked with coloured balls and oranges and long-tailed birds and candles and hung with mistletoe; and now I could see my sister mounting on a chair to set the candles alight. They flickered, and then rose in a strong glow as the old ambiguous symbol swayed slightly in the breeze that always haunted those tall ill-fitting Victorian windows.

"Why 'of course'?" said Alexander.

At that moment we heard the tinkle of the piano. Rosemary was beginning to play a carol. It was *Once in Royal David's City*. I took a deep breath and turned away from the door. I crossed the room to collect my cigarettes which I had left in the bay window. Alexander, who did not seem to expect an answer to his question, had turned the anglepoise back to shine upon his unfinished head. We contemplated it together to the distant sound of the piano. I had known that it reminded me of something, something sad and frightening, and as I looked now at the damp grey featureless face I remembered what it was. When my mother had died Alexander had wanted to take a death mask, but my father had not let him. I recalled with a sudden vividness the scene in the bedroom with the still figure on the bed, its face covered with a sheet.

I shuddered and turned to the doorway. It was quite dark outside now. The snow fell, invisible save in the light from the window, into the depths of its own sleep. Rosemary began to play another verse.

✱ *Chapter Seven* ✱

MY darling Georgie, I have not spent Christmas quite as I expected. On the evening when I last saw you Antonia suddenly announced that she wished to leave me and to get married to Palmer Anderson. I won't tell you the details now, but it looks as if this is what is going to happen. Nor can I tell you exactly what my feelings are. I don't altogether know myself. As you may imagine, I am suffering from shock. Indeed, I feel scarcely sane and nothing seems solid any longer or real for the present. You will understand that there is nothing more I can say just now. I needed to tell you the facts anyway and it is a great relief simply to be writing to you. Hope and fear nothing if you can. Oh, sweetheart, I have never felt more wretchedly incapable of any bright or adventurous destiny. I feel half faded away like some figure in the background of an old picture. Try at least if you can, to restore to me some sense and some vigour. Darling child, your love and your devotion have been so precious to me: support me now with patience. Excuse this cowardly and distracted letter. Your poor discredited prince kisses your feet. I am simply too miserable to think straight. Please bear with me and *go on loving me*. If I can I'll call on you tomorrow at the usual time. If I can't come I'll telephone about then.

M.

I finished the letter and put it hastily into my pocket. Antonia and Rosemary were descending the stairs, still trying to talk both at once.

"And the whole building has oil-fired central heating," Antonia was saying.

I got up from where I had been sitting at the Carlton House writing-table and went over to the fireplace. It was early

58

afternoon, but very dark outside, and the lamps had already been turned on. Two electric fires were burning in the room, but Antonia had insisted on lighting a coal fire as well, to cheer me up, as she put it.

They came in and stood side by side looking at me with the look of tender delighted concern with which women look at babies. The concern was sharpened in Rosemary's case by curiosity, in Antonia's by anxiety. Rosemary in her smart grey unobtrusive London clothes was tiny beside my wife.

"Antonia has been telling me about your flat," said Rosemary. "It sounds ideal. And there's a heavenly view over to Westminster Cathedral."

"Well, you know more about it than I do," I said. Palmer had found me a flat in Lowndes Square. It appeared to be all right.

"But you wouldn't *let* me tell you this morning!" exclaimed Antonia. "Isn't he dreadful?" to Rosemary. "Don't you even want to see it?"

"Not specially."

"Dear heart, don't sulk," said Antonia. "You'll have to make *some* decision soon about the furniture. Rosemary and I have just been measuring curtains, and the landing and Blue Room ones will fit exactly without alteration."

"What luck."

"Well, *I* want to see it," said Rosemary, "even if you don't. Antonia's given me the key and I'm going over there now. Are you sure you don't want to come, Martin?"

"Yes."

"I must be off then," said Rosemary. "I must say I'm *limp* already. I'll drop the key in this evening. 'Bye, Martin darling, 'bye, Antonia." She patted my shoulder and then stood on her toes to peck Antonia's cheek. She and my wife seemed quite wrapped up in each other now.

Antonia saw her to the door. I could hear her saying, "And let me know what you think about the pelmets." The door closed.

I stood by the fireplace watching the flames, and trying to clean out an old pipe which I had found—I occasionally smoked a pipe. I heard Antonia come back into the room. She came across to stand opposite to me. I stared at her and she stared steadily back, unsmiling now. It was the first time we had been alone together since I had returned accompanied by Rosemary. Already, through the secret chemistry of the situation, Antonia and I were two new and different people. We regarded each other with a dismay behind which, in my case, there lurked an abject terror, ready to probe the difference. I felt suddenly dizzy with pain and unable to face whatever scene was to follow. I went back to scraping the pipe. I said, "Well, you've made one person blissfully happy. Rosemary adores catastrophes."

"Martin, darling," said Antonia. She said it lingeringly, with an insistent tenderness of reproach. She stood there before me, her stomach pouting, her hip jutting, her body twisted in such a dear familiar way. A snowy white silk blouse, falling well open, showed off her long neck. Her bun was coiled in a neat golden ball almost as large as her head. I looked at her again and saw her sharply for the first time since our rupture as a separate person and no longer a part of myself.

"You are pleased about the flat, aren't you?"

"Yes, very."

"Don't be cross with me," said Antonia. "It hurts so much."

"I'm not cross."

"Anderson took a lot of trouble to find the flat."

"It's very kind of him, especially when he has so many other things to think about."

"Whatever would he be thinking about, what would either of us be thinking about," said Antonia, "but you? We think of nothing else!"

"Sweet of you," I said. I began to fill the pipe.

"Please, darling," said Antonia, "don't do that."

"Don't do what, for Christ's sake?"

"Be so sort of blank and sarcastic. And please, if you can, be nice to Anderson. He's so terribly worried about what you feel about him and so terribly anxious to please you. You could hurt him dreadfully by the smallest thing."

"I'm not being blank and sarcastic," I said. "I *am* grateful to Palmer. But I do wish everyone would stop scheming for my welfare. I'm perfectly well able to look after myself." I lit the pipe. It tasted foul.

"But we want to look after you!" said Antonia.

As I didn't reply, she sighed and turned away to pull the curtains across the darkened windows. A thick yellow fog had covered London all day, turning the day to night, and filtering into the house to bring even to Antonia's, no longer Antonia's, rose-scented drawing-room a faint bitter smell and a fainter haze. The snow which had lain so thick and beautiful when I left the country was scarcely to be seen in the city, lingering only in diminishing white patches on roofs or on less frequented pavements in long iron-grey streaks of ice. I sat down on the sofa and began knocking out the pipe against the mantelpiece.

Antonia came back to me. "You're making a nasty mark there."

"It doesn't matter now."

"It does matter, Martin. Every single little thing matters."

The cosier, the more enclosed, scene seemed to give her confidence. She reached out and took the pipe away from me. Then she sat down beside me and tried to take my hand. I withdrew it. It was like a strange courtship scene. I said, "No, Antonia."

She said, "Yes, Martin," and laid her hand again on the sleeve of my coat. I began to tremble.

"Isn't it enough," I said, "must you do this as well?"

"It's important, Martin," said Antonia. "Don't flee from me. We must still be able to touch each other."

"Does your psycho-analyst advise this?"

"Please!" said Antonia. "I know you're hurt, Martin, more hurt inside than you will let any of us see. But you mustn't say these bitter things."

"I should have thought that was pretty mild," I said. "But I seem to have set myself such a high standard. Well, I suppose I shall have to keep it up now!" I let her take my hand. I let her quiet me as one quiets an animal.

"*Yes, yes,*" said Antonia, "you will have to keep it up, won't you!" Laughing with relief and gratitude she fell to her knees before me and kissed my hand and drew it to her breast. Then she looked at me steadily. "You are generous, my dear." Her voice was deep and resonant with emotion.

I thought, but did not say, "I'm in love with you." That was too mad. I said instead, "Look, sweetie, we must make those arrangements about the bloody furniture and so on."

"There's plenty of time," said Antonia. She sat back, her arms wrapped round her knees, seeming completely relaxed now. "But we will, of course. There's lots of junk that can go straight to the sale room. You know, the stuff we've wanted to get rid of for years. And the good stuff should divide quite rationally."

That 'we' still came naturally from Antonia's lips. I wondered at her. At the same time, I needed her. The devil of it was that I needed both of them. The thread of intimacy was not yet broken after all between Antonia and myself. I apprehended this fact with a sort of agony. I had only had notice of my death. The stroke had not really fallen yet.

"Look," said Antonia, "could you do a favour for Anderson and me?"

"It seems to be my *métier*."

"Could you meet Honor at the station tonight?"

"Honor?"

"You know, Anderson's sister. She's arriving from Cambridge."

"Oh, Honor Klein. Yes, I suppose so. Only I scarcely know her. Why can't Palmer meet her?"

"He's got a dreadful cold," said Antonia. "He really mustn't go out in this fog."

"Can't she take a taxi?"

"She's expecting Anderson, and he's afraid that if he doesn't come she'll wait indefinitely on the platform in this ghastly weather."

"She doesn't sound very intelligent," I said. "All right, I'll meet her." Antonia's 'Anderson', which had once sounded so curiously formal, now had a ring of hideous intimacy; and somehow the fact of Palmer having a cold irritated me extremely.

Antonia squeezed my arm and moved round to lean her head against my knee. I was beginning to be tormented by physical desire for her. She said, "I feel rather nervous about Honor."

"You've met her before, though. She seems a pretty harmless old don."

"Yes, I've met her," said Antonia, "but I've never *noticed* her."

"Neither have I," I said. "This suggests that she's harmless." I began to stroke Antonia's hair.

"I wouldn't worry," said Antonia, "only Anderson seems a bit worried. He doesn't say much, but I think he thinks that Honor thinks that I'm not good enough for him."

"That's a lot of thinking," I said. "You're good enough for a king, and quite good enough for our Palmer. There's nothing to be nervous about. You're a goddess, and she's just a poor old German spinster. Tell yourself that. What time is the train?"

"Five fifty-seven at Liverpool Street," said Antonia. "Martin, you're an ace. I'm afraid the train's sure to be awfully late because of the fog. Perhaps you could bring her straight to Pelham Crescent. I wonder if you have the faintest idea how good you are?"

"I'm beginning to realise," I said. "It hurts so much, for one thing."

Antonia sat back on her heels. She was consciously, almost shamelessly, exerting her power. She held me a while in the glow of her attention; and I let her so hold me, with a sort of despair, knowing the fruitlessness of taking her in my arms.

"We won't let go of you, Martin," she said. "We'll never let go of you."

I had feared the inevitable breaking of the thread of intimacy. In Antonia's intention this thread, somehow, would never be broken. I felt an abject relief together with a spiritual nausea which made her look to me, for a moment, almost hideous. I was near to breaking down. I said, "You can't have everything, Antonia."

She put her two hands on my knees and leaned forward with glowing eyes. "I can try, my darling, I can try!"

✳ *Chapter Eight* ✳

LIVERPOOL Street Station smelt of sulphur and brimstone. Thick fog filled it and the great cast-iron dome was invisible. The platform lights were dulled, powerless to cast any radiance out into the relentless haze, so that the darkness seemed to have got inside one's head. Excited, strangely exhilarated by the fog, obscure figures peered and hurried past. One moved about within a small dimly lighted sphere, surrounded by an opaque yet luminous yellow night out of which with startling suddenness people and things materialised. The time was five forty-five.

I had got the car out early in case I should get lost on the way. However, flaring fog lights all along Piccadilly and Holborn had kept me crawling steadily on, and I had arrived in fair time. I had already enquired how late the train would be, which no one seemed to know, and had inspected the bookstall at length and purchased a cheap edition of a book about jungle warfare in Burma. I was now sitting in the comparative brightness of the buffet sipping some rather cold tea. I shook out my scarf, which was damp and soggy. I could have wrung the moisture from it. I was chilled to the bone and so dejected that it was almost laughable. With that I felt more than a little mad.

The scene with Antonia had left me stiff and weary, as if I had been beaten, or had come a very long way. I was by now in a state which could only be described as being in love. Yet it was a strange love, whose only possible expression was my acquiescence in her will to keep that thread unbroken between us. At the same time, to consent to this was torture and

66

I felt the tender bond like a strangler's rope. I was confounded by the utter impossibility of violence. Yet violence, veiled with misery, moved within. What most appalled was the sense which I had so clearly had when I was with Antonia of my need for her, my need for *them*; and what I now abjectly craved was to see Palmer and to receive from him some impossible inconceivable reassurance. I was their prisoner, and I choked with it. But I too much feared the darkness beyond.

I looked at my watch. It was five fifty-four, still too early for a drink. I got up and went out to enquire again at the platform where the train was due. Still no one seemed to know how late it would be, and I stood about for a while with my coat collar turned up, breathing the thick contaminated air. It pressed down into my lungs, cold, damp and filthy, doing me no good at all. The place was an image of hell. I wondered if I would recognise Dr Klein. I could not recall her face, and could conjure up only some generalised image of a middle-aged Germanic spinster. I remembered being disappointed at her lack of any resemblance to Palmer. Otherwise she had seemed so true to type as to be without special points of interest. I took a gloomy satisfaction in performing the disagreeable task of meeting her. To be icily and inconveniently here, suffocating on this railway station and faced with the discomfort of a long wait: this was after all the only thing I could do just now to spite Antonia and Palmer. It was for this moment my only weapon. Also it passed the time.

I bought an evening paper and read about how many people had been killed already by the fog. The time was five fifty-nine. I began to think about Georgie and about our meeting tomorrow. I could find somewhere in my heart a warm germ of gladness at the thought of Georgie. Yet I was terrified of seeing her too. I could not at present face anything in the way of a showdown or argument about fundamentals with Georgie. I had been as it were too completely re-absorbed into Antonia. I could think of nothing but Antonia. The pressure upon me of Georgie's needs, any requirement that I should now imagine *her* situation, would be intolerable, and I felt sick at the thought. Yet I did want to see her. I wanted consolation, I wanted love, I wanted, to save me, some colossal and powerful love such as I had never known before. "That train's coming in now, sir," said the ticket collector.

The roar of the unseen train reached a crescendo and then died to a rattle and its nose became visible at the near end of the platform. People began to materialise very rapidly at the barrier, and I concentrated on my, as it now seemed impossible, task of recognising the person I was to meet. Several middle-aged women passed by with strained preoccupied faces and rapidly vanished. Everyone was hurrying and everyone looked ill. It was the Inferno indeed. I began to cough. Dr Klein would be looking for her brother, and I supposed I might identify her by her own searchings and hesitations. But I would have to do it quickly, for if she wandered even a few steps away from the barrier she would be lost in the fog.

When Palmer's sister did at last appear I recognised her at once. The face came back to me with a rush, as so often happens when what one cannot picture appears unexpectedly as something well known. It was not a very pleasant face: heavy, perceptibly Jewish, and dour, with just a hint of insolence. The curving lips were combined with a formidable straightness and narrowness of the eyes and mouth. Dr Klein advanced from the barrier and stood still, looking about. She was frowning, and looked haggard in the lurid yellowish light. She wore no hat and drops of foggy moisture stood already upon her short black hair.

I said "Dr Klein?"

She turned towards me and glared. She had clearly no notion who I was.

I said, "I am Martin Lynch-Gibbon. We have met before, though you may have forgotten. Palmer asked me to meet you. May I carry something?"

I noticed that she was hugging a lot of small parcels, which gave her something of the air of a mid-European *hausfrau*. When she spoke I expected a thick German accent, and was surprised by her deep cultured English voice. I had forgotten her voice.

"Where is my brother?" she said.

"He's at home," I said. "He's got a cold. Nothing serious. I'll take you there at once. The car is just outside. Here, let me take this." I relieved her of the largest parcel.

As she handed it over Dr Klein gave me a keen look. Her narrow dark eyes, which seemed in the strange light to be shot with red, had the slightly Oriental appearance peculiar to certain Jewish women. There was something animal-like and repellent in that glistening stare. She said, "This is an unexpected courtesy, Mr Lynch-Gibbon."

It took me a moment to apprehend the scorn in this remark. It took me by surprise, and I was surprised too how much it hurt. It occurred to me that this was the first judgment I had received from an outsider since I had officially taken up my position as a cuckold, and I was irritated to find that, for a second, I minded cutting a poor figure. It certainly might seem an odd moment to be running errands for Palmer. We walked in silence towards the car through a shadowy and slightly hysterical crowd of arriving and departing travellers and those whose trains were lost without trace.

Outside the fog was as thick as ever, and it took me some time to get the car into the street. The baffled headlights glowed, tiny futile balls, in front of a wall of darkness which their beams could not pierce. We began to proceed at a walking pace along Cheapside. In order to say something I asked, "Was it foggy in Cambridge?"

"No, not foggy."

"Your train was very punctual. We expected it to be late."

A grunt was the reply to this. I said to myself, I don't care what this object thinks of me. The fog came steadily over us in waves and it was extremely difficult to see where one was on the road. People had abandoned their cars here and there by the pavement, and there were a great many obstacles to avoid on the left, while on the right the headlights of approaching vehicles only at the last moment materialised out of the thick darkness. To keep straight along the narrow channel in the middle, seeing traffic lights in time, and not starting to swerve crazily as soon as complete obscurity descended was a feat demanding the utmost concentration. I leaned forward over the wheel, my forehead nearly touching the windscreen upon which the wipers were rubbing a mass of wet grime to and fro. I felt with a sort of exhilaration that we were very likely to hit something pretty soon. Enlivened by this, I said suddenly to my companion, "Well, Dr Klein, what do you think of Palmer's latest little exploit?"

She turned abruptly towards me and the hem of her coat fell across my hand on the gear lever. Before she had time to reply a large lorry suddenly appeared a foot away on my right. I must have wandered over the centre of the road. I braked violently and swerved and must have shaved the lorry by an inch. I said "Sorry." She turned back, gathering her coat about her legs. The apology might have covered either thing.

I turned southward down what I took to be Shaftesbury Avenue. The windscreen was becoming opaque and frosted; I wound down the window on my side and the cold choking air came in. My nose was beginning to drop moisture. I said to her, "Would you mind opening your window and keeping a look out on that side?" She opened the window in silence and we proceeded thus for a while with our heads hanging out on opposite sides. Honor Klein's body sagged and jolted beside me like a headless sack, and I could feel again the rough material of her coat grazing my hand. Great orange flares at Hyde Park Corner showed us the way into Knightsbridge, and by their light I stole a glance at my companion. I saw only her hunched shoulders; and then, revealed momentarily, the back of her leg, turned and braced, a stout crêpe-soled shoe, and the plump curve of her calf clad in a thick brown and white knitted stocking traversed by a dark seam. I returned my attention to the road. That curving seam reminded me just for an instant that she was a woman.

By the time we reached Pelham Crescent the fog had lifted a little. I opened Palmer's big close-fitting hall door, which is always unlocked, and ushered Dr Klein inside. I felt a bond with her now because of our ordeal. The hall was warm and deeply carpeted and after the vapours outside it smelt sweet, a smell of polished wood and new textiles. Breathing was suddenly a luxury. I paused while she took off her coat, and saw above her head the huge tasselled Samurai sword which Palmer had inconsequently suspended above a little rosewood chiffonier which Antonia and I had once greatly coveted.

I wondered if Palmer and Antonia were indeed here, since

we were much earlier than the time I had predicted. I said in a friendly manner, "Would you like to go upstairs first? I'll go and see if Palmer and Antonia are in the drawing-room. Of course you know your way about."

De Klein gave me her unsmiling stare. She said, "You are very hospitable, Mr Lynch-Gibbon, but I have been in this house before." She marched past me and threw open the drawing-room door.

The drawing-room was full of golden firelight and there was a strong resinous smell of burning logs. The black-shaded lamps had been extinguished and the dark furry wall-paper glowed reddish and soft in the moving light. I saw at once and painfully that Palmer and Antonia were indeed not expecting us. They were sitting side by side in two upright chairs by the fire. Palmer had his arm round my wife and their faces, turned tenderly full towards each other were seen clearly in profile, each outlined with a pencil of gold. They seemed in that momentary vision of them like deities upon an Indian freize, enthroned, inhumanly beautiful, a pair of sovereigns, distant and serene. They turned towards us, startled but not yet risen, still gracious in their arrested communion. I came up beside Honor Klein.

Something strange happened in that instant. As I turned to look at her she seemed transfigured. Divested of her shape-less coat she seemed taller and more dignified. But it was her expression that struck me. She stood there in the doorway, her gaze fixed upon the golden pair by the fire, her head thrown back, her face exceedingly pale; and she appeared to me for a second like some insolent and powerful captain, returning booted and spurred from a field of triumph, the dust of battle yet upon him, confronting the sovereign powers whom he was now ready if need be to bend to his will.

The impression was momentary. Antonia leapt up and came forward with cries of welcome. Palmer began hastily turning on the lamps. Honor Klein gave her attention to Antonia, answering her questions about the journey and about the fog in a slow way which seemed at last, in its very laboriousness, a little Germanic.

✳ *Chapter Nine* ✳

I HAD an infernal headache. I had left them early, declining a pressing invitation to dinner, and then had stayed up half the night drinking whisky, and I still felt, as I prepared to leave the office, rather sick and giddy. Last night, strangely enough, I had not felt too dejected; but this, I reasoned out, was because of a particular illusion which had been fostered by the whisky, an illusion to the effect that I was shortly going to *do* something remarkable which would miraculously alter the situation. It was unclear what this remarkable action would be; but as the night proceeded I more and more sensed its magnificent veiled presence. I had not, it seemed, after all been cheated of my moment of power.

Today, however, I could see only too clearly the emptiness of this dream which was but the hollow correlate of my rôle of total victim. There was nothing I could do; nothing, that is, except act out with dignity my appointed task of being rational and charitable: a task whose charms, never many, were likely to diminish as my charitableness and rationality came to be, by all concerned, increasingly taken for granted. More precisely, there was nothing to be done in the near future except to make sensible arrangements with Antonia about the furniture, write a number of letters about the Lowndes Square flat, and see my solicitor about the divorce proceedings: that, and see Georgie.

I was sorry that I had made myself so drunk last night, not only because of the hideous depression of the hangover, but because I felt it would make me stupid in dealing with Georgie. I still had mixed feelings about seeing her, and indeed my opposite wishes had both increased in intensity. On the one hand I felt more than ever absorbed into the idea of Antonia. I wanted to think about her all the time, although this activity was entirely painful. In an obsessed way, what I most desired was to be talking over 'the situation' with Antonia or Palmer, and if either of them had had the time to indulge me that is what I would have been continually doing. On the other hand, the image of Georgie, moved by some pure power of its own, was active within me, and made in my tormented thoughts a cool and even authoritative place for itself. Thither I did feel drawn. Georgie's robust cheerfulness, her good sense, her lucid toughness were perhaps just what I required to pull me out of the region of fantasy which I was increasingly inhabiting and return me to the real world. Yet could I, as things were, rely on Georgie to be cheerful and lucid? What demands might she not now, especially finding me in this weakened state, make upon me? I unutterably wanted some simplicity of consolation. But Georgie too was a person capable of being in torment.

I locked up my desk and put into my brief-case the list of clients whom I had promised to visit in January and the draft of my chapter on the tactics of Gustavus Adolphus at the battle of Leutzen. I had made arrangements so as not to have to come to the office again for a little while. The clients would receive a note to the effect that Mr Mytten, my young assistant, would visit them instead, as I was indisposed. Mytten was at present still in Bordeaux, where it was dangerous to send him since he prolonged his visits so unconscionably, conducting some negotiations with a small house with which we had newly begun to do some business. Mytten was a Roman Catholic, a sybarite and an ass, but he was loyal and a decent judge of wine, and went down splendidly with my more snobbish clientele. I could trust him with the visiting, though not of course with the tasting, and I noted that my next essential engagement was to taste hock, of which we still handled a little, on January 30th. Of course I always politely consulted Mytten and very occasionally listened to his advice on what to buy, but a director of a small wine firm tends to become an omnipotent and jealous deity, and it was on my palate alone that the firm of Lynch-Gibbon depended; and as I had no paternal feelings towards Mytten and did not believe that I could train him to be a second me, the little firm would doubtless perish with me, and the particular piece of reality represented by the discerning taste which my father had so carefully trained and fostered in his son would vanish away forever.

Until the truant Mytten's return my two excellent secretaries, Miss Hernshaw and Miss Seelhaft, could get on perfectly well on their own. I prized these girls exceedingly as they could write accurate and even witty business letters in French and German, and by now knew the business very well indeed, though, quaintly, they had no understanding of wine and praised anything that was offered to them. They had been with me for some years now and I had been very worried in case one or other of them should take it into her head to get married, until the day when I realised, through some imperceptible but cumulative gathering of impressions, that they were a happy and well-suited Lesbian couple.

Today I had, with each of them separately, gone through the painful business of telling them about my divorce: I was made aware that they already knew. So gleefully fast does bad news travel. They stood now by the door waiting without visible impatience to see the last of me. Their faces and attitudes expressed their respective modes of sympathy: tall fair

Miss Hernshaw, long vainly courted by the imperceptive Mytten, swaying moist-eyed and ready to hold my hand, short dark Miss Seelhaft, frowning with concern as she polished her spectacles, darting me glances of brisk commiseration. I left them at last to the *débris* of the Christmas orders and the joys of each other's company and drove my car to Pelham Crescent.

Antonia was wearing a brown cashmere pullover and a string of pearls, neither of which I had seen before. She had never used to buy so much as a handkerchief without consulting me. I noticed too, half relieved, that she was in a state of restless irritation and in no mood to ply me with her tenderness. She jumped up when she saw me and said, "Really, I think she might have waited a bit before dismantling the house!"

"Who?"

"Honor Klein."

I recalled this lady's existence. "I suppose she's taking her own stuff away?"

"Darling, shut the door," said Antonia. "I feel haunted. I suppose she has a right to her own things, but really, when she appeared here this morning it was like being hit by a tornado. Did you see all the junk piled up in the hall?"

"Appeared this morning? Isn't she staying here?"

"No. That was another thing, and after I'd spent ages getting her room ready. She decided last night she wanted to stay in a hotel in Bloomsbury to be near the British Museum or something, and poor Anderson had to take her away in a taxi and he's not at *all* well, and he took ages getting back in the fog."

"How is Palmer?"

"His temperature's still up. It was ninety-nine this morning. I *do* think she's inconsiderate. All the same, I like her."

I laughed at the determined way Antonia said this. "You have to. She's Palmer's sister. I confess, I don't feel myself obliged in this respect!"

"About the furniture, darling," said Antonia, "may we do it tomorrow afternoon? Anderson and I are just off to Marlow. We thought we'd stay at the Compleat Angler, just for the night. It's such a nice warm hotel. Poor Anderson is *so* over-tired, I thought the little change would do him good, and we both hate seeing Honor mauling the house. I'm terribly sorry not to be able to ask you to lunch, but we're having it early in rather a rush and leaving immediately after."

I had introduced Antonia to the Compleat Angler. It had been one of our haunts in the early days of our marriage. "I couldn't anyway," I said. "I'm just leaving town myself. But I'll be back early tomorrow. See you at Hereford Square any time after three."

I told this lie instinctively, as a rejoinder to Antonia's air of somewhat patronising solicitude; and I had the satisfaction of seeing her inhibit her impulse to ask me where I was going. She had, after all, surrendered certain rights. The thread was not broken, but without our notice and without our will the gulf had inevitably grown wider. She sighed; and I took my leave before she could discover the words with which to draw me gently once more towards her.

I closed the drawing-room door upon Antonia and almost fell over Honor Klein, who was half carrying half dragging a large box of books across the hall.

I said, "May I help you?" and together we hauled the box into the big front room which Palmer always called the Library, although it contained only one small bookcase. The room was in disorder now, piled up with tea chests containing books, papers and photographs. A number of pictures were stacked against the wall, including the series of Japanese prints from the study. I noticed too, half hidden by a heap of letters, a framed photograph of what was obviously Palmer as a boy of sixteen. In the dining-room opposite I saw through the door the table laid for lunch and an open bottle of Lynch-Gibbon claret. Only two places were laid.

"Thank you," said Honor Klein. "Now would you mind helping me stack these boxes on top of each other? I shall need the space."

When we had finished this and I wished to take my leave, but could think of no suitable formula, I bowed rather awkwardly and was about to withdraw when she said, "Yesterday you asked me what I thought of my brother's exploit. May I ask what *you* think of it?"

This took me greatly by surprise and I hesitated for words. I was at once aware that I must be very careful what I said to Honor Klein.

She went on, "Do you think they are doing the right thing?"

"Do you mean morally?"

"No, not *morally*," she said almost with scorn. "I mean for their life." She contrived to give the word a metaphysical ring.

I said, "Yes, I do think they are doing the right thing." There was something hideously improper in discussing Antonia's business with this woman. Yet I found suddenly that I wanted to.

"Do you mind if I close the door," she said. She stood with her back to it staring at me with a concentrated calculating expression. She was wearing a dark green coat and skirt which had once had some pretension to smartness and she looked rather less dumpy than she had seemed at the station. Her blunt laced shoes had been polished since yesterday. Her short straight oily hair, a lustrous black, sat like a cropped wig about her pale rather waxen Jewish face. Her narrow eyes were like two black chips.

She said, "I wonder if you realise how much your soft behaviour dismays them?"

I was surprised again. "You are wrong," I said. I added, "In any case I am powerless. If I choose to be civilised it is my own affair." I glared back at her. All the same, there was something refreshing, even exhilarating, even liberating, after so much of the tender and the polite, after Antonia and Palmer's masterly 'wrapping', about this direct talk.

"Civilised!" she said it again with scorn. "As you must know perfectly well, you could get your wife back if you wanted her even now. I don't say that you should have beaten her and kicked my brother; but there was no need to press them so into each other's arms. They are both persons with a great capacity for self-deception. They have enchanted themselves into a belief in this match. But they are both crammed with misgivings. They want to be let off the final decision. They look to you for help. Can you not see that?"

I was amazed. I said, "No, frankly I can't see it. I can best help them by being gentle and I propose to go on being gentle. I am after all in a position to know the truth about both of them." I spoke firmly, but I was very upset by what she had said, and confused, and unsure whether I ought not to be offended. I took a step forward to indicate that I wished to go. But she stood her ground, throwing her head back against the door and looking up at me.

"Truth has been lost long ago in this situation," she said. "In such matters you cannot have both truth and what you call civilisation. You are a violent man, Mr Lynch-Gibbon. You cannot get away with this intimacy with your wife's seducer."

"I am not one of your primitive savages, Dr Klein," I said, "and I do not believe in vendettas." With that I recalled how she herself had been called primitive. Strained back against the door, close to me now, she seemed something black and untouchable.

"You cannot cheat the dark gods, Mr Lynch-Gibbon," she said softly. "Perhaps it is no business of mine if you choose to be powerless and to abandon your wife. But everything in this life has to be paid for, and love too has to be paid for. Why does my brother, who is rich, always charge high fees even to poor patients? Because without payment he could not speak to their condition. Without payment they would be wretched. They would be captives. I believe you love my brother. But you do him no good by letting him off. He wants, he needs, your harshness, your criticism, even your violence. By gentleness you only spare yourself and prolong this enchantment of untruth which they have woven about themselves and about you too. Sooner or later you will have to become a centaur and kick your way out."

I listened to her with great attention. I wanted to understand exactly what she meant. "You said earlier that you thought they both wanted to back out," I said, "but what you say now could imply that if I were violent it might make them happier with each other."

Honor Klein gave a tired gesture. The tension left her body

and she drooped, moving a little away from the door. "Could imply, could imply!" she said. "Where logic breaks down anything can imply anything. While you are all so soft nothing can be clear. It seems to me now that you do not really want your wife back after all. And as I am surprised that you have not yet told me, it is nothing to do with me, your side of the matter. If you want to let them steal your mind and organise you as if you were an infant I suppose that is your affair. All I say is that only lies and evil come from letting people off."

I looked at her harsh and melancholy profile. I said, "I don't imagine that you ever let people off, do you, Dr Klein?"

She turned towards me and suddenly smiled, revealing strong white teeth, her eyes narrowing further to two black luminous slits. She said, "With me people pay as they earn. You have been patient. Good-morning, Mr Lynch-Gibbon." She opened the door.

✳ *Chapter Ten* ✳

"**N**OW you're in a fix, aren't you, you old double-dealer?" said Georgie.

I could have wept with relief. I loved her so much at that moment that I nearly knelt down then and there and proposed. I kissed her hands humbly. "Yes, I am in a fix," I said, "but you'll be kind to me, won't you? You'll let me off?"

"I love you, Martin," said Georgie. "You never seem to get this simple point into your old head."

"And you don't mind if we keep our thing secret still? I just can't cope otherwise, my darling."

"I don't understand why," said Georgie. "But if you want to. For myself, I'd like to publish our liaison in *The Times*!"

"It would hurt Antonia so if she knew," I said. "And the least I can do is make things easy for her. The way we've managed it all is really a remarkable achievement. Without bitterness, I mean. I don't want to add any more strains at present."

"This 'without bitterness' idea just seems to me rather obscene," said Georgie. "And I suspect you of wanting to play the virtuous aggrieved husband so as to keep Palmer and Antonia in your power. But perhaps I underrate your goodness!"

"In my power!" I said. "I'm in *their* power, it seems. No, it's all much simpler. I just want to finish the thing off perfectly without any more complications. If Antonia *knew*, she'd want long intimate talks about it. She'd want to *understand*. And I couldn't bear that. Don't you see, little imbecile?"

"You speak of 'the thing' as if it were a work of art," said Georgie. "Sometimes I think you're a very odd fish, Martin. However, I *do* see, about the intimate talks. Promise you'll never have an intimate talk about me with Antonia?"

"I promise, my darling, I promise!"

"Anyhow, don't worry," said Georgie. "You don't have to *do* anything special, here I mean. It's only me."

"Thank God it's only you," I said, "and thank God *for* you, Georgie. You save my sanity. I knew you would."

"Well now stop looking so *tall*," said Georgie. She stroked down the tip of her nose. The action and the words were beautifully familiar. I blessed her in my heart and sat down at her feet.

Georgie was sitting back in the shabby green armchair in her lodgings. A cold staring afternoon light revealed the room, the humpy half-made bed, the bowl of cigarette ends, the table strewn with opened letters and dirty glasses and half-eaten biscuits and books on economics. She was wearing very tight oatmeal-coloured trousers and a white shirt, and had her hair in a chaotic bun. Her face was pale, and in the creamy transparent pallor of her skin the rose of her cheek glowed faint and deep. A few golden freckles, revealed in the cold light, were scattered on the bridge of her uptilted nose, which she was still absently mauling. Her large blue-grey eyes, lucid with intelligence and honesty, held my gaze steadily. She was wearing no make-up. Yet even as I adored her, looking to see in those eyes which held nothing but good will, beyond the granular iris some more distant shapes of my destiny, I realised that I did not desire her.

I was intensely grateful to her. It now seemed absurd to imagine that, being herself, she could have reacted otherwise, less humanely, with less sheer sense and kindness. I must have been in some irrational state of fear to have been so nervous about Georgie's reactions. I had feared some persecution of her love, the exaction now of pledges half given. But she was all gentleness and filled with so genuine a concern to save me here and now from distress and anxiety; and as I thanked her from my heart I reflected a little guiltily that after all there was nothing very much that Georgie could do to me. Her power was limited. Here at least I was free.

Because of something craven and disloyal in these thoughts, and because of a strange sense of guilt because I did not at that moment desire her, I wished to do after all something significant which would please her. I said suddenly, "Georgie, I want to take you to Hereford Square."

Georgie sat up straight and put her hands on my shoulders. She studied me, grave and intent. "Surely that is not wise."

"If you're thinking of Antonia, she's gone to the country with Palmer. There's not the slightest chance of her turning up."

"It's not exactly that," said Georgie. "Do you really want to see me there, so soon?"

We looked at each other, trying to guess at thoughts.

Georgie added, "Don't misunderstand me, Martin." She meant that her words held no implied expectation of ever living at Hereford Square.

"I don't misunderstand you," I said. "You mean it may upset me to see you there. On the contrary. It will be good and liberating and somehow natural. It will break down some of the doubleness."

"You don't think you will just feel resentment?" said Georgie. "I can see that all this has made you fall in love again with Antonia."

"You're a clever girl," I said. "But no, no resentment. I want to *give* you something, Georgie. I want to *give* you that."

"You want to do something hostile to Antonia."

"No, no, no!" I said. "I'm not in *that* sort of emotional state about Antonia. I just want to break an obsession. I want you to know that Hereford Square really exists." Georgie had never questioned me about my home, and I knew how carefully she had averted her thoughts from all my life away from her.

"*Yes*," said Georgie softly. She stroked my nose now. "I do want to know that it exists. But not yet, Martin. I'm frightened. You will see me there as an intruder. As for breaking down the doubleness, we can't really do that until we stop telling lies."

I didn't want this argument. I said, "It will symbolise breaking down the doubleness. I want to see you there, Georgie. It will do something very important for me to see you there."

"It's odd," said Georgie. "I'm not usually superstitious. But I feel that something disastrous will happen if we go to Hereford Square."

"You make me all the more determined to take you, primitive child," I said. "I tell you, it will *help* me. I need air, Georgie. I need to recover a sense of freedom. Seeing you there will open up a new world." Even as I spoke I realised more fully that what I had thought of as a somewhat bizarre treat for Georgie was in fact, as she had immediately seen, a move of great importance: not something I would give her, but something she would do for me, would do *to* me; and I conjectured, with a thrill both of joy and of fear, that what I had just said might indeed prove true.

The drawing-room seemed mysteriously untouched since the evening of Antonia's declaration, as if a drowsy spell had been put on it at that moment. The Christmas decorations and the cards were still there, covered now with the dust which, since the departure of the daily help whom, contrary to Antonia's wishes, I had turned away, had rained down quietly, a grey sleeping-powder, to dull the glow everywhere. I noticed that the silver was tarnished. Outside the French windows, in the yellowish overcast afternoon, the great magnolia *grandiflora* which occupied most of the small garden drooped, its leaves still pinched and edged by last night's frost. The room felt damp and very cold, and we kept our coats on. My copy of Napier was still on the sofa.

Georgie came in slowly. I could see in her the counterpart of my own emotion. She stared at me, her lips parted, frowning, as if to see whether the power of the room had given me a different face. Then she looked very carefully around, nodding her head as she did so, seeming to count the objects. I was absorbed in watching her, and in the spreading throughout my whole being of the extraordinary experience of seeing her there. I had spoken of 'breaking down the doubleness'. With what a rush it *was* being broken down, and what a vista of open spaces, I felt in those instants, were not now being opened to my astounded gaze. My instinct in bringing Georgie here, and at once, had been a sound one: and what I most apprehended, in the mixture of feelings that possessed me, was the very possibility of loving Georgie more, of loving her better.

I felt this: but felt it in the midst of a considerable and more immediate pain at seeing, in the circumstances of a sort of treachery, the well-loved room again. To lose somebody is to lose not only their person but all those modes and manifestations into which their person has flowed outwards; so that in losing a beloved one may find so many things, pictures, poems, melodies, places lost too: Dante, Avignon, a song of Shakespeare's, the Cornish sea. The room *was* Antonia. It breathed the rich emphasis of her personality. The rose smell was there, barely perceptible, waiting in vain to be warmed to a full fragrance by the blaze of a wood fire. All these things were her, the silky rugs, the plump cushions, especially the mantelpiece, her little shrine: the Meissen cockatoos, the Italian silver cup, the Waterford glass, the snuff box, which I had given her when we were engaged, with the legend: *Friendship without Interest and Love without Deceit.* It was a new and fierce pain to look on all this and see it as something mortal, indeed as something already perished, disintegrated, meaningless and waiting to be taken away. Tomorrow Antonia and I would be dividing up these objects as so much dreary loot, to be stored away in cupboards like guilty secrets or desecrated by the labels of the auctioneer. I touched the Waterford glass with my finger: and in its ring I heard the echo of a voice saying *You do not really want your wife back after all.* I answered the voice in my heart: a bond of this kind is deeper and stronger than wanting or not wanting. Wherever I am in the world and whenever I am I shall always be Antonia.

I sat down on the sofa. Georgie turned from looking out of the window and came towards me. The untidy bundle of her hair was contained in the upturned collar of her coat and she kept her hands deep in her pockets as for some time she stared down at me with a look of almost hostile tenderness. She said at last, "Do you hate seeing me here?"

I said, "No. I can't tell you how entirely good for me it is to see you here. But there's such pain too."

"I know," she said, her voice deep, weighted with understanding. "Don't be angry with me because of the pain."

"I am far from that. I feel more like kissing your feet. You've put up with so much from me." As I spoke these words I felt myself, obscurely yet positively, upon the road towards making Georgie my wife. I had told her once that secrecy was essential to our love. Seeing her in this room, and thus joining the two halves of my life, seemed to prove me wrong and her right. The lies should indeed be done away with: and so far from breaking the texture of my love for Georgie this would set it free to be something stronger and purer than anything I had yet known. Gratitude to her, gratitude for her loyalty, her reason, her sheer kindness to me, possessed my heart.

"Ah, you're hating me!" said Georgie. She was still staring down at me intently, as if to wrest the thoughts out of my head.

"If you only knew how wrong you are!" I said. I gave her back a steady unsmiling stare, and felt pleasure at the idea of surprising her, rewarding her, with my better love. God knows, she deserved it.

I got up and began to collect the Christmas cards from the piano. Beneath them it was thick with dust. The business of clearing up had begun.

"It's so strange and moving to be here!" said Georgie. She had begun to roam about the room again. "I can't think what it's like. It's like possessing you retrospectively. No, not quite. But you've no idea how completely I assumed that I would never see this place. I *will* now come to believe, and this will be better, so much better, that in the past, all that time that you were away from me, you really went on existing. It was too painful to believe at the time. But I knew that not to believe it was a failure of love. Now, with your help, I can put that right. I shall love you better, much better, Martin, in the future.

She came to a standstill in front of me. I was deeply affected by the way in which her words echoed my thought. I sought for, but could not yet find, some eloquence by which to draw her closer in a preliminary exchange of vows.

I threw the pile of Christmas cards on the floor and led Georgie with me towards the mantelpiece. I said, "I want you to *touch* everything. I want you to *touch* all these things."

She hesitated. "It would be sacrilege. I should suffer for it!"

"No," I said. "It will be good sacrilege. You bring me closer to reality. You have always done that for me."

I took her hand and laid it on the Meissen cockatoo. We held each other's eyes. Georgie drew her hand back. Then after a moment she rapidly touched all the other objects on the mantelpiece. I took her hand again. It was marked with dust. I kissed it in the palm and raised my eyes to her again. I could see she was on the point of tears. I began to take her in my arms.

At that moment I heard a sound which made my heart violent with fear even before my mind had understood it. It was the familiar sound of a key turning in the front door. Georgie heard it too and her eyes became wide and hard. We stood thus for a second, paralysed. Then I pulled myself roughly out of the embrace.

It could only be Antonia. She had changed her mind about going to the country, and had decided to come and look the furniture over before our interview tomorrow. In another moment she would come straight into the drawing-room and find me with Georgie. I could not bear it.

I acted quickly. I took Georgie's wrist and pulled her over

to the French windows. I opened them and then drew her into the garden and round a little to the side of the house so that we should be invisible from the room. I whispered to her, "Go out of that little gate and you can get back into the square. Then go straight home and I'll join you."

"No!" said Georgie, speaking softly but not whispering, "No!"

Panic possessed me. I had to get her away. I felt horror and nausea at the idea of an encounter between Antonia and Georgie at Hereford Square: there was something here horrible, almost obscene. I put all my will into my voice. "Go at once, damn you."

"I don't want to," said Georgie, in the same tone. She glared at me. Our heads were close together. "Let me meet your wife now. I won't be made to run away!"

"*Do as I tell you*," I said. I took her arm and applied a pressure until she winced.

She pulled her arm away and turned. "I haven't any money."

I gave her a pound quickly from my wallet, made a violent gesture of dismissal, and went back into the drawing-room. To my relief the room was still empty. I closed the doors quietly. I did not look back to the garden.

I waited a moment. There was a profound silence. What could Antonia be doing? I wondered if I perhaps had been mistaken after all. I walked across the room and out into the hall. Honor Klein was standing just inside the door.

The appearance, so unexpectedly, of this absolutely im-mobile figure had something of the uncanny, and she had for a moment the snapshot presence of a ghost. We stared at each other. She was hunched up inside her overcoat and her troll-like face was still moist with the raw air outside. She did not smile or speak, but regarded me with a steady tense meditative gaze. I felt, at seeing her, relief mingled with a profound dismay and a certain deep unreasoning fear. I felt her as dangerous. I said, "May I help you?"

She threw her head back, pulling her coat open at the neck. "You mean, Mr Lynch-Gibbon, why the hell am I here."

"Precisely," I said. I never seemed destined to achieve politeness with Palmer's sister.

She said, "The explanation is this. Your wife told me that you would be away today. I needed to have a certain key to a bureau. This key is in my brother's wallet. This wallet he lent to your wife for the paying of some bill. She put it into a basket which she accidentally left here when she called in yesterday. As my need was urgent, and as you and she were both to be away, she lent me your front door key. So here I am. And there is the basket."

She indicated a basket standing under the hall table. On the hall table I saw Georgie's handbag and two books on economics. I picked up the basket and handed it to her.

"Thank you," she said. "I am sorry I disturbed you." Her gaze seemed to pass slowly over Georgie's bag.

"Not at all," I said. I experienced a sudden fierce desire to detain her. I wanted to know what she was thinking. But I could not find the words. I felt lame and foolish before her. She too seemed for a moment to want to stay. But as neither of us could find the means to prolong the situation she turned about and I opened the door. As she passed me I bowed.

I went back into the drawing-room. The garden was empty. I slipped the copy of Napier into my pocket. I found I was breathless. I leaned on the mantelpiece and began to stroke one of the cockatoos. The gritty dust came off on my hand.

✳ *Chapter Eleven* ✳

THE next thing was that Georgie was not at her place. I had gone straight round there by car after I had recovered my wits, and banged on the door, but there seemed to be no one in. I then went to her room at the School, but she was not there and had not been there. I rushed back to her lodgings. There was still no reply. I went back to the School again and wasted time asking people. I felt both upset and offended, and after a while I returned to Hereford Square and spent the rest of the evening making a list of furniture, and telephoning Georgie, without result, at intervals. I did not seriously think she had been kidnapped or run over. I imagined that she must have been affronted by the way in which I pushed her off. I hated this idea; but felt confident of bringing her round fairly easily. It was not a pleasant evening, however. I drank a great deal of whisky, and went to bed.

I woke late the next day to hear the phone ringing. How well one sleeps when one is in grief. It was not Georgie. It was Antonia. She said she was glad to find me back, and asked if I would come to Pelham Crescent before lunch instead of her coming to Hereford Square in the afternoon. I agreed to this. Since I had made a fairly complete list of our belongings the matter could be as well discussed there as here. I telephoned Georgie's number again and got no reply. I decided I would call on Antonia, leave the furniture list with her, go to Georgie's, and come back to Antonia later on. I felt, still, hurt and cross rather than seriously anxious at Georgie's behaviour.

After I had washed and shaved I telephoned Georgie again,

and tried the School, still with no results. When I was about to leave the phone rang again, but it was only Alexander to say that he and Rosemary were in London. He had come up to speak at a debate at the Institute of Contemporary Arts, and had stayed last night at Rosemary's flat. He wanted to know when he could see me. I told him I would ring him back.

It was a sunny morning, the first for a long time, frosty and very cold, but bright and clear with a light which, as it made the white crystals shine upon the leaves in the Hereford Square garden, reminded me of Austria, snow, skis, and old happiness. The painful elation which I had experienced yesterday at seeing Georgie in my house had vanished without trace; I was depressed, cross, weak and terribly on edge. As I entered Palmer's front door I felt a sort of confused craven relief. At least here were people who would be gentle with me.

There was no one in the drawing-room. Then as I heard from Palmer's study the sound of Antonia's voice I knocked on the door. I opened it and went in. Antonia and Palmer were both there. Antonia was dressed in a quilted check housecoat which was new to me. Her hair hung down over her breasts in two plaits in a fashion which I had not seen her use and which disturbed me very much. She was tall, Greek. She was standing at the end of the divan, leaning with one hand on Palmer's desk. Palmer was sitting on the divan facing the door. He was wearing his loosely woven French jacket, a blue shirt and a purple cravat. He looked sleek, clean, agile, young, a little raffish. In the bright sunny light I saw both their eyes fixed on me with concern, with a certain excitement, Antonia's big soft and tawny, Palmer's blue clear and cold. Behind them on the wall was the row of empty marks where the Japanese prints had been.

I realised instantly that something odd had happened. Neither of them greeted me, they simply stared, not smiling, and yet with a certain gentle retaining solicitude. I closed the door. For a wild moment I imagined that they were going to tell me that they had changed their minds about getting married. I took an upright chair from the wall by the door and placed it in the centre of the carpet and sat down on it facing them. "Well, my friends?"

Antonia shook her head and half turned away. I began to feel rather alarmed.

Palmer said, "Shall we tell him?"

Antonia, without looking at me, said, "Yes, of course."

Palmer gave me his level cold stare. He said, "Martin, we have found out about Georgie Hands."

This took me so terribly off my guard that I instantly covered my face with one hand. I drew it away quickly, to change the gesture of weakness into one of surprise. I felt sick. I said, "I see. How did you learn this?"

Palmer glanced up at Antonia, who had by now turned her back to me. He said after a moment, "We'd rather not tell you just now. Anyway that doesn't matter."

I stared back at Palmer. His limpid expression contrived to be tender and stony at the same time. He sat very straight and square, looking at me across the length of the room.

I said, "What have you found out?"

Palmer again looked back towards Antonia. She spoke over her shoulder. "Everything, Martin. The child, everything." Her voice was rich with emotion.

I wished I could feel anger. I felt simply devastating guilt. I said, "Well, there's no need to make such a fuss about it."

Antonia made an inarticulate sound. Palmer kept me in his

cool stare and shook his head very slightly. There was silence.

I said, "I think I'd better go. I brought a list of furniture for Antonia to look at." I threw the list on the floor beside me and made to rise.

"Wait, Martin," said Palmer, in a voice that made me wait. After a moment, during which he seemed to wait for Antonia to speak, he said, "I'm afraid we can't just leave this thing. Well, use your common sense, Martin, of course we can't. We have to talk about it. We have to react in an honest way. We can't pretend not to mind! Antonia has a right to hear from you on this."

"To hell with Antonia's rights," I said. "Antonia has forfeited her rights."

"Martin," said Antonia, who had not yet turned to face me, "do not be rude and unkind as well."

"I'm sorry I said that," I said. "I'm suffering from shock."

"Antonia is suffering from shock too," said Palmer. "You must be considerate, Martin. We don't want to be unpleasant or censorious. But we must have this thing right out. See?"

"I see," I said. "Well, suppose you go away and let me talk to Antonia."

"I think she would prefer me to be present," said Palmer. "Is that correct, dear?"

"Yes," said Antonia. She was holding her handkerchief to her mouth. She turned about now and sat down on the divan beside Palmer, dabbing her eyes but still not looking at me. Palmer put an arm round her shoulder.

"Look here," I said. "What is there to talk about? You apparently have the facts and I don't deny them. Do we have to have the bloody court-martial as well?"

"You misunderstand us, Martin," said Palmer. "There is

no question of a court-martial. Who are we to be your judges? On the contrary, we should like to help you. But you must realise two things: first, that we both love you very much, and second, that you have deceived us on a matter of very great importance."

"Martin, I can't tell you how it hurts," said Antonia, still in a voice of tears, looking at the floor and twisting the damp handkerchief.

"I'm sorry, my dear," I said.

"Ah, but are you?" said Palmer. "We thought we knew you, Martin. We have just had a surprise. I will not say that we are disillusioned, but I will say that we are distressed. We have, in a sense, to start again. We have lost our grip. We have to see where you are, we have to see *what* you are. We are not trying to blame you, we are trying to help you."

"I don't want your help," I said, "and as for blame, I can do that job myself. I'll talk to Antonia, but not to both of you."

"I'm afraid you must talk to both of us, Martin," said Palmer. "We are both wounded and we are both concerned. For our sake as well as your own you must talk to us, and talk to us frankly."

"How *can* you have told such lies, Martin?" said Antonia. At last she managed to look at me. She had shed her tears and was more controlled now. "I was so *surprised*," she said. "I know I sometimes tell lies myself, but I thought you were so truthful. And I thought you loved me so much." She choked on the last words and put the handkerchief to her face again.

"I did love you so much," I said. "I do love you so much." I could not stand much more of this. "I just loved Georgie too."

"And love her," said Palmer.

"And love her," I said.

"Honestly," said Antonia, "I just can't think how you were capable of it." A rational indignation was saving her from tears.

"Christ, one can love two people," I said. "You ought to know that."

"All right," she said, "all right. And that you should deceive me—well, I don't exactly understand it, but I can imagine it. But when Palmer and I told you about us, that you should not have been honest *then* . . . I can't conceive how you could sit there pretending to be virtuous and let us carry all the guilt. It's not like you, Martin."

"No, indeed, it isn't like you," said Palmer, "yet it must belong to you. Even psycho-analysts get surprises. We were very straight and honest with you. It simply didn't occur to us to deceive you. As Antonia says, you might at least have been truthful then. However, it humbles one. We must just try again to understand you. For understand you we will."

"I can't explain," I said, "though there is an explanation. It doesn't matter." I felt sunk in confusion and guilt. I could not possibly make clear to them the compulsion under which I had treasured the secret of Georgie. Understanding was out of the question; and indeed how passionately, just then, I did not want to be understood.

"But it does matter, Martin," said Palmer. "It matters very much. And we are in no hurry. We can talk about this all day if necessary."

"Well, I can't," I said. "What do you want to know? Georgie's twenty-six. She's a lecturer at L.S.E. She's been my mistress for nearly two years. We had a child and got rid of it. That's the lot."

"Oh, Martin," said Antonia, and she was quite in control

by now, "don't pretend to be a cynic and not to care. It doesn't ring true at all. We know you love this girl and we want to help you. We know you haven't it in you to take a mistress without loving her deeply. I confess it was a shock to me to learn this. But I can get over it and I know how to be generous. Of course I'm jealous. It would be impossible not to be. I've already talked all this out with Anderson. But I think I really and truly do want what's best for you. Only you must be more frank and simple with us now. Please."

"Antonia has been very honest with herself and with me," said Palmer. "You know how very much she loves you. She cannot but be shocked, not only by your deceit, but by the very existence of this girl. And it is natural, and indeed proper, that this revelation should arouse her love for you in an active and jealous form. Which is, for all of us, a painful situation. But she has behaved rationally, finely, and you need fear no resentment from either of us. In fact we want, as it were, to give you our blessing. So you see how wrong you were, and how unjust to us!"

"We'll see you through, Martin," said Antonia, who had been nodding her head throughout the previous speech. "Who knows but that this strange tangle may not be for the best in the end for all of us? We'll stand by you and Georgie. This was really what I wanted to say. I'm sorry I seemed so upset and cross. It did distress me terribly that you deceived me. But indeed I do believe that you loved me all the time. So do not be guilty or worried, darling Martin."

"I won't be guilty or worried, I'll be raving mad," I said. "I don't want you to see me through. I want to be left alone by both of you at long last."

"You are mistaken about your wishes," said Palmer. "You don't so easily escape the toils of love. The fact is that this discovery has cast a shadow on us all, and we must all work to remove that shadow."

"You mean I must be tidied up so that you and Antonia can go ahead?"

"You must be, as you put it, tidied up for your own sake also," said Palmer. "A lot of lying *must* be compensated for by a lot of truth-telling. I'm sure Georgie will agree with us. And then we shall be much happier, all four of us."

"You were on about all three of us some time ago," I said. "Now it's all four. Why do you leave your sister out? Let's have a quintet."

"Come," said Palmer a little stiffly, "be serious, Martin. You must take some responsibility for what you've done. As I said, we've got to understand you. And we shall understand you a good deal better after we've met Georgie."

"Over my dead body."

"You will have to be reasonable in the end," said Palmer. "After all, you are hardly in a position of strength. So you may as well be reasonable now. Antonia has only just heard of this young woman. It is very natural that she should wish to meet her. And you should both be thankful that she will do so in no spirit of anger."

"I'm told she is beautiful and clever," said Antonia, "and young: which is a lovely thing for you, Martin. Can you not see that I mean what I say? Can you not be generous enough to receive the gift of my goodwill, my blessing?"

"I tell you I shall go mad," I said. "You talk as if you were arranging my marriage. After all, for Christ's sake, you're not my parents!"

Palmer smiled his broad white American smile and drew Antonia closer to him.

❊ *Chapter Twelve* ❊

I CLOSED the door behind me. I said to Georgie, "Antonia knows. How did she find out?"

When I escaped from Palmer and Antonia I went straight round to Covent Garden. But I did not call on Georgie at once. I spent twenty minutes sitting in a pub and trying to collect myself. I was shivering all over and found it very difficult to think. What I chiefly felt, and this seemed strange, was guilt, overwhelming annihilating guilt. Yet there was no rational reason why Antonia and Palmer's discovery of the fact should make me feel guilt which the fact itself had not made me feel. I experienced too an obscure dismay at the extent to which, in a moment, those two seemed to have established over me a moral dictatorship even more complete than that which they had enjoyed before. It appeared to me that just this was what they wanted; and looking back on the scene, although it was true that Antonia *had* been upset and felt genuine pain, yet there had been a sort of excitement in her manner too. To have me presented as so easy, so defence-less, a quarry to a mingled power of censure and of love excited her, gave her a sort of sexual thrill.

When I turned my thoughts to Georgie I was no better off. A veil of guilt seemed to divide me from her, and with it a sense that the blow of discovery had at least crippled, if not killed, my love for her. An opening of that love to the world would strengthen and purify it, I had thought: and this might indeed have been so had I been able to make the revelation in my own time and in my own way, with dignity and a serene face. But to be had up like that by Palmer and Antonia, to have the thing thrust at me as a crime, and at the same time stroked and cosseted in their benevolent imagination, was to make it appear to me merely obscene: and it occurred to me to wonder inconclusively whether this too were not precisely in their intention. What had happened was just what I had wanted not to happen. I had been right, not Georgie. The effect of being so accused was to call up a positive fountain of guilt which covered now with its nauseating tar my whole love for Georgie which had seemed so simple and so clean. Yet I knew that this was deeply unfair to her; and I told myself that my mood would change.

I wondered too how it had all come out; and the fantastic idea came to me that Georgie herself had betrayed us. Yet after a while I could not believe this. I could not see her being so disloyal, nor could I see her carrying out an action which required, which must require, so much of the histrionic. The thing might have come out in hundreds of ways. Since Antonia's own revelation I had become careless. Something, a letter perhaps, must have been found. I finished my drink and mounted Georgie's stairs. At least it was a sort of going home.

"Well," I said, "how did she find out? Do you happen to know?" I found myself, on confronting Georgie, cold and almost angry with her. How angry I was with myself did not bear contemplating.

Georgie was wearing an old skirt and a shapeless jersey. She looked as if she had been up all night. She stared at me gloomily, scratching her nose, and then cleared a space in the mess on the table, pushing the books and papers into a dusty heap. The room was both cold and stuffy. She sat on the table. She said, "I expect Honor Klein told her."

This was so unexpected I gaped at her and then sat down

in the armchair as if I'd been pushed over. "However did *she* know?" I asked.

"I told her," said Georgie. She sat there gravely, very pale and dignified, one black-stockinged leg curled under her. She adjusted her skirt and returned my gaze with a face of iron.

"I see," I said. I was blushing and breathless with anger and shock. After a moment, when I felt able to speak again, I said, "As you may imagine, I am utterly astonished. Would you mind explaining, please?"

"After you pushed me out into the garden," said Georgie, "I didn't go home. I felt too angry. I'll tell you more about that in a minute. I went to the University Library and tried to read something, but it was no good. Well, then I had a coffee and went home. I felt bloody miserable, and I rang you up, but you weren't there."

"I was out looking for you," I said.

"Anyway," said Georgie, "I'd just put the phone down when the door-bell rang. I thought it was you. Well, it was Honor Klein. She looked pale and as grim as hell. I asked her in and gave her a drink and we made some conversation. Then she suddenly asked me about you."

"Good God," I said, "just like that?"

"Yes," said Georgie. "So I told her."

"You told her everything?"

"Everything."

"Why?"

"Because it was impossible to lie to her," said Georgie. She straightened her leg and massaged her ankle. Then she slithered slowly off the table and hobbled to a cupboard where she found a bottle of gin. There seemed to be no clean glasses. She looked exhausted.

"You're insane," I said, "and what's more you're a treacherous little bitch. You let that woman bully you."

"I was tired of the bloody lies," said Georgie. "And I was so angry with you about what happened in the afternoon. It would have been so much better if you'd let me stay and see Antonia. I simply loathed that whispering and being shoved out the back, as if you'd been caught kissing the housemaid. I *hated* it, Martin." Her voice was harsh and cracked with emotion. She took two used glasses from the mantelpiece.

"It wasn't Antonia," I said. "It was Honor Klein."

"I see, I see," said Georgie slowly. She spilt some gin and began soaking it up with a paper handkerchief. "Then *that* was how she found out. I wondered. I left two books with my name in on the hall table."

"But why should she guess just *this*," I said, "and why should she trouble to follow it up and make you confess?"

"As for guessing just *this*," said Georgie, "anyone might. She probably heard us whispering. Why she should have followed it up beats me."

"You didn't ask her?"

Georgie laughed a dry grunting laugh.

"Of course not! As I told you, she carries too many guns. And anyway after spilling the beans and sitting in silent communion with Honor every time you telephoned I was practically a stretcher case." She added slowly. "It was a relief, all the same."

"And it didn't occur to you to ask her to keep quiet? Well, I suppose you couldn't."

"You suppose rightly," said Georgie. "If you can see me going down on my knees afterwards, asking her not to tell on me, you know me better than I know myself!"

"I simply can't understand you," I said. "You know how important it was to me not to let this be known, especially now. I simply can't cope with Antonia's knowing it. I can't cope with the *way* she knows it. You just don't know what this is like. I'm in torment. And you go and blurt it all out to some bloody stranger just because she was your supervisor at college!"

"Indeed," said Georgie, stammering, her voice beginning to shake, "you *don't* understand me and you've never tried very hard. I put up with things being secret when they had to be, but I loathed it. I suffered all the time, every day, every bloody day. But I offered you this suffering, even gladly, because I loved you. And I never spoke to you about it. Then when it didn't have to be secret, and you still kept on—it made me feel as if you were ashamed of me. It began to poison things. Oh, I don't mean that you should instantly have married me—why should you? But there was no need to keep me so deeply buried. And you *ought* to have told Antonia then. I began to feel I didn't exist. Oh, I love you, I love you entirely! I wish I didn't. But I feel utterly poisoned all the same. I would never have blown the gaff of my own accord. But when Honor Klein came like that it was like a message from the gods. I *couldn't* have told lies then, I would have died of it!"

She was practically in tears. She poured out some gin, jarring the bottle on the edge of the glass, and then slopped some water in after it. As I rose she handed it to me. My own anger had soured into despair.

"Christ, darling," I said, "you don't know what you've done. But it doesn't matter. It's all my bloody fault anyway. I should never have put you in this position at all."

"You're saying you don't love me and you never loved

me," said Georgie, and the tears brimmed over her eyes in a great flood.

"Oh God!" I said. I put the drink down and went to her. She stood stiffly with her hands on the table while I put my arms round her. The tears dripped onto her blue jersey.

"You know perfectly well I love you, little imbecile," I said. "Please be rational now and *help* me. I know I don't make myself clear. It's just that there's something *terrible* for me about those two knowing. They were eating me up before. Now, if they choose to, they can assimilate me entirely. But I can't expect you to understand all this. You'd have to be me. You've got to help me, Georgie." I shook her to and fro until she put a hand on my arm. She took a paper handkerchief for her eyes and poured out some more gin. She drank a little and handed the glass to me.

The familiar ritual steadied us both. I drew her limp warm being against mine. She laid her head on my shoulder. Our bodies, at least, were old friends.

"What is so dreadful about the *way* she knows?" said Georgie. "You see, I *do* want to understand."

"Oh, something to do with the way it's all hideously caught up in intimacy and love. You'd have to see it. It's like the nursery. For instance, she's dying to meet you."

"Is she?" said Georgie, jerking back from me and brushing the moisture from her jersey. "Well, that's fine. I'm dying to meet her."

"Don't be silly, darling," I said. "Don't *you* start."

"When you took me to Hereford Square," said Georgie, "you took me through the looking glass. There's no going back now. I've had enough of having things around that I'm afraid to think of."

"Well, I'm not going to introduce you to Antonia, and that's that."

"Antonia, this is Georgie Hands. Georgie, my wife." I found these incredible words passing my lips. I was able to speak without stammering or choking. No one fainted.

The interview took place in Palmer's drawing-room. The purple velvet curtains were drawn now upon the evening and the dark wallpaper covered with furry black roses, lit by a dancing firelight, surrounded us like a wicked forest. Dark-shaded lamps upon distant tables cast a narrow light upon Palmer's collection of crystals, which emitted here and there a mysterious but significant ray. Antonia stood on the thick black rug by the fire. In front of her on a low mosaic table was the tray of drinks and three glasses. Warned by telephone, she was ready.

Antonia, who had taken more than usual pains with her appearance, was wearing a dark green dress of light Italian wool which I had bought her in Rome once. She wore no jewellery and had her great golden hair done in a plain bun. She stood there, plump, tall, one hip thrown out and one hand upon it turned back at the wrist, an elegant, anxious, tired, older woman, and at that moment, and in the particular quality of her nervousness, to me infinitely familiar and infinitely dear.

Georgie in her shabby brown skirt, blue pullover and black stockings looked like a child. She had, with a defiant deliberation, made no change in her appearance. She wore no make-up. Her hair was plaited and twisted carelessly, a little absurdly even, to the top of her head. She was very pale, and the pallor emphasised the limpid clarity of her complexion.

She bowed a stiff little bow to Antonia, who fluttered, not deciding whether to extend her hand. Both women were breathing quickly.

Antonia said, "Will you have a drink?" Her voice was deep with nervousness. "Do sit down, please." She began to pour out some sherry.

"No, thank you," said Georgie.

"Don't be silly," I said.

No one sat down. Antonia stopped pouring and looked at Georgie with a sad appealing conscious look. Her big tawny eyes were pained. She was very very anxious to please. She said in a tense little voice, "Don't be angry with me."

Georgie shook her head and made a gesture with her hands which seemed to set Antonia's remark aside as being unmentionably inappropriate.

I said, "Well, *I'll* have a drink, Antonia." My terror of a 'scene' was overwhelmed by the dreadful tender pain of seeing them together.

She gave me the glass and poured out two more, placing one for Georgie at the far end of the little table which extended between them. I took my place in the middle facing the fire.

"May I call you Georgie?" said Antonia. "I feel as if I know you already."

"Certainly," said Georgie, "if you want to."

"And will you call me Antonia?"

"I don't know," said Georgie. "Sorry. I don't think I can. But it's of no importance."

"It's of importance to me," said Antonia.

"Oh, break it up!" I said. I could not bear Antonia's tone of tender insistence.

"Martin, *please*." said Antonia. Still looking at Georgie,

she put her hand on my sleeve and left it there. I could feel her trembling. I was penetrated with pity for her.

"Look," said Georgie. The muscles of her nose contracted. "I wanted to see you, since you wanted to see me. I felt it was right, and a matter of taking seriously what one has done. But I doubt if we can really talk to each other."

"Don't dislike me, Georgie," said Antonia. She bent her appealing look upon Georgie, and I could feel her intimate insistent will bent upon the girl. It was almost palpable, like a warm electric fan.

"Why ever should I?" said Georgie. "You are much more likely to dislike me."

I quietly removed my arm from Antonia's pressure.

"Ah, you mustn't feel any guilt!" said Antonia.

"You misunderstand me," said Georgie. "I was just replying to your remark. I wasn't implying anything else. I don't feel guilt. I realise that I may have harmed you. But that is quite another thing."

I could feel Georgie's stiffness. She seemed with it almost a marionette. She was stiff as a piece of wood with her anxiety to be accurate, to be truthful, to be precise, and to express no emotion whatsoever. In the face of Antonia's dewy radiance she was utterly closed and cold.

"Don't be so harsh with me, my child," said Antonia. She was desperate to establish a relationship. She wanted here, to meet her special need, to soothe and calm her, the warm human contact.

"Sorry," said Georgie. "I wish you well. Perhaps you wish me well. It's just that it's difficult to talk."

"I do wish you well, I do!" said Antonia, clutching on to this. "I wish you both so well. I hope you and Martin will be very very happy. Do believe me, this will always be near my heart."

"Leave me out of it, Antonia," I said. I could not bear that she should seem ridiculous to Georgie. A protective love for Antonia overwhelmed me, a desire to carry her away and hide her, to shield her from the cold young stare of a more exacting sincerity.

"Whatever can you mean, leave you out?" said Antonia, laughing a little and fixing her hand again on my sleeve. "How can you, between *us*, be left out, my dear? Isn't he absurd?" She turned with a gay feminine appeal to Georgie again.

"Martin means there's nothing to discuss and some subjects are better not touched on," said Georgie. She was rigid with strain. She kept a wide-eyed level look on Antonia and did not glance in my direction. She was conscious of Antonia's hand.

"But, Georgie, there is *everything* to discuss!" said Antonia.

"Perhaps we'd better go now," I said. "You've clapped eyes on each other, which was what you wanted to do." I put my glass down, releasing myself again from the tender clutch.

"Oh, don't go!" said Antonia with a wail. "I haven't had anything like enough of simply *looking* at Georgie. You must forgive me, child. You mustn't be embarrassed by the way I go on, must she, Martin? I mean well, I really do! Please sit down and drink some of your sherry."

No one sat down and Georgie did not pick up her drink. She turned towards me, wanting another prompting to go. If I was by then afraid that she might pity Antonia her look should have reassured me. She was far too anxious about herself, about being accurate, about preserving, as only the young are ruthless enough at such time to do, the dignity of exact statement. "I think I ought to go," she said. "Will you come with me, Martin, or stay here? I honestly don't mind which you do. It was kind of you to ask me," she said to Antonia. "I am glad to have met you. I think it is a good thing for both of us."

"My dear child, I am so glad too," said Antonia. "You must learn to be patient with me. You *will* learn."

"I doubt if we shall meet again," said Georgie. "But, as I say, I am glad to have seen you. It makes things more honest. I did not enjoy deceiving you. I wish you very well. And now I must really go."

"No, no," cried Antonia, "and don't speak of our not meeting again, why, that would be too cruel! When you are married to Martin we shall often meet. I love Martin still, you know, I do. In some ways I love him better than ever."

"That is nothing to do with me, Mrs Lynch-Gibbon," said Georgie, "and as for my being married to Martin, it seems to me very unlikely that this will ever happen. In any case it is no one's business but our own. I hope I haven't been rude. If I have, I apologise. I must go. Thank you very much for asking me." She bowed again her stiff puppet bow and began to walk away.

While Antonia raised her cry of protest the door opened to admit Palmer. He raised his hands in a gesture of surprised delight, and then spread them wide, advancing on the hesitating Georgie like a father greeting a long-lost child.

"Why, I nearly missed her!" he cried gaily. "A patient delayed me. They are so demanding! Forgive me for being so informal, Georgie Hands. I believe we have a lot of friends in common."

"She knows your sister," I said. I came up behind Georgie, ready to pilot her out. I had had more than enough.

"I saw you at a party once," said Georgie, "but you wouldn't remember me." She held out her hand.

"Then I am the poorer for that!" said Palmer. "Please don't go. Do stay and have another drink. We can at least start to get acquainted." He retained Georgie's hand, which she left woodenly in his grasp while he stood back, extending his arm and looking at her with admiration.

"We must be off," I said.

"Well, Martin," said Palmer, still holding Georgie and turning to me, "you *are* a lucky man! No, I must insist on my rights. Georgie, I forbid you to talk of going yet!"

A sound behind us made us turn. Antonia was holding her handkerchief before her face. She took another deep breath and uttered a long sob.

Palmer released Georgie and I pushed her past him. As he approached Antonia I hustled Georgie on towards the door. Antonia uttered a terrible long trembling wail and then sat down in the chair in a storm of weeping. I led Georgie out, leaving Palmer to use whatever were now the most up-to-date psychological methods for dealing with hysterical women.

✳ *Chapter Thirteen* ✳

I SIMPLY had to see Antonia again. It was with her, as we left Pelham Crescent, that the weight of my love and concern remained. I could no more separate my being from her than if she had been my mother; and the confrontation of the two women had made me feel, perhaps momentarily but with desperate sadness, the concreteness of my bond with her, the abstractness of my bond with Georgie. Yet how much Antonia exasperated me. I felt, every twist and turn of it, Georgie's exasperation, her so fastidious curling up. At the same time I resented this wincing in Georgie, resented even her cautious, scrupulous, after her own fashion dignified, approach to a judgment. I had to depart with Georgie; but I had to return to Antonia.

I took Georgie home in the car. We were both silent, exhausted really. Once inside she offered me supper, and I stayed to eat bread and cheese. Georgie was no cook and I had no heart for cooking anything myself. We ate the bread and cheese, wolfishly and with surly looks, washing it down with whisky and water. I felt I could not bear any display of emotion just then from Georgie; I wanted to get away. She taxed me, as we were finishing our meal, with just this, and I could not find the protestations which would console her. She spared me her tears. But it was in both our minds that she had said "it is unlikely that he will marry me". For her, I think, these words were a barrier between us which she wished me now lovingly and tempestuously to remove. For me they constituted rather a kind of moratorium, a momentary neutral zone where I could, and how very much in my weariness I needed it, absolutely rest. I had not got it in me to produce for Georgie the passionate reassuring speeches which she wanted. Her words had been intended as a provocation. I accepted them gratefully and in silence as a resting place.

Just before I left we achieved a sort of peace together, lying down for a moment beside the gas fire, forehead to forehead and foot to foot. Georgie's so familiar face, close to mine, in repose at last, her big eyes gentle now, her mouth relaxed, resting from my kisses, was a beloved landscape. Without words we gazed and murmured each other into quietness, until it was as if we had talked in detail for a long time, so spiritual a thing is the human face.

I left Georgie taking aspirins and promising to go to bed at once. I did not suggest and she did not demand that I should remain with her. The prospect of a night together, so eagerly grasped in the old days, was now a problem and not a prize. We were both in a state of emotional exhaustion, and what we really needed for the moment was a rest from each other. In addition I required, with anxiety and with eagerness, to see Antonia once more, however briefly, before I went to bed. I drove the car back to Palmer's house.

It was beginning to be foggy again. A yellow sulphurous haze hung about the street lamps of Pelham Crescent imposing its own infernal curfew, and my steps as I crossed the pavement left moist sticky traces. There were no traffic noises here. The place was sunk in the stricken silence of the gathering fog. The great London night contracted about me into a cold brown kernel, where the damp curled and crept, diminishing, and already too opaque to return an echo. I hurried up to the door and stepped quietly into the warm fresh-smelling hall. I had stayed long with Georgie. The time was a little after ten o'clock.

The lights were on in the hall and on the upstairs landing. I listened. There was no sound of voices. I crossed to the drawing-room door and opened it. The fire was burning brightly but there was no one there. I turned the lamps on from the door. The room came into being before me, still, yet tense with its own sinister life. I closed the door behind me and stood there a while. Something of Palmer and Antonia was present, some tall shadow of them, which illicitly and with an almost guilty relish I enjoyed, simply standing in the empty room. I moved towards the fire and realised then that I was a bit drunk. I had had no lunch and precious little supper and I had consumed, with Georgie, a formidable amount of whisky. I sat heavily into an armchair and reflected on how pleasant it was to be alone and not to have to think of ways of justifying myself.

I became aware that I was filled with undirected sexual desire. I wanted somebody. I supposed, after a little while, that it was Antonia that I wanted. I had certainly not wanted Georgie. I had envisaged with a trapped gloom the possibility that she might suggest our going to bed together; I had accepted gratefully her obvious desire to be, for the moment, rid of me. I had not had, for her, the right words, the proper consolations. Later, I knew, I would be able to soothe and delight her with these. Now, however, with a resentment which I knew to be unjust, I was prepared to keep her in suspense and to greet her weary disappointed dismissal with a sigh of relief. No, it was about Antonia, in a sad and confused way, that my imagination now played; and it was evident to me that I had not yet accepted that I had lost her. It was as if recent events represented a mock barrier between us, an element as it were in a flirtation, over and past which I would later sweep to a reunion. I imagined myself, ultimately and safely, at home in her arms.

I shook myself out of these dreams. There were places where my thoughts must not go; and as I then reflected how few places were left where they *could* now go without incurring pain or guilt I decided that I needed some more whisky and recalled that Palmer kept some in the sideboard in the dining-room. Leaving the lights on I crossed the hall. The dining-room door was closed. I opened it and went in.

The room was not dark and my hand hesitated on the electric light switch. Candles were burning still in the silver candlesticks on the long table, making of the room a cave of warm dim luminosity to which my eyes became in a moment accustomed. I stood still, a little surprised, and closed the door behind me. Then I saw that there was someone sitting alone at the far end of the table.

It was Honor Klein. As I saw her the consciousness returned to me, but without being distressing, that I was somewhat tipsy; and I stood there for a moment longer leaning against the door. I could not see her clearly. But I apprehended at once, and it struck me as a trifle strange, that she was not particularly concerned about my arrival. It was like an arrival at the shrine of some remote and self-absorbed deity. She was plunged in thoughts of her own.

I came slowly down the length of the table. I saw as I came that Palmer and Antonia had dined. Again there were the two places set, and the bottle, this time of Lynch-Gibbon Château Malmaison 1953, almost emptied. Two table napkins lay in disarray beside the places and there was a wide scattering of crumbs upon the polished surface beneath which the light of the candles seemed to burn again. As I approached Honor

Klein I saw that without moving her head she was following me with her eyes. It was like the animation of a corpse. I looked down at her with a sort of fastidious surprise and then found that I had sat down beside her.

I said, "Excuse me, I was looking for Palmer's whisky. Where are they anyway?"

"At the opera," said Honor. She spoke in an abstracted tone, as if I had only a small corner of her attention. She stared ahead of her now toward the candles. I wondered for a moment if she was drunk, but decided probably it was only I who was drunk.

"At the opera," I said. It occurred to me as scandalous that Palmer and Antonia, after the scene in which I had taken part in the drawing-room, should have gone out to the opera. Antonia ought to have been waiting for me to come back. I resented this indifference to the tempo of my own drama.

"What's on?" I said.

"*Götterdämmerung.*"

I laughed.

Presently I got up and went to the cupboard to look for whisky. As I passed behind her I saw something lying upon the table. It was the Japanese sword, encased in its scabbard of lacquered wood, which usually hung in the hall. Honor Klein had evidently been continuing her dismantling activities. There was no whisky but I found a bottle of excellent brandy. I returned to the table with the bottle and two glasses. "You'll join me?"

With a sort of effort she gave me her glance. Her face, in which I now apprehended a fugitive resemblance to Palmer, had a slumbrous look which I could not decipher. It might have been sheer weariness, it might have been resignation. She said after a moment, "Thank you, yes, why not." I realised, but without understanding and without curiosity, that somehow, in some way, she was *in extremis*. I poured out the brandy.

We sat in silence for a while. The room was beginning to seem abnormally dark. Perhaps some of the fog had drifted in from outside. One of the candles began to flicker, and its flame foundered sizzling in a sea of melted wax. As I saw it go I felt frightened and then wondered if I had rightly identified the thing which clutched at my heart.

I said to Honor Klein, "You didn't waste much time in having me brought to justice."

She kept her eyes on the candles and smiled very slightly. "Was it unpleasant?"

"I don't know," I said. "I suppose so. Everything is so unpleasant nowadays it's hard to tell." I found I could talk to her with remarkable directness. Our conversations were refreshingly lacking in formality. As I spoke I reached out automatically toward the sword, which lay with the blunt-ended scabbard towards me; but Honor Klein drew it away a little and I left my hand upon the table to fiddle with the bread crumbs.

I wondered if I should ask her why she had made Georgie confess, but found that I could not bring myself to do so. A nervous shrinking which was not exactly dislike made me hesitate to probe the motives of such a being. Therewith some vague yet powerful train of thought led me to say, "I'm a broken reed after all."

I was not sure why I said this, but some subterranean affinity with the thoughts of my companion must have prompted it, for she replied at once, "Yes. It doesn't matter."

We both sighed. My hand moved restlessly upon the table. I began to stare at the sword and to want very much to get hold of it. Honor was holding it in a possessive predatory way, her two hands on the scabbard, like a large animal holding down a small one. She faced the candles looking pale and rather haggard, her eyes screwed up as against a great light, and I tried in vain to detect what it was, other than a certain elusive air of authority, which made her resemble her brother; for the fact was that Palmer was beautiful while she was very nearly ugly. I contemplated her sallow cheek which shone dully like wax, and the black gleaming hair, oily, straight, and brutally short. She was a subject for Goya. Only the curve of her nostril and the curve of her mouth hinted, with a Jewish strength, a possible Jewish refinement. I said, "Is the sword yours?" and as I spoke I put my hand on the end of the scabbard.

She started a little and said, "Yes. It's a Japanese Samurai sword, a very fine one. I used to have a great interest in Japan. I worked there for a time." She drew the sword away again.

"You were with Palmer in Japan?"

"Yes." She spoke as out of a deep dream.

I wanted her to know that I was present. I said, "May I see the sword?"

I thought for a moment that she was going to ignore me. But she turned towards me as if after taking thought. Then she twisted the thing about on the polished surface of the table. I expected her to offer me the hilt, but instead, as I reached for it, she took the hilt in her own hand and with a swift movement drew the sword from the scabbard. At the same time she rose to her feet.

The sword came out with a swishing clattering sound and the disturbed candles flashed for a moment in the blade. She laid the scabbard on the table and let the blade descend more slowly until it lay a long her thigh. Its bright surface showed against the dark material of her dress as with head bowed she gazed down along its slightly curving length.

When she spoke her voice was dry. She might have been in the lecture room. "In Japan these swords are practically religious objects. They are forged not only with great care but with great reverence. And the use of them is not merely an art but a spiritual exercise."

"So I have heard," I said. I moved her chair out of the way so as to see her better and made myself comfortable, crossing one leg over the other. "I am not attracted by the idea of decapitating people as a spiritual exercise."

Somewhere, seeming at first to be inside my head, I heard a small sound. Then I realised it was a very distant peal of church bells; and I brought to mind that it was New Year's eve. Some nearer bells took up the peal. We both listened for a moment in silence. Soon it would be the turn of the year.

Honor let the sword droop towards the floor. She said, "Being a Christian, you connect spirit with love. These people connect it with control, with power."

"What do you connect it with?"

She shrugged her shoulders. "I am a Jew."

"But you believe in the dark gods," I said.

"I believe in people," said Honor Klein. It was a rather unexpected reply.

I said, "You sound rather like a fox saying it believes in geese."

She laughed suddenly, and with that she laid her other hand upon the hilt and drew the sword upward with surprising swiftness to describe a great arc at the level of her head. It made a sound like a whip moving. The point came down within an inch of the arm of my chair and then descended again to the floor. I resisted an impulse to move back. I said, "You can use it?"

"I studied it for several years in Japan, but I never got beyond the beginning."

"Show me something," I said. I wanted to see her moving again.

She said, "I am not a performer," and turned away again toward the table. In the distance the church bells continued their mathematical jargoning.

The remnants of Palmer and Antonia's dinner lay derelict under the falling candles. She drew towards her their two crumpled table napkins and looked at them thoughtfully. Then with one hand she tossed one of the napkins high in the air into the darkness of the high-ceilinged room. As it descended the sword was already moving with immense speed. The two halves of the napkin fluttered to the floor. She threw up the other napkin and decapitated it. I picked up one of the pieces. It was cleanly cut.

As I held it, looking up at her, I suddenly recalled the scene in the drawing-room when I had first seen Honor Klein confronting the other two like a young and ruthless captain. I laid the piece of linen on the table and said, "That was a good trick."

"It was not a *trick*," said Honor. She had been standing before me, still holding the hilt in a two-handed grip, and looking down at one of the severed napkins. I saw that she was breathing deeply. Now she moved her chair back to the table and sat down. For a moment or two she lifted the sword, moving it as if it had become very heavy, and cooled her forehead on the blade, turning her head slowly against it with a caressing motion. Then she laid it down again on the table, still keeping one hand on the hilt. I looked at the corded hilt, long and dark, continuing the gentle sinister backward curve of the blade, the inner casing, which seemed like snake-skin, decorated with silver flowers, appearing through the diamond-shaped slits of the black cordage. Her large pale hand was firmly closed about it. I felt an intense desire to take the sword from her, but something prevented me. I put my hand on the blade, moving it up towards the hilt and feeling the cutting edge. It was hideously sharp. My hand stopped. The blade felt as if it were charged with electricity and I had to let go. No longer now attending to me she moved the sword back and laid it across her knees in the attitude of a patient executioner. I realised that the church bells had become silent and it was the New Year.

✳ *Chapter Fourteen* ✳

ANTONIA rang me up early in the morning. She insisted on my coming over at once, which was why I did not go to see Georgie sooner. When I arrived I found Antonia feverish, excited, very loving. I spent the whole morning with her and stayed to lunch. Palmer kept out of the way. It was a profitable morning and I felt by the end of it more at ease with Antonia than at any time since her original revelation. She certainly worked hard. She made me tell her the whole story of my relations with Georgie in detail; and although the idea of doing so had filled me, beforehand, with repulsion, when it came to it I poured it all out with relief, and, as I talked Antonia held my hand. It was, with a vengeance, the intimate talk which I had promised Georgie I would never have; and as I thus betrayed her I felt an invigorating increase of my freedom.

I attempted to portray honestly to Antonia the exact state of my doubts and hesitations about Georgie, and the effort made to do so cleared my mind. Antonia was extremely sympathetic and perceptive. I could feel, and I felt it with tenderness and almost with amusement, her subtle anxiety lest I should keep anything back, lest I should, at a certain point, suddenly regret my frankness and check the flood of revelation. She wanted to know *everything*, she wanted, oh so lovingly, to draw back the stream of my life towards her, she wanted to *hold* me and Georgie in her hands, to gaze down upon us with solicitude and complete understanding. I did not deny her. She was overjoyed.

We agreed that it was probably best that I should go right

away for a short holiday, not even to think things over but simply to rest; and indeed I was worn out. We considered Brittany, Venice, Rome, though without deciding. What she chiefly urged upon me was the desirability, the necessity, of waiting calmly, even for a long time, before approaching a decision. It was absurd to distress myself with such problems when I was, after recent events, so upset and so tired. I must look after myself and spoil myself a little; I needed rest: and Antonia promised herself, during my absence, the pleasure of getting to know Georgie better.

We also managed, and this too relieved my mind, to make some minimum decisions about furniture, such decisions anyway as would enable both of us to move certain essentials out of Hereford Square; and now for the first time I began to picture as a reality my life in the Lowndes Square flat. I mentioned this to Antonia and she congratulated me. As the time came for me to go she clung to me, covering me with kisses, and I let her have her way.

"Dearest Martin, come round again to see us tonight after dinner, will you, please? Anderson so especially wants to see you. Just to see you, you know. And now that I feel so much happier, tomorrow is far too far away!"

"All right," I said, "I'll drop in. I'll bring you some wine if you like. The '57 Château Lauriol de Barny is good, and I think you and Palmer haven't tried it."

"Oh, do that!" said Antonia. "After all, you must still educate me, mustn't you? Darling, you will often see me alone, won't you, in the time to come?"

I said that I would, and also now for the first time envisaged this as being perhaps not too painful to be possible. When I left her we were both exhausted but feeling better.

I reflected, as I walked through the cold misty afternoon

toward Georgie's lodging, that on the whole I was grateful to Georgie for having forced my hand. That Antonia now knew about it did relieve a certain pressure which although I had endured it stoically enough in the past I now recognised to have been a pain. It was indeed better to be free of the lies; and although I was still very unsure what this revelation might not have done to my relationship with Georgie, it was at least plain that nothing very honest or clear could have been settled between us prior to it. There was now, I felt, a beginning of sanity. Yes, I was grateful to Georgie; or rather, I further reflected, to Honor Klein; and as I climbed Georgie's stairs I saw again the strange image of Honor Klein sitting with the Samurai sword across her knees. The image returned to me with a certain resonance of meaning which, as I neared Georgie's door, I diagnosed as arising from the fact that I must have dreamt about Honor last night. But I could not recall the dream.

Georgie was not alone. I could hear voices as I approached and I waited a while before knocking. The stairs and landing were being painted and looked unfamiliar, and as I stood there I stared at a pile of painters' litter, and tried with an envelope to rub some wet paint off my hand. The place had an alien smell. Eventually, as the visitor showed no signs of departing, and gay laughter seemed to indicate that things were indeed going on nicely, I knocked on the door and after a suitable interval went in. Georgie was sitting by the gas fire dispensing coffee to a guest. The guest was a man. It was my brother Alexander.

When I appeared they both started up and we all stared at each other. Georgie put her hand to her breast. I could scarcely believe what I saw and I had the sense as in a nightmare of being involved in something both wildly improbable and relentlessly inevitable. This had to happen. Yet how could it have happened? And for a wild moment I wondered whether I hadn't long ago introduced Georgie and Alexander to each other and *forgotten* about it. Then I wondered if I were going mad. I sat down on a chair near the door and said "Why are you here?" to my brother.

Alexander twisted his long form and gave me a deliberately rueful and guilty look. In his smart dark grey London clothes he looked elegant, taller, a thought more degenerate. He said, "I met Georgie at lunch today. I'm sorry, Martin."

"Why are you saying sorry?" said Georgie. "It's not very polite! And there's nothing to apologise about." She was flushed and excited. I guessed she had had a good deal to drink.

"Well, it's a shock to Martin, naturally," said Alexander, turning back to Georgie. They stood one at each end, leaning against the mantelpiece and looking at each other. "I'm sure he would prefer to have introduced us himself."

"I asked him often enough!" said Georgie, laughing harshly. "He's only got himself to thank."

"You two seem to have been getting on splendidly," I said. "May I ask how you ran into each other?"

Georgie's nostrils expanded rabbit-like then contracted, and she stroked the tip of her nose with a forefinger. She was wearing her best black corduroy coat and skirt and her hair was piled artfully and with care. "Honor Klein introduced us."

"That bloody woman again," I said. "I wish people would just stop interfering with my affairs!"

"If people interfere with you it's because you like it," said Georgie. "You're dying to be interfered with. You're a sort of vacuum into which interference rushes. Anyway, it wasn't anything to do with you. Why do you assume everyone is so interested in your doings? I asked Honor to introduce me to Alexander and she kindly did so. She invited me to lunch and I accepted. I'm a free agent after all!"

"I wonder if you know how much you're hurting me," I said. "Yes, I suppose you do!"

"Go easy, Georgie," said Alexander.

"I can do without kind words from you," I said to my brother. "Do you know that Georgie is my mistress?"

"Yes," said Alexander. "She has told me." He gave me his gentle solicitous apologetically ironical stare.

"Don't flatter yourself," I said. "She tells everybody. But you must have had a delicious conversation. And now will you clear out?"

"You're being beastly, Martin," said Georgie. "It's not Alexander's fault. And of course you should have introduced us long ago. I know all this is unfortunate in a way, and it's a great pity you turned up just now. But I've felt so bloody miserable lately and so damnably tied up, I wanted to take some action on my own, I wanted to feel a bit free. I didn't do it to hurt you, but just somehow to ease myself. And anyway it's not so important."

"Now *you're* being rude!" said Alexander.

"You knew bloody well it would hurt me," I said. "But perhaps we can continue this chat when my dear brother has gone."

"Don't be so excitable, Martin," said Alexander. "Surely you can carry the thing off without all this shouting? Look, have some coffee. Georgie, get him another cup. Do have some sense of proportion, Martin."

"It's kind of you to act as host to me in my own house," I said.

"It's not your house," said Georgie, pouring out another cup of coffee. "That's the point!"

"Please don't be angry," said Alexander.

"All right," I said. "But go."

Alexander dropped his hands and bowed to me in a way that was half ironical, half submissive. He turned to Georgie and with a rueful admiring stare he took her in. She stared back evenly, unsmiling, but with a candour and a presence more telling than any smile. They must have had a good talk. Then as if unable to help himself he reached out a hand and drew it back over her head from the crown down toward the nape of the neck. She remained perfectly still, but her eyes widened slightly. He murmured, "Yes. I wonder if that was the head I was waiting for?"

"Go," I said, "go, go, go."

"Ah, well," said Alexander. "Georgie, thank you. Martin, sorry. Good-bye." He bowed this time to Georgie and left the room. I closed the door behind him.

I went over to Georgie and struck her hard on the cheek with my open hand.

She stepped back, but with dignity, and her face became scarlet. I had never struck her in anger before. She turned her back to me and said in a thick voice, "The reign of terror has started."

I turned her round again to face me, holding her by the shoulders. Her eyes were filled with tears, but she had control of herself. She glared at me furiously and then fumbled for a handkerchief.

"All right," she said, "all right, Martin, all right, all right."

"It's not all right," I said.

"You don't understand," said Georgie. "It was all much more accidental than it seems. I just said that to Honor Klein on the spur of the moment, about wanting to meet your brother. Then I forgot about it and I was quite surprised when she rang me up and suggested this."

"You ought not to have gone," I said. "Oh well, it doesn't matter." I sat down on Georgie's bed. I felt sunk in misery and confusion.

"It does matter," said Georgie. "Martin, I'm miles nearer the edge than you've got any notion of. I can't tell you how much I've suffered not only from the lies but from feeling so *paralysed*. I had to do something of my own. I feel twice as real now. I was just stopping being free. And for me that's stopping existing. I was getting to be no good to either myself or to you. You've got to *see* me, Martin. I'm to blame. I've never been quite and entirely myself with you. The situation didn't let me be. The untruthfulness infected every-thing. I must break out a little. Do you see at all?"

"Yes, yes, yes." I said. "It doesn't matter."

"Don't keep saying that," said Georgie, "and stop looking so bloody dejected, for Christ's sake."

"Anyway," I said, "the era of lies is over. We'll tell everybody now."

Georgie was silent. I looked up at her. She looked at me strangely, her face, still marked with tears, poised and with-drawn, beautiful in a new way, and older.

I said, "You don't want it told now?"

"I'm not sure," she said.

"Will you marry me, Georgie?" I said.

She turned away and drew in a sharp breath like a cry. After a moment she said, "You don't mean it, Martin. You're just a little crazy at the moment and jealous. Ask me again later if you still want to."

"I love you, Georgie," I said.

"Ah, *that*." She gave a dry laugh.

"Oh Christ," I said, and buried my face in my hands. I felt Georgie's arm about my shoulder. We rolled back on to the bed and I took her in my arms. We lay quiet for a while.

Georgie said, "Martin. You said you used to pass your girls on to Alexander. Are you sure it wasn't that he always took them away from you?"

"Yes," I said, "that was how it was, in fact."

"Martin, I love you so much," said Georgie.

I buried my head in her shoulder and groaned.

✳ *Chapter Fifteen* ✳

I WAS back again at the door at Pelham Crescent. I was also drunk. It was late and the fog was gathering again. It struck me, as I handled the heavy crate of wine, that I was shuttling to and fro with an increasing speed between the various poles of my situation and was indeed by now all over the place. I got the door open and got the wine through into the hall. I simply had to come back.

I had found myself unable to make love to Georgie. I had stayed with her too long, drunk too much, and ended up abjectly in tears. I left her with relief, and I think she felt relief too at my going. We did not speak seriously again, but treated each other with great gentleness, like a pair of invalids.

Now it was essential for me to see Palmer and Antonia. It was after eleven o'clock, but the crate of wine which I had promised to bring served as an excuse. I assumed that I would find them up. I knocked on the drawing-room door and looked inside. The room was dark except for the subdued glowing fire. Then I heard Palmer's voice calling from upstairs, "Who is it?"

"It's Martin," I said. My voice sounded hollow, like someone talking in a cavern. I added, "I've brought the wine."

Antonia's voice said, "Come and see us."

I said, "Have you gone to bed? I'm sorry to come so late."

"It's not late," said Palmer's voice. "Come on up. Look, bring three glasses and one of the bottles. We simply must see you."

I found three glasses and took a bottle of the Château

Lauriol and began to mount the stairs. I had never been upstairs in Palmer's house before.

"We're here," said Antonia's voice. A stream of golden light showed the open door. I paused in the doorway.

An enormous double bed faced the door, its white headboard festooned with trails of gilded roses. The snow-white sheets were parted. A pair of lamps, mounted on tall carved ecclesiastical candlesticks, also gilt, shed a soft radiance from either side. There was a scattering of rosy Persian rugs upon the white Indian carpet. I stepped in.

Palmer was sitting on the side of the bed. He was wearing a cream-coloured embroidered robe of Chinese silk and, it was evident, nothing underneath. Antonia was standing beside him well wrapped in her familiar cherry red Jaeger dressing-gown. I closed the door.

"How very sweet of you to bring the wine!" said Antonia. "Are you all right?"

"I'm fine," I said.

"Let's have some straight away!" said Palmer. "I love a dormitory feast. I'm so glad you've come. I've been looking forward to you all the evening. Oh dear, there's no corkscrew! Do you mind fetching one, Martin?"

"I always carry one," I said. I unfolded it and opened the bottle.

"I'm afraid we're offending against all your canons!" said Palmer. "Do you mind drinking it cold? Do pour out three glasses and then put the bottle by the fire."

I set the glasses upon a little table of pink marble beside the door and poured them out. I set the bottle down carefully beside the electric fire which was set low down in the wall. The muted yellow pattern in the satin wallpaper flickered in my eyes. I returned to the glasses.

Antonia got on to the bed and knelt her way across on to the other side, supporting herself on Palmer's shoulder. She sat there, curling her softly slippered feet under her, well enveloped in the glowing red gown. Her hair, which had been contained in the lifted collar, spread now a little on to her shoulders in flat heavy coils of faded gold. Without make-up she looked older, paler, but her face was tender, alive, maternal, as she kept her tawny eyes upon me, her big working mouth half smiling, posed and attentive. Palmer opposite to her was calm, relaxed, formidably clean, looking in his embroidered robe, with his small neat head, like some casual yet powerful emperor upon a Byzantine mosaic. One long leg, slim and very white, scattered with long black hairs, crossed over the other, was revealed by a slit in the silk. His feet were bare.

I said, "Ares and Aphrodite."

"But you are not Hephaistos, are you, Martin?" said Palmer.

I advanced and gave them the wine, first to Palmer and then to Antonia. I said, "I can hardly get higher than this."

"You are very high indeed," said Palmer, "and we love you for it. This constitutes an apex."

"That suggests a descent on the other side," I said.

"Let us call it a plateau," said Antonia. "People live on plateaus."

"Only people with a good head for heights," I said. I raised my glass to them and drank the wine. It was cold and tasted bitter. I was troubled by Palmer's naked body under the silk robe.

"Antonia told me of your talk," said Palmer. "I felt quite jealous at being left out, but I simply had to see patients this morning. I think you are being very wise. A complete holiday, a complete rest, that is what you need. Have you decided where you are going?"

"I've changed my mind," I said. "I don't think I'm going away after all."

Palmer and Antonia exchanged glances. Antonia said in her softest voice, "Darling, I do think you should go. Believe me, believe *us*, it is what is best for you."

"Isn't it odd," I said. "Here I am bringing you wine in bed. Instead of which I ought to be killing both of you."

"Martin darling, you're drunk," said Antonia. "Shall I order you a taxi to go home in?"

"Don't bother," I said, "I have the car." I moved toward the claret bottle to give myself some more. Somehow or other my foot came into contact with it and it tilted soundlessly over. A big red stain spread on the white absorbent carpet. I said, "Damnation!"

"Don't worry, my darling," said Antonia. "It'll come out!" She jumped up and went through a white communicating door into the bathroom. In a moment she was squatting at my feet deluging the carpet with water from a bowl. The stain faded to a pale pink.

"And if it doesn't come out," said Palmer, "we'll put a rug over it. I forbid you to worry about it, Martin. But, my dear fellow, can you get yourself home all right? Shall I drive you?" He sat there smiling and swinging his naked leg.

"No, of course not," I said. "I'm perfectly capable. I'm terribly sorry about the carpet. I'd better go. I've left the crate in the hall. Will it be all right there?"

"If you wouldn't mind putting it in the cellar," said Palmer. "Don't think of unpacking it, just leave it there. Our maid comes at some unearthly hour, and what with paper boys and milkmen and other mysterious persons who come and go when Antonia and I are asleep, it would be better to have it out of the way. It's very kind of you indeed."

"I'm terribly sorry," I said. I looked down on Antonia who was still mopping the carpet.

She rose quickly and kissed me on the cheek. "You're not to worry. Is he, Anderson? Promise?"

"I promise," I said with an embarrassed laugh. I began to back towards the door.

Antonia sat down again on the bed and they both watched me go. The light from the candlesticks shone upon her golden head and his soft silver one. They watched me, smiling, she infinitely soft and tender, he candid, confident, brilliant. Across the white bed their shoulders leaned together, and they glowed at me out of a centre of white and golden light. I closed the door on them as one closes the door of some rich reliquary or glorious triptych. The light was left within.

❋ *Chapter Sixteen* ❋

I STUMBLED cursing down the cellar steps. The crate was infernally heavy. I got it to the bottom and kicked it. The bottles rattled reproachfully. An electric light, unshaded but dim, showed the bleak musty cavern that was Palmer's cellar. The place seemed darker than usual and a sulphurous odour of fog mingled with the smells of rotting wood and cold damp stone. I sat down on a broken kitchen chair. I had hurt my foot kicking the crate.

I found that I had thrust my glass into my pocket, and it occurred to me that I might as well drink some more wine. Reaching out from a sitting position I got hold of the neck of a bottle and hauled it from the crate. I took a little time unfolding my corkscrew again and getting the bottle open. I poured out some wine, slopping it over my trousers and on to the floor. I drank it quickly and poured out some more.

It was cold in the cellar and the smell which I had identified as fog seemed to be getting stronger. I shivered and turned up the collar of my overcoat. I found myself wondering what the inside of a gas chamber could be like. The wine was cold too, harsh and unlike itself, a strange unfamiliar potion. It left an ill taste on my tongue. My head was spinning a little and I had an uneasy sensation in the stomach which was either fear or indigestion.

There was a sudden noise very near by. I jumped up hastily and retreated a few steps across the uneven cellar floor. My heart struck against my side like a gong. A figure had appeared on the cellar steps. For a moment in the obscurity I could not see who it was. Then I recognised it as Honor Klein. We stared at each other. My heart knocked still, and for a moment I had the strange experience of seeming to stand outside and see myself, a tall stooping figure, my coat collar turned up, my hair wild, my eyes staring, and the wine half spilt. I found it difficult to speak.

Honor Klein came down another two steps. She said, "Oh, it's you. I saw the light on and I thought it might be my brother." She stood there, hands deep in the pockets of her tweed coat, looking down at me broodingly, her eyes narrow, the line of her mouth equally hard and straight.

I said, "Your brother is in bed with my wife." I added, "I just took them up some wine in bed."

Honor Klein went on brooding at me. Then her face relaxed slightly and her eyes opened a little with an ironical light. She said, "You are heroic, Mr Lynch-Gibbon. The knight of infinite humiliation. One does not know whether to kiss your feet or to recommend that you have a good analysis." She said it as one might say "a good thrashing".

I said, "You kindly introduced my mistress to my brother. That was charming of you."

"She asked me to," said Honor Klein after a pause.

"And why did you do so with such alacrity? I cannot credit you with a kind heart."

The mockery had left her face and as she stared at me through the gloom the grimness of her expression seemed more and more weighted with melancholy. Her face was heavy and surly, like a face in a Spanish religious painting, something looking out of darkness, barbarous yet highly conscious. She said, "Oh it doesn't matter. I did it on the spur of the moment. I thought it was time for her to see a new face."

"It matters to me," I said. "I wonder if you have any idea

what a destructive person you are? I should be grateful if you would keep your hands off my business in future."

"We are not likely to meet in the future," said Honor Klein. "I am going back to Cambridge almost at once."

"You speak as if it were the North Pole," I said. "I wish it were! And I'm not the only one who'll heave a sigh of relief."

"What do you mean?"

"Palmer and Antonia aren't exactly delighted to have you hovering over them like a carrion crow."

Honor Klein looked at me and her face twisted for a moment. Then she said, "You are drunk, Mr Lynch-Gibbon, foully drunk, and even when you are sober you are stupid. Good-night." She turned to go.

I said, "Wait a minute."

What happened next may seem a little improbable, but the reader must just believe me that it did occur. She paused and turned round again to face me. I set my foot on the lowest step and seized her arm roughly. Then I pulled her down towards me. She came stumbling, and for a moment we stood together at the foot of the steps, me breathing hard and crushing her arm in my grip, she tense and glaring at me. I had in retrospect the illusion that her entire face, then and during the moments that followed, had become black.

She pulled away from me with a sudden violence, trying to free her arm. It was odd that she did not seem particularly surprised. As she pulled I changed my grip and began to turn her about, twisting her arm behind her back. At this she kicked me very hard indeed in the shins. I pushed her wrist upward towards her shoulder blade and captured her other hand. I could hear her gasp with pain. I was behind her now and her weight came backward against me as I increased my pressure. She kicked me again, very painfully.

I relaxed my grip and curled one leg round hers, at the same time pushing her violently forward. She fell on her knees, and I fell half on top of her, losing hold of her arm. We rolled over each other on the floor. I gave her my weight, trying to find her wrist. On her back now, she came against me with both hands pushing and clawing, and endeavoured to drive her knee into my stomach. She fought like a maniac; but it was remarkable too that throughout our brief battle she did not cry out once.

We were both impeded by our overcoats, and I was also impeded by being extremely drunk. She was even stronger than I would have expected. But it took me only a moment to get hold of her wrists. I crushed them both together in one hand, leaning my weight upon her until she became still. I could see her face just below mine, the black hairs on her upper lip, the white of her teeth. I lifted myself a little and with my free hand struck her three times, a sideways blow across the mouth. She closed her eyes and tried to turn her head away. I saw that clearly in retrospect too.

After I had hit her the third time I began to wonder what I was doing. I let go and rolled off her. She got up without haste while I got myself into a sitting position. My head, suddenly asserting its existence, felt terrible. She brushed down her coat and then without looking at me and still without haste she mounted the cellar steps.

I sat quiet for a minute feeling extremely confused. Then, holding my head, which felt ready to break open, I got shakily to my feet. I got myself up the steps and into the hall. The front door was open and outside, hung like a blanket a yard from the opening, was the fog, yellow, opaque, infernal, completely still. I stood in the doorway. In the hollow damp silence I could hear the echo of receding footsteps. I went down into the street, ran a little way, and stopped to listen. My footprints lay behind me, a reeling progress, upon the damp pavement. With a choking sigh more profound than silence the fog enclosed me. I opened my mouth to call out to her but found that I had forgotten her name.

✳ *Chapter Seventeen* ✳

DARLING, I'm sorry I was so drunk yesterday—and I do hope I didn't make a beastly stain on the carpet. You and Palmer were sweet about it. You must let me pay to have it cleaned. I think after all I shall go away, though I'm not sure where to. So don't expect to hear from me for a bit. I'm perfectly all right and you're not to worry about me. I'll make the arrangements about moving the furniture before I go. I'll be glad when that part is over. I may have seemed churlish, but don't think I'm not deeply grateful for your concern. I may yet need your help; and I would be a fool to be indifferent to having, still now, your love. Though I'm not sure after all that I understand what generosity is. However, even if what I manifested was something else, it was like enough to it and might become changed into it in time without anyone noticing, don't you think? Forgive me and bear with me.

M.

My dearest child, I'm sorry I was so drunk yesterday. I hope I didn't tire you out. I should have gone sooner. This is just a little note to say that I may perhaps go away for a while, so I won't see you in the nearer future. I think honestly that this may be a good thing, as I am afraid that if we meet now we may quarrel. As I said yesterday, I am not really aggrieved about Alexander. I have quite got over that: and I do believe you when you say you love me. But I just feel too bloody miserable and mixed up to be able to see you without fretting terribly about taking decisions which I do not feel myself competent to take at present. You understand. It may seem unreasonable to ask you to love me all the same and to love me especially: but nothing here is reasonable, and in love nothing is ever reasonable. So, selfish, inconsiderate and sorry for myself, I ask just that.

Your M.

Dear Dr Klein,

I literally do not know how to apologise for what happened last night. What form of words can I use to say how very deeply I regret my extraordinary conduct. You will have concluded, indeed you did, if I remember, conclude that I was drunk. Mad would perhaps describe it better. And perhaps all I can do by way of apology is to offer you some explanation, however crude, of how I could have behaved in so eccentric a fashion. Before this however let me express the hope that I did not seriously hurt you. Indeed, I am speechless with contrition. I can only trust that, since you have seen much of the world, you experienced no damaging shock, however profound the dislike and contempt which my actions cannot but have provoked in you.

As you know, I have been under an extreme strain of late; how extreme, I did not fully know until yesterday. You said once earlier on that I was a violent man. I plead guilty to this charge, and to having, as I now realise, grossly over-estimated my powers of control. It was both unfortunate and unjust that you, an innocent party, should have had the benefit of my violence. I spoke wildly last night when I implied that you had harmed me. Your actions in my regard were, I fully realise, without malice and indeed without interest: I would be a fool in any case to imagine that I could have inspired any concern in you which could find expression in animosity. It is just that I am feeling thoroughly persecuted at present and because you arrived at a moment when I was particularly strained and irrational I flew at you.

Yet also it was no accident. I owe it to you here to attempt to understand myself. Indeed I am grateful to you, because in some way, and not only by occasioning last night's outburst, you have helped me to see what has gone wrong. I love my wife and I still desire her. I also love your brother. As may or may not have been obvious to you—it was until lately by no means obvious to me— my feelings for Palmer are of no normal intensity. I have never been in the accepted sense, a homosexual, but certainly my attachment to Palmer has something of this colour; and it is an odd thing, though it may be for all I know a phenomenon well known to clinical psychology, that Palmer's liaison with my wife has increased rather than diminished my affection for him. The situation implied, therefore, or perhaps I should say however, a two-way jealousy: yet it has been a long time before I have become aware of this implication. It may be suggested that my slowness was due to a preoccupation with moral principles, and indeed at the conscious level I believe that I did make moral efforts, if such things are ever really made, in the direction of what I understood to be generosity and compassion. A more profound and plausible explanation may however be found in the particular rôle which Palmer and Antonia have played towards me, and with which I have so readily co-operated. I mean of course the rôle of parents. It was, I fear, not by chance that I married a woman considerably older than myself; and when that woman turned her affections toward a yet older man, to whom I was already related in a quasi-filial manner, the stage was set for my regression to the situation of a child.

But children, as we know, are savages, and their immature love for their parents is often with difficulty distinguished from hatred. Of such hatred and such violence you were for a moment the innocent, yet as I have said not the accidental, victim. Although naturally I entertain no personal feelings toward you whatsoever, not even, as I have explained, those of the slightest resentment, your connection with Palmer made you serviceable as a symbol, you became as it were the joker in the pack whom I could imagine momentarily to be the object of my fury. I should add that it was, needless to say, an ephemeral fury, fully expended, as I deeply regret, upon you: I have, I must assure you, no real ill-feeling toward Palmer. Indeed this solitary outburst has helped me, by making me more profoundly conscious of myself, to purge my imagination of evil humours and to render myself more truly like the generous person whose part I have endeavoured to play. I say this in case you should, after last night's exhibition, feel any apprehension of possible violence to your brother. I assure you sincerely that there is no such possibility.

It only remains for me to apologise to you very humbly and to hope that even if, as I fear, you find my conduct inexcusable, you will at least, if you have had the patience to read this letter, find it somewhat more comprehensible.

I am yours sincerely

Martin Lynch-Gibbon

Dear Honor Klein,

I am afraid there is little point in trying to explain my conduct of last night, and scarcely any point even in apologising. I was, as you observed, very drunk, and I behaved like a wild beast. I can only say that I am not only as shocked at myself, but also as amazed, as you could possibly be. I cannot account for it; nor would you be interested in a rigmarole of implausible hypotheses about the state of my psyche. It is enough to have assaulted you without boring you into the bargain. I must, however, write this letter to send, though without any hope of its being acceptable, my very humble and very sincere apology. I dare to hope that I did not seriously hurt you. If I caused you any pain, I assure you that my contrition burns me more sharply than the harshest blow. I cannot think what came over me; nor can I at all conjecture what your state of mind about me can now be. It would hardly need saying, were it not that I fear I have consistently behaved badly to you, but you are to me an object of profound respect, not only because you are Palmer's sister but because you are you: and I feel a most biting regret at having forfeited, I must fear forever, the possibility of your good opinion. I will not prolong this letter. I hope, contrary to your prediction, that we may meet again: though I shall certainly not offer you my company in the forseeable future, nor of course will I expect any answer to this communication. I am very sorry indeed for my shocking behaviour.

Yours sincerely

Martin Lynch-Gibbon

Dear Honor,

I am sorry that I behaved to you like a beast and a madman. I cannot offer any explanation—nor is this indeed in the ordinary sense an apology. I feel that things between us, after last night, have passed beyond the region of apologies. I want to write to you something brief and something honest to be, as it were, in lieu of posturings of regret which might not be entirely sincere. I have in the past felt resentment against you, even dislike of you, and not entirely without cause. Ever since you appeared on the scene you have, for reasons which remain obscure to me, behaved towards me with hostility, and in two instances you have deliberately done me harm. I am not aware that I have in any way merited this treatment at your hands. I am at present passing through a time of great anxiety, indeed a time of great misery, and might have hoped at least to escape irresponsible persecution from strangers.

I am not saying of course that the fact of what I have called your persecution (which may indeed be the result of thoughtlessness rather than malice) in any way excuses or warrants my throwing you on the ground and beating you about the head. I only write down here what occurs to me when I set myself the task of apologising; I only write down what seems to me to be the truth. You are, I add, and for all my resentment I can see this clearly, a person worthy of my respect and one who pre-eminently deserves the truth. I am confident that you will prefer this truthful letter to a conventional apology. I hope that I did not hurt you much. I believe that, since you know the world even better than I do, you will not have suffered serious shock or even experienced serious amazement. I hope we shall meet again and that this incident may serve as a stepping stone to an understanding of each other which has so far been, on both sides, conspicuously lacking.

With my good wishes,

M. L.-G.

I sealed up the letters to Antonia and Georgie. I brooded

for some time over the three versions of my letter to Honor Klein, and finally, with some misgivings, chose the second one. I was tempted to write a fourth version, and the notion of there being some further development of my thought which demanded expression became very compelling indeed. Yet when I reflected more I could not see what that further development could possibly be like. It remained, though maddeningly present, shrouded in darkness. I eventually gave up, copied out Honor's letter and sealed it, and went to the post. The fog had cleared. When I returned I ate some biscuits and dosed myself with whisky and hot milk. I felt totally exhausted, having put more intellectual effort into the letters to Honor than I had expended since I wrote *Sir Eyre Coote and the Campaign of Wandewash*; yet I was quieted by an irrational feeling of having done a good morning's work. I went upstairs to lie down and fell into the most profound and peaceful sleep that I had experienced for a long time.

* Chapter Eighteen *

I WAS in torment. Two days had passed, but I had not been able to make up my mind either to leave London or to see Antonia or Georgie. A taboo seemed set upon the two women. It was as if in writing to them I had had the intention of clearing the decks for something, for some drama or some event; but what this could be I did not know, although a continual tension and expectancy affected me positively with a physical ache. In addition I felt sick, unable to eat, and if in desperation I drank alcohol I was afflicted with prompt internal pains. I could neither lie comfortably in bed nor find anything to do with myself if I got up. Reading was impossible, and a visit to the cinema almost reduced me to tears. I visited the office twice and had a talk with Mytten and arranged one or two routine matters, but to keep my mind upon these things was practically an agony. I took my temperature and found it exasperatingly normal. I could not conceive what was the matter with me and it was not until half way through the third day that I found out.

Alexander rang up just before leaving again for the country and we talked for some time on the phone. Our relations were such that scarcely any 'patching up' was either possible or needed. We simply fell back, half articulately, upon an old understanding. He was cautious, rueful, tactful, I was morose, ironical, complaining. We left it, with relief, at that. I was less pleased to receive a call from Rosemary who was now installed once more in London and very eager to come and organise my life. I felt I could not bear at present to see Rosemary and face her bright bird-like inquisitiveness. She suggested that she should come over and pack up my Minton dinner service and one or two other things which she said must on no account be trusted to the removal men. I said that she might do this, and added that I had not yet made any removal arrangements. She replied that this was just as well, as she knew of an excellent firm and would arrange it all for me. She arrived within half an hour and in a business-like conversation it was agreed that I should go as soon as possible to camp at Lowndes Square, not waiting until the arrival of the furniture. I had no desire to witness the gradual dismantling of the house. I was grateful to her: and as her tasks seemed sufficiently to delight her without the addition of my company I took myself off. As I shut the hall door I could hear Rosemary, her precise little voice ringing with authority, telephoning instructions to Harrods for the immediate delivery at my flat of the best available kind of camp bed.

London was misty, with a golden sun-pierced mist in which buildings hung as insubstantial soaring presences. The beautiful dear city, muted and softened, half concealed in floating and slightly shifting clouds, seemed a city in the air, outlined in blurred dashes of grey and brown. I walked, inevitably, by the river. As I turned on to Victoria Embankment I saw that the tide was in, and upon the surface of the fast flowing water itself there played a warm light, turning its muddy hue to an old gilt, as if some pure part of the sunlight had escaped to play here under the great vault of the mist. The strange light suited my mood and as I sauntered slowly along beneath the shadowy cliff of New Scotland Yard I began to feel, if not relieved of pain, at least a little more able to collect my wits.

It was too cold to sit down, but I paused every now and then to lean on the parapet, and as I passed each damp dolphin-entwined lamp-post I felt a little nearer to something. Yet I did not seem to be making any famous progress with my troubles. I felt on the whole a thorough nausea about recent events. That I should have had some time to 'open up' my relation with Georgie seemed inevitable: yet I detested both the moment and the manner of this particular revelation, and there were times when I wondered whether my love for Georgie was strong enough to support the sheer weight of mess and muddle under which I felt it now laboured. All the same, when I had found her with Alexander my sense of possessiveness had been immediate and violent: a possessiveness which lingered on now as a sort of aching resentment. It was odd that I felt no urgency about seeing her. What I really wanted most just then was to put Georgie in cold storage. It is unfortunate that other human beings cannot be conveniently immobilised. Do what I might, Georgie would go on thinking, would go on acting, during my absence and my silence. This thought caused me pain, but still did not galvanise me into the simple action of ringing her up.

To turn my mind to Antonia was no less painful. One thing which I had in the last day or two realised was that I was very far indeed from having unravelled my thoughts and feelings concerning my wife. That I had so readily jumped at a way of enduring, as it were acting my way through the situation, had, it now seemed, merely postponed the moment of a more radical and more dreadful estimate of what had happened. It occurred to me particularly that I had never taken sufficient trouble to find out exactly what Antonia herself was thinking and feeling. To have attempted it would, of course, have been exquisitely painful, and it was partly to shun just that trial that I had so jumped at my rôle, that I had accepted with such completeness the picture of things which Palmer and Antonia had seemed to be offering. I could not have borne, given that I despaired at once, to have kept things 'open' between Antonia and myself. But perhaps it was just my terrible mistake to have despaired at once. Was it a mistake, or was it indeed the acting out of some hidden desire? Whichever it was, it had been, I now felt, my duty to enquire more closely, at whatever cost to myself. It had been suggested that Antonia and Palmer were, for all the appearances, really in two minds. What was certain was that my alacrity had helped to stabilise their union; and as I thought this I wondered whether in some way my rôle was just now destined to change, and that having, as Palmer put it, reached an apex, I was now about to undertake some remarkable descent.

I greatly regretted too that I had been so frank with Antonia about Georgie. My own former instinct, which Georgie had endorsed, that an intimate talk about her with Antonia was something to be avoided, seemed now to have been a sound one. That intimate talk had done nothing but damage: damage to me since I had thereby in some way blunted my love for my dear mistress, damage to Georgie since she was not only betrayed but put positively in danger of being in Antonia's power, and damage to Antonia since she had been thereby disturbed and excited and filled with schemes which could in the end only do harm. I was well aware, and it gave me a twisted gloomy satisfaction, that Antonia was very far from having made herself emotionally independent of me. She needed to have, and had indeed almost announced this as a programme, both Palmer and, in a subordinate rôle, myself. The discovery of Georgie's existence had been a bad shock and a challenge; and although I was sure that Antonia imagined herself to be inspired by nothing but ingenious and affectionate benevolence, she was certainly determined to hold, to organise, to gain power over, the matter of Georgie and me: and if in the process the matter of Georgie and me suffered shipwreck Antonia would not be exactly heartbroken. She would then set herself, with oh such enthusiasm and satisfaction, to the task of consoling me.

I watched, where a long golden streak had opened in the mist, the water flowing under Waterloo Bridge. A concealed sun was shining on the great white buttresses. And I thought about Honor Klein. I had in fact really been thinking about her all the morning. It was with something of an effort that I had given my mind to other matters, even to other people. For this was at present the magnetic centre of my swinging thoughts, and with a puzzlement which it was something of a luxury to indulge I found myself brooding on Palmer's curious sister. I was sorry now that I had sent her the second letter, though I was very relieved that I had not sent her the first one. The second letter was a poor trivial affair, making but little of what had been, after all, a somewhat remarkable occasion. The third letter would have been in many ways more suitable; or I regretted, rather, that I had not taken time and trouble to write the fourth one, whatever that would have turned out to be.

The third letter was certainly the most sincere, since I felt curiously little remorse about the scene in the cellar. The only thing I regretted, paradoxically, was that I had not been sober, although of course if I had been sober the scene would not have occurred. But I recalled the scene itself even with a certain satisfaction: satisfaction mingled with some more obscure and disturbing emotions. I kept returning with wonderment to the thought that I had now *touched* her: 'touched' was putting it mildly, given what had happened. But it seemed, perhaps for that very reason, almost implausible in retrospect; and although I could picture her face screwed up with pain and fury, although I could see her black oily hair rolling in the dust and hear her gasp as I twisted her arm yet further, I could not altogether recall any sense of the contact of my flesh with hers. It was as if the extreme untouchability, which with a kind of repulsion I had earlier felt her to possess, had cast, on this sacrilegious occasion, a cloak about her. It was as if I had not really touched her.

I was beginning to feel rather sick again. I walked on under Waterloo Bridge and saw through the tilting, slightly lifting, mist the long gracious pillared façade of Somerset House. Receding, swaying, variously browned and greyed, it seemed like a piece of stage scenery. Below it upon the river, clear yet infinitely soft and simple as in a Chinese print, two swans sailed against a background of watery grey light, swept steadily downstream in the company of a dipping branch of some unidentified foliage. They receded, turning a little, and disappeared. I walked on, and then paused by the parapet looking out to where in the much-curtained distance the great form of St Paul's must be. I could now just descry the ware-houses directly opposite across the river, their fronts touched by diffused but increasing intimations of sunlight. The task of peering through the mist was becoming exasperating and painful. I cannot see, I cannot see, I said to myself: it was as if some inner blindness were being here tormentingly exterior-ised. I saw shadows and hints of things, nothing clearly at all.

I turned back from the swirling tawny flood with its shadow palaces to look for reassurance at the solid pavement, and I saw that I was standing near a telephone box. I looked at the telephone box; and as I looked it seemed to take on a strange sudden glory, such as is said to invest the meanest object in the eyes of those who claim to experience the proof of the existence of God *e contingentia mundi*. Like one of Köhler's apes, my cluttered mind attempted to connect one thing with another. Very dimly and distantly, but hugely, it began to dawn upon me what the nature of my ailment was. It was something new and something, as I even then at once apprehended, terrible. My pain was that of a perhaps fatal illness. I moved toward the telephone box. My hands trembled so much that it was only at the third attempt that I was able to dial the Pelham Crescent number correctly. The maid answered. Dr Anderson and Mrs Lynch-Gibbon had gone away for the week-end, and Dr Klein had gone back to Cambridge.

❊ *Chapter Nineteen* ❊

CAMBRIDGE by moonlight was light blue and brownish black. There was no mist here and a great vault of clear stars hung over the city with an intent luxurious brilliance. It was the sort of night when one knows of other galaxies. My long shadow glided before me on the pavement. Although it was not yet eleven o'clock the place seemed empty and I moved through it like a mysterious and lonely harlequin in a painting: like an assassin.

When the idea had come to me that I was desperately, irrevocably, agonisingly in love with Honor Klein it had seemed at first to shed a great light. It was clear to me that this, just this, was what so urgently and with such novelty of torment ailed me, and also that the thing was inevitable. Inevitable now Honor certainly seemed to be, vast across my way as the horizon itself or the spread wings of Satan; and although I could not as yet trace it out I could feel behind me like steel the pattern of which this and only this could have been the outcome. I had never felt so certain of any path upon which I had set my feet; and this in itself produced an exhilaration.

Extreme love, once it is recognised, has the stamp of the indubitable. I knew to perfection both my condition and what I must instantly do about it. There was, however, as I began to realise as soon as I was safely stowed in the train at Liverpool Street, much cause nevertheless for anxiety, or rather for terror, and also for puzzlement, or rather for sheer amazement. That I had no business, with two women on my hands already, to go falling in love with a third, troubled me comparatively little. The force that drew me now towards Honor imposed itself with the authority of a cataclysm; and as I felt no possibility of indecision I had, if not exactly no sense of disloyalty, at least no anxieties about disloyalty. I was chosen, and relentlessly, not choosing. Yet this very image brought home the insanity of my position. I was chosen, but by whom or what? Certainly not by Honor, whose last words to me, still ringing like a box on the ear, had been far from flattering. I had never felt so certain of any path; but it was a path that seemed likely to lead only to humiliation and defeat.

Yet even this did not yet trouble me very much. The thought that, *whatever* my reception, I would see Honor again was, in the frenzy of need and desire which had now come upon me, enough. I was perhaps moreover a little the dupe of that illusion of lovers that the beloved object *must*, somehow, respond, that an extremity of love not only merits but compels some return. I expected nothing very much, I certainly expected nothing precise, but the future was sufficiently open, sufficiently obscure, to receive the now so fierce onward rush of my purpose. I had to see her and that was all.

What had more occupied my mind, as the train drew near to Cambridge, was wonderment at the nature and genesis of this love. When had I begun, unbeknown to myself, to love Honor Klein? Was it when I threw her to the cellar floor? Or when I saw her cut the napkins in two with the Samurai sword? Or at some earlier time, perhaps at that strange moment when I had seen her dusty, booted and spurred, confront the golden potentates who were my oppressors? Or even, most prophetically, when I had glimpsed the curving seam of her stocking in the flaring orange lights at Hyde Park Corner? It was hard to say, and the harder because of the peculiar nature of this love. When I thought how peculiar it was it struck me as marvellous that I had nevertheless such a deep certainty that it *was* love. I seemed to have passed from dislike to love without experiencing any intermediate stage. There had been no moment when I reassessed her character, noticed new qualities or passed less harsh judgments on the old ones: which seemed to imply that I now loved her for the same things for which I had previously disliked her heartily; if indeed I had ever disliked her. None of this, on the other hand, made me doubt that now I loved her. Yet it was in truth a monstrous love such as I had never experienced before, a love out of such depths of self as monsters live in. A love devoid of tenderness and humour, a love practically devoid of personality.

It was strange too how little this passion which involved, so it seemed, a subjection of my whole being had to do in any simple or comprehensible sense with the flesh. It *had* to do with it, as my blood at every moment told me, but so darkly. I preserved the illusion of never having touched her. I had knocked her down but I had never held her hand; and at the idea of holding her hand I practically felt faint. How very different was this from my old love for Antonia, so warm and radiant with golden human dignity, and from my love for Georgie, so tender and sensuous and gay. Yet, too, how flimsy these other attachments seemed by comparison. The power that held me now was like nothing I had ever known: and the image returned to me of the terrible figure of Love as pictured by Dante. *El m'ha percosso in terra e stammi sopra.*

It occurred to me later as remarkable and somehow splendid that one thing which I never envisaged in these early moments was that my condition was in any way bogus or unreal. Wherever it might lead, it was sufficiently what it seemed and had utterly to do with me: I would not, I could not, attempt to disown it or explain it away. If it was grotesque it was a grotesqueness which was of my own substance and to which, beyond any area of possible explanation, I laid an absolute claim. I had no idea what I would do when I saw Honor. It seemed quite likely that I would simply collapse speechless at her feet. Nothing of this mattered. I was doing what I had to do and my actions were, with a richness, my own.

I glided, motley and all, into the great checkered picture of King's Parade. Beyond the slim street lamps the great crested form of King's chapel rose towards the moon, its pinnacles touched to a pallid blue against the starry distance beyond. The moon-shadow of the Senate House lay with a thicker obscurity across the grass until dispelled by the lamplight. The majesty, the familiarity, of these buildings seemed to add solemnity to my rite, as when old patriarchs come to grace a marriage. I felt by now extremely sick again and practically suffocated with excitement and with something which I supposed must be desire. I turned into the street where Honor Klein lived.

I checked the numbers and could see ahead the house which must be hers. There was a single light on upstairs. The sight of that light made my heart increase its pace so hideously that I had to slow down and then to stop and hold on to a lamp-post while I tried to breathe evenly and quietly. I wondered if I had better wait a while and attempt, not to calm myself which was impossible, but simply to organise my breathing so as to be sure not to swoon. I stood for a few minutes and breathed steadily. I decided that I must wait no longer in case Honor should take it into her head to go to bed. I knew she could hardly be in bed at this hour, and pictured the upstairs room as a study. Then I pictured her there sitting at a desk surrounded by books. Then I pictured myself beside her. I advanced to the door and leaned against the wall.

There was a single bell. I had not until that moment envisaged the possibility that she might have lodgers. In any case there was only one bell and I pressed it. I heard no sound within and after a moment I pressed the bell again. Still no sound. I stepped back and looked up at the lit curtained window. I returned to the door and pushed it gently, but it was locked. I peered through the letter box. The hall was in darkness and there was no sound of approaching feet. I held the letter box open and pressed the bell again. I decided that the bell must be out of order and I wondered what to do next. I might either call out, or bang on the door, or throw stones at the window. I stood meditating on these various courses for a little while, and they all seemed insuperably difficult. I was uncertain whether I could control my voice sufficiently to produce the right sort of cry, and the other methods were too brusque. In any case I did not relish a head thrust from a window, a confused encounter at a street doorway. What I really wanted was to slink quietly into some room and find myself at once in Honor's presence.

It then occurred to me that just this was precisely what I might be able to manage. I noticed a little gate at the side of the house which doubtless led into the garden. I tried it and it was open. I passed down a narrow passageway of mossy bricks which divided the houses and found myself in a small garden. I stepped back a little. Above the black shape of a drooping tree the high moon revealed the back of the house, which was in darkness. French windows of a lower room gave on to the garden. I tiptoed back across the grass and put my hand against the windows. Here I had to pause again to subdue a wave of sheer panic. My breathing, even my heartbeat, must I felt already be audible through the house like the panting of an engine. I tried the doors, got my finger into a crack and pushed them sharply away from me. They gave; I was not sure whether they were unlatched anyway or whether my violent push had broken some weak fastening. I opened them wide with both hands.

A dark room gaped before me, very faintly illuminated by the remains of an open fire. By now I scarcely knew what I was doing. My movements took on the quality of a dream. Things melted before me. I crossed the room and opened a door whose white surface I saw glimmering in the darkness. I came out into the hall. A little light from the street lamp in front, coming through the open door of one of the front rooms, showed me the stairs. I began to mount the stairs, leaning hard on the bannisters and stepping softly. Once on the upper landing I could see the line of light under the door of Honor's room. I hesitated only a moment.

I advanced to the door and knocked. After so much breathless silence the sound of the knock seemed thunderous. I let it die away and then as there was no reply to it I opened the door. For a moment the light dazzled me.

I saw opposite to me a large double divan bed. The room was brightly lit. Sitting up in this bed and staring straight at me was Honor. She was sitting sideways with the sheet over her legs. Upwards she was as tawny and as naked as a ship's figurehead. I took in her pointed breasts, her black shaggy head of hair, her face stiff and expressionless as carved wood. She was not alone. Beside the bed a naked man was hastily engaged in pulling on a dressing-gown. It was immediately and indubitably apparent that I had interrupted a scene of lovers. The man was Palmer.

I closed the door and walked back down the stairs.

✳ *Chapter Twenty* ✳

I TURNED a light on in the hall, finding the switch instinctively, and went back into the room through which I had come. I turned the switch here and various lamps came on. I vaguely took in a white book-lined room with chintz armchairs. I went over and closed the French windows which were hanging ajar. It appeared that I had broken the fastening after all. I pulled the curtains which were also chintz. I turned back towards the fireplace. On a low table before it stood a tray with two glasses, a decanter of whisky and a jug of water. I poured out some whisky, spilling a good deal of it on the table. I drank it. I poured out some more, poked up the fire a bit, and waited.

Ever since the moment near Waterloo Bridge when I had come to consciousness of my condition, I had felt like a man running towards a curtain. Now that I had so suddenly and with such exceedingly unexpected results passed through it I felt dazed and in great pain but also curiously steady. I had entered the house like a thief. I stood in it now like a conquering general. They would come, they would have to come, to attend upon me.

I felt this steadiness, this setting as it were of my feet sturdily apart; yet with it I was in a confusion amounting to agony. I had so rapaciously desired and so obtusely expected to find Honor alone. The simple fact of her not being alone was a wrench almost separately felt, even apart from the nightmarish significance of who her companion was. From *this* there shivered through me a violence of amazement not distinguishable from horror; and I felt as a physical pain the

shock of what I had done to *them*. How naively had I imagined that Honor must be free; I had even, it now occurred
to me, imagined that she must be virgin: that I would be the
first person to discover her, that I would be her conqueror
and her awakener. Caught in the coils of such stupidity I
could not yet even begin to touch with my imagination the
notion that she should have had her brother as a lover.

Palmer came in. He shut the door softly behind him and
leaned against it. He was wearing a dark silk dressing-gown
and as was again apparent was naked underneath it. He was
barefoot. He leaned back against the door and looked at me
with a steady wide-eyed gaze. I looked back at him meditat-
ively, looked into the fire, looked at him again. I willed myself
not to shiver. We remained so in silence for a minute. Then
I poured some whisky into the other glass and motioned
Palmer to approach.

He came forward and took the glass and stared into it for
a while. He seemed to be quietly and carefully deciding what
he was going to say. I resolved to let him begin. His first
words surprised me. "How did you know I was here?"

I hesitated and my mind began to waken up. This remark
revealed two things, two doubtless interconnected things:
that Honor had not told Palmer about the episode in the
cellar and that Palmer imagined that I had come to Cambridge in pursuit of him. If he had known of the cellar episode
he would surely at least have conjectured that I might have
come in pursuit of Honor. Although my passion for Honor
was something so improbable and out of nature yet, given the
fact of my violence, a psycho-analyst particularly would be
likely to have guessed at it. But no such idea seemed to be in
Palmer's head and he appeared to believe that I had come
suspiciously on his track, that I had come positively to unmask

him. My first and overwhelming sensation was gratitude to Honor. I could not but regard it as somehow significant and propitious that she had not told her brother. My second and more obscure apprehension was that I was in possession of an advantage which I must not lose.

I said, "Need we go into that?" I hoped he would not press me.

"Well, it doesn't matter," said Palmer. "You've found out what you came for and that's what's important. Does Antonia know?"

I thought a moment. "No," I said.

"Are you going to tell her?"

I was completely cool by now. I said, "I don't know, Palmer. I honestly don't know."

Palmer turned to face me. His voice was deep with earnestness and his countenance had a stripped quality which I had never seen before. He put his whisky on the mantelpiece and took a step towards me. For a moment he put his two hands on my arms, pressing me slightly. Then he let them drop to his sides. It was a supplication. He said, "This is desperately grave, Martin. There are some things we must get clear."

Looking back on the scene I felt admiration for the way in which, from the start, Palmer took it that something catastrophic and irrevocable had occurred. He did not attempt— and indeed it would have been difficult—to explain away the scene I had witnessed upstairs. Nor did he attempt to minimise its importance or cover it with any veil of distracting mystification. He faced me frankly as one faces a conqueror or a judge; and as our interview progressed it was with a certain sick giddiness mingled with an agony of compassion that I so felt, for the first time, the scales of power inclined in my direction. We were indeed on the other side of the mountain.

I said, out of an immediate sympathy for him, "Palmer, I'm sorry."

"Don't," said Palmer. "You've acted cleverly, resolutely, doubtless properly. I didn't know you had it in you. Let's have no nonsense here. It's just that what has happened may prove fatal. And I want us at least to understand each other."

"Please," I said, "in one way at least don't misconstrue me. I don't disapprove of incest. I don't think that you're committing any sin by embracing your sister: that is, not any sin that arises from that fact that she's your sister."

"You are being frivolous as usual," said Palmer. "You don't disapprove of it. You feel total horror of it. You are trembling with horror at this very minute. But your feelings are not important. The person we must think of is Antonia."

"And Honor," I said. I saw again the vision of her dark breasts; and I felt in a sudden agony her presence close to me in the house and the probability that if she did not detest me already she would detest me for this. I found I was indeed trembling and with an effort made myself still.

"Honor is my business," said Palmer. "Honor will be all right in any case. She is a great person. What is at stake is Antonia's happiness. I will not say exactly her sanity. But a revelation of this kind could disable her for life."

"You are positively suggesting," I said, "that I say nothing of this to Antonia?"

"Of course I am positively suggesting that. It is not, you understand, like the revelation of an ordinary unfaithfulness. We have to do with something which can shake the mind to its foundations. Antonia stands on the brink of a new life and a new happiness. Either she goes forward into that—or she suffers a shipwreck from which, given her temperament, she may take years to recover. It depends on you which of these things will happen."

"What about you?" I said. "Are you also on the brink of a new life and a new happiness, with her?" I eyed him closely. I was trying to see him as a man desperately fighting himself free from a binding obsession. I could see nothing. He retained his wide-eyed resolute look which by its very frankness revealed nothing.

"I want Antonia," said Palmer, "and I want only Antonia. And let me say to you in the profoundest and most faithful seriousness that what you saw tonight will have no sequel. *No sequel.* Do you believe me, Martin?"

"But it had antecedents," I said.

"That is not your business."

"It might concern Antonia."

"If you are here to torment and blackmail me," he said, "you had better go at once. But if you want to understand what you are doing before you do it, then stay." He was desperate to keep me with him.

"Sorry, Palmer," I said. "I have no desire to torment you, you know that perfectly well. I am confused and shaken and I honestly don't know what I shall do."

"If you imagine," said Palmer, his voice becoming sharper, "that you can get any advantage for *yourself* out of destroying Antonia's peace of mind, if you imagine that you can settle down again happily with her after—"

"Oh *shut up*," I said. "It's enough that my marriage has been wrecked. Don't now accuse me of selfishness because I hesitate to shield an adulterer who has got himself into a muddle."

"You are the adulterer," said Palmer. "Stop thinking of yourself and think of Antonia. I *beg* you, Martin, to reflect carefully. Do not be offended at my words. You and I know each other too well to play at scoring points. As I have said, the thing has no sequel."

I wanted, in this perhaps unique moment, to find out something more. I sought for the right words. I said, "I think I have a right to know a little more. I conjecture that you have had a long-standing liaison with your sister. Many things point to it. Am I to understand that now by mutual consent it is coming to an end?"

Palmer was silent, staring and breathing hard. Then he moved away from me and put one hand to his brow for a moment. I found the gesture, the sign of weakness. infinitely touching. He spread his hands. "I have nothing to say here," he said. "There are things which are not one's own property. I have told you what is relevant. If Antonia is never told you may be quite certain that I shall never betray her by thought or deed. What you saw tonight was an ending. Indeed your arrival sealed it as such. But it was an ending in any case."

"If I had not appeared there *might* perhaps have been a sequel?"

"No, I have told you *no*," said Palmer impatiently. "Martin, have the grace to understand plain words."

"I don't know how much to believe you," I said. "I don't say this to persecute you, but just to express what is the case. And I don't know what I shall do. I can tell you now that I think it is very unlikely that I shall tell Antonia. But I can't at the moment promise not to tell her."

"You will be wise and generous not to tell," said Palmer. He had recovered himself and gazed at me, dignified, his cropped head thrown back, his dressing-gown falling open to reveal a white chest shadowed with grey hair. He looked touchingly old, an old warrior.

I said, "My arrival at any rate has sealed the end of my friendship with you." I said this to provoke him, indeed in some wild need myself of comfort.

Palmer, and again I admired this as I remembered it, took it full in the face. He replied quietly, "We shall have to see about that, Martin. This has been a terrible shock for both of us—we do not yet realise how terrible. We shall begin to realise it tomorrow morning. And you will find that it is scarcely less of a shock for you because you saw what you expected to see. There are some things which imagination cannot do for one. After such an experience a friendship, if it is to survive, must be very deeply altered and reorganised. It remains to be seen whether our friendship can be so altered. I hope sincerely that it can—and for myself I shall make every effort to see that it is."

"Provided I don't tell Antonia," I said.

He looked at me sombrely. "If you tell Antonia we are all done for."

In the silence that followed I finished my whisky, and then addressed myself to departure. With a strange spontaneous formality I bowed to Palmer. He inclined his head; and as I left the room I saw him with head still bowed staring into the fire. He caressed the fender with a naked foot. But even as I closed the front door I could hear him emerging from the room and making for the stairs.

As I stopped for a moment to look back at the lighted window I wondered in what terrible and unimaginable colloquy those two were now wrapped.

❊ *Chapter Twenty-one* ❊

I FOLLOWED my sister up the steps. Outside the house the fog was golden yellow, thick with sulphurous grains. It was hard to breathe. I hurried after her retreating figure which had become almost at once invisible. It was exceedingly cold and our footsteps made a small crackling sound as they crushed the thin layer of ice which had formed upon the paving stones. When I caught her up I took her ungloved hand in mine and pressed it against my side to warm it a little, but it remained cold and limp. She walked a little faster than I did and as I began to hurry she always hurried a little more. Her face was averted from me, but I could see the drops of moisture upon her short black hair which seemed like a bedraggled cap set with small gems. The pavement seemed to become more thick with ice so that our feet no longer broke through the crystalline layer. The ice was stronger. At last very gently and without difficulty we began to skate. Her hand was warmer now as we began to move at first slowly and then faster upon the wide expanse of ice which showed yellow in the baleful winter light, its edges lost to view. As we moved effortlessly onward I turned her a little to face me. She had shaken the water from her hair which seemed now to be a furry hat, and in her high black skating boots she looked to me like a Cossack. But her face was sad. I drew her closer and we began to waltz together on the endless ice. As we danced I attempted to embrace her: but I was impeded by the sword which hung down stiffly between us, its hilt biting into me and causing a sharp pain. I lowered my hand and put it upon the hilt and felt immediately her hand trying to prevent me. We moved more slowly in a circle as I increased my pressure and then broke suddenly through her restraining grip. The sword came out with a rush as still facing each other we drew apart. Over her shoulder I could see on the far horizon a tiny figure approaching. Steadily as he approached she receded until for a moment they were the same size, stiff and rounded like twin images in the middle distance. Then as she dwindled away to nothing he glided on towards me with increasing speed, his huge Jewish face growing like a great egg above the silken wings of his gown. I swung the sword in an arc before him but as it moved the blade came away and flew upwards into the winter darkness which had collected above us. Clinging in fear and guilt to what remained in my hand I recognised my father.

I woke up shivering. It was dark. The blankets had fallen to the floor and the camp bed felt damp as well as very hard and cold. I had a sharp pain in my stomach, doubtless the result of drinking a great deal the night before. Or was it still the night before? I got up, found my dressing-gown, and switched on the light.

The naked bulb lit up a scene of gloomy disorder, the gaunt camp bed with its trail of blankets, the bare floorboards, my suitcase disgorging towels, underwear, packets of letters and an electric razor. My jacket and trousers lay in a heap where I had drunkenly fallen out of them. The half-empty whisky bottle stood in the corner. There were various cigarette ends. The glass which I had just overturned with my foot rolled slowly across the floor until it came to rest against a leg of the bed. It made a hollow sound. The famous oil-fired central heating seemed to be making little impression on the temperature of the room. I turned on the electric fire which was set into the wall and it glowed in the bright light with a cheerless pallor. The demon asthma, defeated when I went to bed by drink and sheer exhaustion, was present still, and I could feel it squeeze my chest like a broad band wound about me and gradually tightening. Intermittent whines and gurgles issued from my lungs. I tried to breathe slowly. I knotted the belt of my dressing-gown and opened the window, but shut it at once after one sniff of the cold thick air outside. I looked out.

Far below me in a kind of dark, Lowndes Square slumbered in the haze of its street lamps out of which black trees soared almost to the level of my window. I could not make out whether the diffused light in which I saw the shapes below was a twilight or whether it was simply the glow of lamplight spread out upon the night. The sky was dark and thick. I wondered what time it was. My watch had stopped and the telephone was not connected yet. In what I could discern of the Square there seemed to be no one about. Perhaps I had only slept for an hour or two. What was certain was that I could not now sleep again. I turned back to the room.

Palmer had of course been right. It was only on the following day that the full shock came to me. I had returned to London in a daze, had come straight to Lowndes Square and had then slept until late. That had been, assuming that it was now after midnight, yesterday morning. When I woke I woke to a state of terror and despair which was unlike anything I had ever experienced. I had tasted despair in the past, but as I remember it had always had a fairly clear cause and a clear nature. This present thing was confused and irrational and its very obscurity was a source of fear. I was frightened to be alone with it and yet there was no one to whom I could run. I could not even make out what part in my condition was played by horror of incest. I had never consciously felt any aversion from the idea of an embrace of siblings. Yet perhaps it was just this idea at work in my soul through some pattern which I could not discern which brought about this almost tangible sense of darkness. What was strange too was that this particular horror, whatever its source, was now indissolubly connected with my passion for Honor, so that it was as if the object of my desire were indeed my sister.

During my interview with Palmer my sense of Honor's proximity had been as it were diffused, a trembling in the atmosphere which was not quite a sound but which if it had been audible might have been a shriek. Now afterwards my thought of her, focused, was a round pain to the periphery of which the torn fragments of my being adhered like rags of flesh. I could indeed hardly put a name to my state, so unlike was it to anything which I had experienced previously when in love. It seemed as if this condition had with those no common feature. Yet I could not think what else to call it if it was not love which so brought me to my knees.

I could not without agony recall the mounting level of my intention and its terrible climax. Something still remained to torment me of a kind of dream which I had had of some miraculous and magnificent encounter with Honor in which the lurid light of battle which had so flashed over our past meetings should be transformed into, or rather finally seen as, the glow of a violent love. I had dreamed of her as free, as alone, as waiting in her still slumbering consciousness for me, reserved, separated, sacred. The so different truth of the matter could scarcely be contemplated. I had not for a second conceived of her possessing a lover; and at the idea that she had taken to her in that rôle her brother my fascinated and appalled imagination reeled. In any woman this could be, if it existed, no trivial passion, and in such a woman this dark love could not but be something of colossal dimensions. Some sign of how great it was I could indeed now in retrospect see, interpreting in the light of my knowledge Honor's bewildering conduct.

I thought of myself as in every sense lost, sunk without trace in a love which now seemed tinged with insanity, and deprived altogether of hope. I attached little importance to Palmer's statement that what I had seen would be without a sequel. It seemed as if Honor's will alone, bent upon Palmer, must bring all that she wished to pass. I had of course no intention, had never had any intention, of speaking to Antonia. Antonia seemed to me as unconnected with this as if she were a complete stranger. She seemed too, for such monstrous knowledge, too flimsy and too small. I could not have spoken to Antonia about my falling in love and so I could not speak to her about this which was inseparably a part of my falling in love. No one would ever know about it. But I could not see Palmer, even married to Antonia, as ever free from the clutches of that tawny-breasted witch the vision of whom, her jagged black hair in disorder, her face stern and angelic above her nakedness, never ceased now to be before me; and I felt equally that I was cursed for life, like men who have slept with temple prostitutes and, visited by a goddess, cannot touch a woman after.

I spent the day in a sort of limbo. I could not eat anything, nor could I rest because of a dreadful aching and tingling in the limbs. I walked about in Hyde Park, returned to the flat, and set out again at once through fear of being alone. The misty park was desolate as a moon landscape but at least there were forms of human beings upon it here and there. I thought a little bit about Georgie, but her figure, seeming already to belong to a remote past, looked so sadly upon me that I could not endure to contemplate it. I could not ask Georgie to console me because I loved another, nor could the old love, poor pathetic thing as it now seemed, heal me of the new. I drank a great deal and went to bed about nine o'clock in a desperate desire for oblivion.

I wondered now if I should not try after all to go to sleep again. There was nothing I could do with myself waking. I pulled the blankets back on to the camp bed and lay down on top of them without switching out the light; but the ache had come back into my limbs and I knew it was useless to attempt to rest. I got up again and began to hunt for my asthma tablets, tilting the rest of the contents of my suitcase out on to the floor. I found them, and retrieved the glass which turned out to be cracked. I trailed out to the kitchen and began gloomily to wash a plastic mug which had been left behind by the previous tenant.

A strange sudden sound echoed through the flat. It was close by, and yet I could not locate its direction. It seemed to come from everywhere at once. I jumped, with a violent trip of the heart, and then stood rigid listening to the silence and wondering what I had heard. The sound came again. After a terrified moment I realised that it was the door bell which I had not heard before. I adjusted my dressing-gown and went into the dark corridor, leaving the door open behind me to give some light. I fumbled with the catch of the front door, my hands trembling with nervousness, and eventually got it open. The lights were on on the landing. It was Antonia.

I stared at her with an idiotic surprise and my heart beat faster as if I already knew that she brought bad news. She had her back to the light but her darkened face seemed to stare as madly as my own. Without speaking I turned back toward

the lighted sitting-room and Antonia followed me in, closing
both doors behind her.

I moved over toward the window and then turned back to
look at her. She looked wild. She wore a scarf over her head
from which great strands of greying gold hair escaped on to
the collar of her tweed coat. She seemed to be wearing no
make-up and was extremely pale. Her big mouth was drooping as it sometimes did before she cried.

I said, "What time is it, Antonia?"

"Ten o'clock."

"In the night or in the morning?"

"In the morning," she said, staring at me with wider eyes.

"But why is it so dark?"

"It's foggy."

"I must have slept for twelve hours," I said. "What is it,
Antonia?"

"Martin," said Antonia, "did anything odd happen when
I was away?"

My breath came short. "Odd?" I said. "No, not that I know
of. Where were you, anyway?" I had not even wondered till
now. I had not had a thought to spare for her.

"I went to see mother," said Antonia. "She hasn't been
well. I'm sure I told you. I wanted Anderson to come too,
but he had to go to Cambridge to fetch away his things."

"Why did you ask if anything odd had happened?"

"Well, something must have happened," said Antonia,
"or else I'm going mad."

"You're not the only one," I said. "But I still don't
understand."

"Did you see Anderson at the week-end?"

"No."

"Well, something's happened to him."

"What?"

"I don't know," said Antonia. "It's like in stories when someone is possessed by the devil, or in science fiction. He looks the same and yet he seems to be a different person. It's as if a different personality inhabited him."

"This must be nonsense," I said. "Sit down, for heaven's sake, Antonia, and stop looking as if you were going to scream."

"But he *is* changed," said Antonia, her voice rising. "He's turned against me." She was staring at me as if she positively wanted to infect me with her own craziness.

" 'Turned against you'?" I said. "Come, come, Antonia. And please don't be so intense. I'm not feeling at all well myself. Now just tell me quietly and in detail what the hell you mean. And do *sit down*, for Christ's sake."

"It isn't anything very definite," she said, "and yet it's overwhelming. Something must have happened. He behaves quite differently to me, he's cold and he looks at me in such a terrifying way as if he were thinking about killing me. Of course I got quite tearful, and that seemed to annoy him more. Then he went away for ages in the middle of the night. And Honor Klein has come back to the house and she seems to be everywhere at once like a sort of black cloud. And honestly, Martin, I'm frightened." She ended with a little whine and sat down on the camp bed, getting out her handkerchief.

"Pull yourself together," I said. "You must be imagining all this." I was exceedingly shaken to see my own fear mirrored in her unconsciousness, in her innocence.

"It was such a shock," said Antonia. The big tears now coursed down her face. "I could hardly believe it at first, I thought I must be imagining it too. But he kept *watching* me, and so *cold*. As if I'd committed a crime. I wonder if anyone has told him some story about me?"

"What story could anybody tell?"

"Oh, I don't know," said Antonia. "Something about me and Alexander for instance. You know the way people love to invent things. Somebody must have done something to put him against me. There must have been some misunderstanding. You haven't done anything, have you, Martin?"

"No, of course not," I said. "I haven't seen Palmer. Anyway you know perfectly well I wouldn't do anything like that." Palmer must be on the rack, wondering if I had told Antonia. The thought did not displease me.

I became aware of a faint hissing sound behind me. It increased, and I turned to the window. It had started to rain. Looking at the greyish yellowish sky I saw it now as daylight. I turned back to the lighted room and the lifted frightened face of Antonia. The place was as bleak and lurid as a prison cell.

"Perhaps he's going mad," she said. "Martin, did you know that his mother was insane?"

"No, I didn't," I said. "Was she? That's interesting."

"He only told me quite recently," said Antonia. "Last week, before—" She sobbed, wiped her face slowly all over with the handkerchief and sobbed again.

I stood, hands in the pockets of my dressing-gown, watching her cry. I pitied her, but only as an unconscious extension of my own dilemma.

"So Honor Klein is there," I said.

"I hate that woman," said Antonia. "She was supposed to be going back to Cambridge, but there she still was and now she's actually living in the house. She gives me the creeps."

"Me too," I said. The door bell rang and we both jumped.

I looked at Antonia, and her wide eyes followed me to the door. I crossed the hall and flung the front door open. It was the removal men.

I told them to dump the stuff anywhere and returned to Antonia. She was standing up now, examining her face in her pocket mirror. She had dabbed a little powder on to her nose and was now rubbing her cheeks which were still shiny with tears. She pushed the scarf back off her hair and gave an exhausted sigh. She looked haggard.

"Darling, do use your common sense," she said. "You may as well have the stuff put in the right rooms." She seemed a little recovered and went out to organise the removal men. A few minutes later two giants came shuffling in carrying the Carlton House writing-table with the Audubon prints stacked on top of it. I told them where to put it. When they had gone I cut the string which held the prints together and began to lay them out against the wall in a row: the puffins, the night-jars, the gold-winged woodpeckers, the Carolina parrots, the scarlet tanagers, the great crested owls. The uprooted familiar things affected me with a sad sick feeling as if I were dimly remembering that someone had died. I could hear Antonia's voice in the hall instructing the men. What was my sickness? I stared through the prints, unable to focus my eyes upon them, into another world. Behold her bosom and half her side, a sight to dream of not to tell.

Antonia came back into the room and shut the door. She was carrying the Meissen cockatoos one in each hand. She put them on the two ends of the mantelpiece. She said, "That's all for this room, I've told them. Oh, the bird prints, yes, you've taken them. I'd somehow forgotten that they were yours." She looked at them sadly and began to take off her coat.

"We rather forgot about mine and yours, didn't we?" I said. "I'll give them back to you."

"No, no," said Antonia. "I don't want them. You must have your own things."

"Well, you must come and help me arrange them," I said. "You will, won't you?"

Antonia looked at me. Her face contracted, and she shook her head, trying to speak. Then she said, "Oh, Martin, I'm so miserable!" She began to wail with a low keening sound, and sat down heavily on the bed rocking herself to and fro. For a while I watched her.

The door bell rang again. Antonia's weeping stopped as if at the turn of a switch, and as I passed her she clutched my hand for a moment. I gave her a reassuring squeeze and went on out into the hall. Someone was silhouetted in the open doorway. It was, of course, Palmer.

Ever since Antonia had arrived I had been expecting him, and it was with an extraordinary exhilaration that I now saw his tall figure confronting me. I could not see his face properly, but I could feel my own becoming expressionless and bland. I was glad he had come.

Palmer said, "Is Antonia here?" His voice was low and harsh and there was emotion in him.

I said, "Yes, do you want to see her?"

"I've come to take her away," said Palmer.

"Really?" I said. "But suppose she doesn't want to go?"

Antonia had opened the sitting-room door and the light now showed me Palmer's face, the straight tense line of his mouth and his eyes practically closed. It was the face of a man in danger and I exulted at the sight of it. Antonia said in a clear voice, "Come in here, please." The removal men were coming up the stairs again carrying the Chinese Chippendale chairs. I could hear them bumping on the banisters. I went back into the sitting-room and Palmer followed. I closed the door and we all looked at each other.

Palmer said to Antonia, "Please come with me, Antonia." He spoke in a cold dead manner and I could see what she meant about his having changed into another person. He must by now be certain that I had told her.

She hesitated, looked at me, looked at Palmer, and said in an almost inaudible voice, "All right."

"You're not going," I said to her.

Palmer said, "Just keep out of this, will you, Martin? You've meddled enough in things you don't understand." He was looking at Antonia.

"You meddled in things *you* didn't understand," I said, "when you destroyed my happy and successful marriage."

"It wasn't happy and successful," said Palmer, still staring at Antonia. "Happy husbands don't keep little girls as mistresses. Put your coat on, Antonia."

"She isn't going with you," I said. "Can't you see she's afraid of you?"

Antonia stood paralysed, swaying a little, her shoulders twisted, looking from one to the other of us with big alarmed eyes. She did in fact look the picture of terror.

Palmer said, "Martin, you and Antonia will do as I tell you."

"Not any more," I said. "Poor Palmer. Now get out."

The notion that I was shortly going to hit Palmer came to us all at the same time. It showed in Antonia in a sudden excited moistening of the lips, and in Palmer in a relaxing of his expression, a return of the wide-eyed stripped look which he had worn in Cambridge. He stopped looking at Antonia and turned to face me.

He said softly, "You are a destroyer, aren't you." Then he said to Antonia. "Use your reason. I want to talk to you, and not here."

I said, "For Christ's sake go."

Palmer said, "Not without her," and stepped forward towards Antonia, who moved back against the window, her hand coming up to her mouth. He put his hand on her arm as if to pull her and she gave a little cry at the contact. I followed him and dug my fingers into his shoulder. He turned and knocked my grip roughly away, and as his hands came up I hit him in the face as hard as I could. He lost his balance and fell heavily. Antonia stepped over him and ran from the room. The fight, such as it was, was over.

Violence, except on the screen, is always pathetic, ludicrous and beastly. Palmer got slowly to his knees and then man-œuvred himself to a sitting position with his back to the wall. He kept his face covered with his hand. I squatted beside him attentively. I noticed that the glass of one of the prints was cracked. I felt no anger against Palmer now, just a satisfaction in what had happened. The rain was still hissing down outside the window. After a minute or two I said, "Are you all right?"

"Yes, I think so," said Palmer through his hand. "No serious damage. It just hurts like hell."

"That was the general idea," I said. "Let me see." I gently pulled his hand away. Palmer's face, contracting against the light, showed me the beginnings of a splendid black eye. The eye was closed completely and the area round it was raw and swollen. A little blood marked the place on the cheek where my fist had arrived.

"I haven't anything to treat you with," I said. "You'd better go home. I'll get you a taxi."

"Give me a handkerchief, would you?" said Palmer. "I can't see anything at the moment."

I gave him one and he held it to his damaged eye while he got laboriously to his knees again. I helped him up and brushed down his clothes. He stood there like a child while I did so. I kept my hands upon him and he did not move away. It was like an embrace. What I experienced in that moment was the complete surrender of his will to mine. Then I felt him trembling. I could not bear it.

I said, "I'll give you some whisky." I poured some into the cracked glass. Palmer sipped it with docility.

Antonia said from outside, "The men are going. Could you pass me some money? I haven't enough."

I found a few shillings in the pocket of my jacket, and said to Palmer, "Could you lend me five bob, by any chance?"

He put the whisky down and, handkerchief still to eye, fished inside his coat. He gave me the silver, and I passed it all through the door to Antonia. I could hear the men departing. I wanted Palmer out of the house.

I said, "I'll go down with you now. We can pick up a taxi at the door."

He nodded. I pulled on my trousers and jacket over my pyjamas and we went out. There was no sign of Antonia. In the lift Palmer dabbed his eye and said softly to himself, "Well, well, well . . ." I escorted him to the street, holding his arm, and a cruising taxi appeared almost at once. The rain was still falling relentlessly. When he was in the taxi we both tried to think of something suitable to say and Palmer said "Well" again. I said, "I'm sorry." He said, "Let me see you soon," and I said, "I don't know." The taxi drove off.

I crawled back to the lift. I felt I wanted to go away somewhere and sleep. I didn't even know whether Antonia was still in the flat. It occurred to me that it was for Honor and not for Antonia that I had hit Palmer. Or was it? I reached the door of the flat which was still wide open. I went through into the sitting-room. Antonia was standing near the window. She seemed calm. Hands behind back, head thrust forward, she surveyed me and her tired face was alive with a sort of provocative quizzical concern. She must have liked my hitting Palmer. Perhaps if I had hit Palmer on day one everything would have been different. Everything was certainly different now. Now I had power, but useless power.

"Well, that appears to be that," said Antonia.

"What appears to be what?" I said. I sat down on the camp bed and poured some more whisky into the glass. I was trembling now.

"You've got me back," said Antonia.

"Have I?" I said. "Good show." I drank the whisky.

"Oh, Martin," said Antonia in a shaken voice, "darling, darling Martin!" She came and fell on her knees in front of me, clasping my legs, and the great crystalline tears which she used began to pour again. I stroked her hair with one hand in an abstracted way. I wanted to be by myself and to think what I was going to do about Honor. It struck me as a bitter paradox that my flight to Honor had had the result of reconciling her and Palmer, Antonia and me: whatever vision it was that she through the brother and I through the sister had momentarily had it seemed likely now to perish. It was that that would have no sequel. I went on drinking the whisky.

"Martin, you are so *familiar*," said Antonia. "It seems silly to say this when I ought to be saying much more splendid things to you, because you've been wonderful. But it's just this that strikes me! You know, I *was* afraid of Anderson, right from the start. It was never quite right, there was something a little forced. Do you know? I might even never have gone on with it if you had resisted. But no, you've been marvellous, you've been perfect. And it's so much better for me, don't you think, to have tried it and come through, and come back—if I'd dropped the idea at the start I would have been so tormented, wondering if perhaps there might have been something in it."

"But aren't you in love with Palmer any more?" I asked. I stared at the sleeve of my pyjamas which protruded damply from under my jacket. I had got soaked in my dash to the taxi.

"It seems callous, doesn't it," said Antonia. "But somehow yesterday and last night—I can't tell you what it was like. I felt he hated me. He is a demon, you know. And love can die quickly, I think, just as it can be born quickly. I fell in love with Anderson in a flash."

"Heigh-ho," I said. "All's well that ends well." I noted in a spiritless way Antonia's perfect assumption that I wanted her back. There was something almost magnificent about it. But I could not play out the grand reconciliation scene which she obviously wanted.

"Martin," said Antonia, still on the floor, "I can't tell you what joy and *relief* it is to be able to talk to you again. Though we never really lost touch, did we? Wasn't that quite miraculous, the way we kept in touch?"

"Pretty good," I said. "That was mainly your doing. Anyway, now we needn't worry about the Audubon prints."

"Darling!" She hid her face against my knees, weeping and laughing. The door bell rang.

I was in no mood for further visitors, but I went to the

door. A wild idea occurred to me that it might be Honor. It was Rosemary.

"Martin dear," said Rosemary in her precise manner, business-like as soon as the door was six inches open, "I've come about the *curtains*. There's a problem about the shape of the *pelmets*, whether you want wavy ones or straight ones, and I thought I'd better ask you and have a look again myself on the spot. Good, I see your stuff has come. We can do a little arranging straightaway."

"Come in, flower," I said. I led her to the sitting-room.

Antonia had dried her tears and was powdering her nose again. She greeted Rosemary. I said to Rosemary, "I don't think we need bother about the pelmets. Antonia and I are going to stay married after all, so everything can now go back to Hereford Square."

If Rosemary was disappointed, she concealed it gallantly. She said, "I'm so glad, oh I'm so glad!" Antonia flew to her with a little cry and they began kissing each other. I finished the whisky.

❋ *Chapter Twenty-two* ❋

MY darling Georgie, you will have been impatient, anxious, perhaps angry, because of my silence. I am sorry. I have been in hell lately. I didn't know that there were so many varieties of torment. I've been sampling a few new ones. Anyway. You will have heard about me and Antonia. I can't "explain" this. It happened not exactly against my will, but without my will. And I have to accept it. I cannot now reject Antonia; you have no conception how broken she is, I would not have believed it. I *have* to look after her. I am certain of that. I wonder if you understand. All this is strange and unexpected to me beyond words and in many ways bitter too, but it has to be endured. You must forgive me, and forgive this inconclusive, you may even feel evasive, letter. I cannot see you at present. I have to give my energies to putting together again something which I thought to have been completely smashed. It can never be whole. But for the moment at any rate I must give myself completely to it. What I have to offer you, Georgie, I honestly *do not know*. This is not a way of saying "nothing", but is the truth. I love you, my child, and I believe that you love me, and in a loveless world this is at least something. I can only selfishly ask you to go on loving me in whatever way you can—and I for my part, when my mind is more at peace, will give you what I can, whatever that may turn out to be. I cannot conceive of our friendship coming to an end—and precisely because I believe in our friendship I dare to write such an unsatisfactory letter. But an unsatisfactory letter is, here, the only honest letter. Let me have a little note in return to say you have received this. I hope you are well. I kiss you.

M.

I completed this not only unsatisfactory, but in some ways dishonest, missive under the frank and friendly eye of Miss

Seelhaft, who at her desk across the room was making copies of the latest price list. Mytten was away visiting a bibulous titled client; he had been persuaded, not with difficulty I dare say, to stay over the week-end. Some very serious tasting of Lynch-Gibbon wines was apparently taking place. Mytten excelled at those methods of business, especially favoured in the wine trade, where the matter in hand is introduced with leisurely indirectness and a sale takes place almost at an unconscious level, so little reference has there been to the crude details of commerce. Such methods, however, demand time, and Mytten always took his. I was not displeased at his absence.

Miss Seelhaft looked up every now and then to see if I was all right. She and Miss Hernshaw, once again informed of my fortunes before I came to tell them, had with a perfect tact combined discreet congratulation with respectful solicitude. They gave their nod to the conventions, but did not pretend not to notice the extent to which I was worn out and wretched. They were full of little kindnesses and generally treated me as an invalid, while at the same time welcoming me back to work in a manner which in less intelligent girls would have showed as patronising. We all, they strenuously and I with a languid acquiescence, kept up the fiction that the business had scarcely been able to carry on without me.

I sealed up the letter to Georgie. I wondered what she would make of it. There is a time limit to how long a spirited young person can be kept in cold storage. Georgie's time must be approaching the end. But there was nothing I could do. I could not face seeing Georgie just now. If I saw her I could not tell her the truth—and neither could I bear to lie to her face to face. It was true that I didn't want to lose her. I wanted her love. I was not so flush with love that I could afford to dispense with it. But I did not yet want to make the effort required to decide that I could not merit, and therefore could not ask for, that love. I wanted, frankly, not to have to think about Georgie at all for the present. There were other matters which rapaciously claimed my soul. Miss Hernshaw, who played mother to us, came in at that point with the tea. As she passed Miss Seelhaft she brushed her arm against her friend's shoulder as if by accident. I envied them.

I went home by tube. It was odd, this feeling of being integrated once again into the ordinary life of London. For over a week now I had been going to the office every day and returning at five thirty to Hereford Square, just like in the old days; and as I hung from my strap in the swaying train, reading the short story in the *Evening Standard*, I was sometimes tempted to think that I had been the victim of a rich and prolonged but now completed hallucination. Yet I had not dreamed it. The constant pain was enough of a reminder.

Antonia's mood of exaltation was over. It had not lasted long; and now she appeared to be, as I had said to Georgie in the letter, simply broken. I found the spectacle of this brokenness extremely pathetic and moving, and I had not been insincere in telling Georgie how much Antonia now needed and claimed my attention. The house at Hereford Square still seemed grey and derelict; after having been half slaughtered it had not yet come back to life. We had brought back the pictures and the smaller objects by car, but the rest of the stuff that had gone to Lowndes Square was still there, and Antonia to whom I had left the task of organising its removal had not yet had the energy to attend to it, so that notable gaps, especially that caused by the absence of the Carlton House writing-table, figured to us as visible scars. How deep were the invisible scars we were only just beginning to learn.

We nursed each other. Antonia, who looked much older and whose face had developed an expression of sulky irritability which was new to it, showed a tendency to crossness which she tried visibly to control. We had sharpish exchanges followed by periods of strenuous solicitude. We were perpetually enquiring about each other's health, fetching hot-water bottles, boiling milk, making tea, and dosing each other with aspirins and phenobarbitone. The house even smelt like a hospital. The fact is we were both exhausted, and yet with nerves sufficiently on edge, both required each other and found rest impossible together. For myself, what mainly sustained me was feeling sorry for Antonia. It was not a pure compassion, but a feeling, I very well knew, compounded with the vindictive. She was aware that she had made me suffer; but she would never know the extent and the nature of the suffering for which, no doubt irrationally, I could not help somehow blaming her. We were both defeated.

It was in some ways fortunate that during this time Antonia was so extremely self-absorbed. She assumed wearily and completely that I was content to accept a return to our former situation. Georgie's name was not mentioned; and I could not make out whether Antonia was now indifferent to my infidelity, or believed that it had ceased. It seemed, strangely, most likely of all that she had simply *forgotten* about Georgie. I could not quite suppose, mad as we both then were, that she had literally forgotten; but it seemed as if her tired and confused spirit could only deal with a few matters at a time, and evidently Georgie was not one of them.

Palmer's name was not mentioned either. We both knew that it would have to come up. But we were resting. There was no sign of life from Pelham Crescent. Those two had vanished as if they had never been. Antonia suggested of her own accord that she might go down and stay with Alexander at Rembers. I would have been glad enough to have her looked after yet off my hands. But it turned out that Alexander was not at Rembers, but was in London on some mysterious ploy of his own, and in fact we saw very little of him. Rosemary turned up regularly, bringing flowers, fruit, magazines and other toys for invalids, but neither of us was glad to see her. So, with pity and with exasperation, we lived side by side, each of us sunk in our own thoughts.

In so far as it was possible to do so I thought about Honor the whole time. She filled my consciousness to the brim. She became the atmosphere which I lived and breathed. I endlessly went over our various encounters in my mind and marvelled at how necessarily and how vastly she now, after so little acquaintance, existed for me. But what I chiefly clung to was one thing: she had not told Palmer about the scene in the cellar. At least she had not *then* told him; and with that, as my thoughts ran frantically again and again through the same circuit I measured with despair the gap between then and now. Then I had been free and thought that she was. Now I was caught, and somehow more profoundly and irrevocably caught than before, while she—I did not know what to think. At times I attached importance to the idea that Palmer had, through his relation to Antonia, been trying to free himself from a burdensome obsession. At other times I felt equally certain that the strange pair, after Palmer's abortive experience, had become even more united. In any case there was nothing I could do. I did not seriously envisage leaving Antonia. I had her, and definitively so, on my hands. Nor did I even know, though this was somehow the least of my concerns, exactly what picture of me was present in Honor's mind. In spite of evidence to the contrary, and coming back again to the fact of her silence to Palmer, I was confident that I existed for Honor. Yet, and I concluded it for the hundredth time, I was powerless. And yet, starting out again for the hundred and first time, I could not stop thinking about Honor and with every reason for despair, somewhere, through some minute cranny, there filtered a ray of hope to make in the dark labyrinth of my bewildered thoughts a little dim twilight.

Of course my mind returned continually with fascination to the fact of incest. I even visited the public library and read up everything I could on the subject. The psychological literature was scanty and unsatisfactory, and I soon turned my attention to mythology where, with a curious gratification which was almost consoling, I noted the frequency of brother and sister marriages, particularly among royalty and gods. Who after all was fit for a royal brother except his royal sister? The progeny of such unions, I also noted, was various, often monstrous. When not so engaged my imagination, in an incompetent and frustrated manner, followed the liaison of Palmer and his sister back into their childhood. I reflected too, though not to much purpose, on the insane mother. What lurid illumination I thus engendered served merely to display with a vividness which prostrated me the figure of Honor, aloof, frightening, sacred, and in a way which I now more clearly understood, taboo.

It was still raining. It had been raining for days. I arrived at Hereford Square, shook the water off my overcoat and hung it up, and tramped into the drawing-room. A bright fire was burning and the lamps were all on. The curtains were not yet drawn and I could see outside in the light from the window the dripping form of the magnolia tree. Antonia, who had been reading by the fire, jumped up to welcome me.

She had a Martini all ready mixed, and a bowl of cocktail biscuits on the little table. She kissed me and asked me what sort of day I had had. I told her and began to sip my drink. I sat down heavily on the sofa. I was now, all the time, unutterably tired as if simply keeping alive was a terrible effort. Absentmindedly I picked up my latest volume of *The Golden Bough*.

"Must you read over your drink?" said Antonia sharply. "I've been alone all day, except for Rosemary coming in this morning, which was hardly a treat."

"Sorry," I said. I put the book aside.

"And why are you reading mythology all the time now? You never used to. You haven't even looked at that book I got you on the war in the Pacific."

"Sorry, darling," I said. "I'll read it next." I closed my eyes.

"And don't go to sleep either," said Antonia. "I want to ask you to do something for me."

"Anything you like," I said rather sleepily, "What?"

"Will you go and see Anderson for me?"

That woke me up. "Why?" I said. "To achieve what? And why don't you go yourself?"

"I don't want to," said Antonia. "God knows what exactly I feel about Anderson. Sometimes I think I hate him. But I'm quite clear that the whole thing is utterly over."

"Then why should I see him?" I said. But my heart burnt with desire.

"Simply to finish it off," said Antonia. "And there are practical things. There are a lot of my belongings at Pelham Crescent, which you might bring away, or arrange for a van to take, I suppose, as you wouldn't be able to get them all into the car."

I said, "Do you want me to find out whether Palmer still loves you?"

Antonia looked at me wearily, as if from far away, through infinite grey curtains of gloom and resignation. She said, "He can't love me, or else he wouldn't have given up just because you put your fist in his eye."

This seemed true; and I was reminded again of Antonia's innocence. Her connection with Palmer and Honor, since she did not share in the knowledge that was crucial, seemed flimsy and abstract compared with mine. *How* connected I was I felt through my bones and my blood as I contemplated the possibility of seeing them again. I had known, of course, that it would come to this, I had known that I *would* see them again. It was perhaps just this certainty, secretly at work in my imagination, which had shed the little glimmer of hope. But, resting, I had averted my attention.

"You're sure you want me to do this, not you?"

"Yes," she said, and sighed heavily. "It's an unfinished business. I shall be relieved when it's done and you and I can settle down to living a normal life again."

She sounded so dejected that I got up and leaning over her kissed her on the brow. I remained, leaning a little on her shoulder, my cheek touching her crown of golden hair. It was fading into grey. One day, without having noticed the transition, I would see that it was gold no longer.

✳ *Chapter Twenty-three* ✳

ONCE it had been settled that I should go on an embassy to Pelham Crescent I wanted to put it off for as long a possible. When it came to it I was scared stiff. It was not just that I was positively frightened at the idea of perhaps seeing Honor again, and that when I pictured being in the same room with her my whole body became cold and rigid. It was also that this embassy represented in all probability my last chance. My last chance of *what* I was not very clear about, but certainly fear, curiosity, expectation, even hope clung about the prospect of the visit. Though if I believed in a miracle I could not at all conceive what that miracle might be. So it was that I played a little for time. I could, in the darkness and uncertainty into which we had been plunged by the mute withdrawal of the other two, just about do with, live with, the image of Honor: an image which might however become for me at any moment altogether a Medusa. For deprived utterly of hope I did not see how I could manage; and I feared like death that utter deprivation.

But Antonia was impatient, and I could get from her a grace of only three days. Resolved at last, she wanted to make a quick end. Our discussion had taken place on a Monday. It was agreed that I should write to Palmer simply suggesting that I should come to see him at six o'clock on the following Thursday. This gave him time to reply; and in fact I received a postcard, brief but bland, by return to say that the time was suitable. By nine o'clock on the Wednesday evening I was already in a state of almost unbearable agitation and could settle to nothing. Not even a recently discovered book of

Japanese legends, wherein brothers and sisters regularly lay together and procreated dragons, could retain my attention; and I would at last in desperation have gone to the cinema, only I feared that at the sight of anything sad or touching I might break into audible groans. Antonia was equally restless and had been in a mood of nervous irritation throughout the afternoon. We both wandered morosely about the house passing and re-passing each other, profoundly connected yet unable to touch, in a silent mutually hostile hay.

I was worried that I had heard nothing from Georgie, who had not yet replied to my letter. Pain at this neglect, a particular pain separable from my other troubles, persisted, and I had had the intention of writing to her again that very evening. But when the time came I was unable to. The figure of Honor stood between us. I could not *see* Georgie any more. I could not, at that moment, even distantly envisage going to call on her; and to write now without suggesting a meeting seemed insuperably difficult. So I postponed thinking about Georgie, as indeed I was now postponing everything, until after my visit to Pelham Crescent.

I had just made another round of the house and was wondering if I could decently go to bed and whether if I did I would have another attack of asthma. Antonia had now got the entire contents of the linen cupboard out on to the stairs and was quite unnecessarily folding and sorting them. I stood on the landing for a while and watched her in silence. The telephone rang.

"I'll go," I said, and took a long stride down over the piles of linen. "Be *careful*," said Antonia. I entered the drawing-room, closed the door, and picked up the receiver, as I always did now, with the expectation of something strange. It was Alexander.

I was pleased to hear his voice. "Hello, you ruffian," I said. "Why are you neglecting us? Antonia's dying to see you. You've no idea how dull we've become. Do come and cheer us up."

Alexander sounded confused. He said, yes, he'd love to come and he was sorry he'd been elusive, but first of all he had something important to tell me and he had better not beat about the bush.

"Beating about the bush," I said, "is exactly what you *are* doing. What is it?"

"I'm going to get married."

I was shaken. I said, "Well done, at last, brother. Who is she? Do I know her?"

"Well, you do, actually," said Alexander. "It's Georgie."

I laid the phone down on the table. Distantly I could hear Alexander talking still. I put my hand over my face.

With a hideous rush, like blood returning to a crushed limb, I was invaded by my old love for Georgie; and in that instant I realised how very much I had all the same, all the same, all the same, relied upon her faithfulness. I had been mad.

I picked up the phone again and said, "Sorry, I missed that last bit."

"I said, I suppose it's no use hoping that you won't be displeased, even angry. But I hope too that in the end you'll wish us luck. Do you want to see us, or would you prefer not?"

"I'll wish you luck now," I said, "and of course I want to see you. I can't think why you imagine I'd be displeased. I'm afraid I had nothing left for Georgie except a bad conscience. You're a cure for both of us. Honestly, I'm delighted." With a fluency that amazed me lies and treachery streamed from my lips. I was in extreme pain.

"You're an ace, Martin," said Alexander. "Would you mind breaking it to Antonia?"

"I'll tell her surely," I said. "But won't you both come round to see us now, this evening? Where are you, anyway? Is Georgie with you?" I felt such misery, and such frenzy, at the news, I wanted now only to fall upon the knife, to get the major shock over as rapidly as possible.

"Yes, she's here," said Alexander, "and sends her love." He muffled the phone for a moment and I could hear him saying something indistinguishable. "We're at Gloucester Road station in fact. We've got to make another phone call, but we could be with you in ten minutes if you'd really like to see us." Alexander was obviously eager to get it over too.

"Of course we would," I said. "It's an occasion for champagne. Come as soon as you can. Tell Georgie I'm very pleased with you both!"

"Thanks, Martin," said Alexander. "I thought you'd blow me out of the water."

"Admit you're a fast worker!"

I heard Alexander's relieved laugh at the other end. "I knew what I wanted for once."

I replaced the receiver and stood there by the table staring out at the black uncurtained garden. It had stopped raining and in the silence I could hear the water dripping from the magnolia. Antonia came in.

She saw my face and said, "Christ, what is it?"

"My dear brother Alexander is getting married to Georgie Hands."

"*No!*" said Antonia. Struck by the vehemence of that *no*, its tone of utter bewildered rejection, I looked at her face. It had become in an instant a wrinkled mask of pain. Antonia minded.

195

I said, "Well, I expect it's all for the best. You ought to be pleased. It removes temptation from my path."

Antonia drew her breath in sharply as if for an exclamation. But she said nothing. She turned her head away and I thought for a moment that she was going to burst into tears. I was surprised at her reaction. She must have laid more store than I realised by her tender sentimental friendship with my brother. But of course she was in an over-excited state.

I said, "I asked them to come round now to drink some champagne. They're at Gloucester Road. They should be arriving in a few minutes. I hope that's all right by you."

"You asked them round *now?*" said Antonia. Her face, screwed up with distress and anger, was positively ugly. "You perfect fool! Have you no consideration? I'm going out." She turned to the door.

"Dear Antonia," I said, "don't be cross with me. I didn't know you'd mind. I should have asked you. I'll entertain them alone if you like. But do please stay."

She stared at me for a moment almost with hatred. Then she left the room, clapping the door sharply to behind her. I heard her feet going heavily up the stairs. I waited, mastering a physical pain of jealousy so severe that it almost doubled me up. The bell rang. I went out into the hall.

Wrapped in their big overcoats, against the damp blue night whose air blew warm and fragrant in through the doorway, they stood tall and indistinguishably close together. "Come in, you disgraceful pair," I said.

They entered in silence and I helped them off with their coats. Alexander was wearing a stiff smile which must have been a duplicate of my own. I led the way into the drawing-room and by the fireplace we spread out and looked at each other's faces. It was, for all three, an effort. The shock was extreme. I could see Georgie trying to control a grimacing smile which kept returning. She was not able to prevent the blood from rushing visibly to redden her two cheeks. After the first quick glance she avoided my eye. Alexander watched us both tensely, ruefully; but he had, and could not conceal, the air of a successful man.

"Well, Martin," he said, "so you forgive us?"

"Of course, lunatics," I said. "There's nothing to forgive." I went forward and kissed Georgie on her burning cheek. It was not easy. I felt her shiver. I shook Alexander by the hand. I said, "You're bloody lucky."

"I know it," he said humbly, and cast a quick look at Georgie. He added, "Life can be very sudden, can't it? But the fastest things are often the surest things. Once we got the idea we needed little convincing!"

I had no desire for these sentiments and confidences. I wanted to get past the moment of hearing Georgie's voice. I turned and said to her more roughly than I had intended, "Come on, Georgie, speak up. It's only your old friend Martin. So my headlong brother carried you off?"

"Yes," said Georgie in a low tone, still not looking at me.

"Well, you're lucky too," I said. "Come and sit by the fire and we'll all have some champagne. And you can stop looking as if you'd been caught stealing the till." I plucked Georgie's sleeve and drew her to the sofa. This time I was really magnificent. They both sat down.

Alexander said, "We'll soon stop looking hangdog. We're terribly glad we've told you. Where's Antonia? Have you told her?"

"Yes, indeed," I said. "She's delighted too. She's just powdering her nose. She'll be down in a minute." I hoped this was true.

Georgie was looking at Alexander. She stretched out her long legs in a deliberate attempt to relax. Her breath came slowly and deeply. She was thinner and paler, wearing a black tweed pinafore dress with a high-necked striped blouse. Her hair, cascaded on top and carefully pinned, was immaculate. She seemed, with so much neatness, beautifully older. Alexander, with a cautious veiled tenderness, returned her look. The sense of my exclusion was for a moment almost unbearable; and I had a sudden repetition of an impression which I had had before in relation to Palmer and Antonia. They simply wanted me out of the way. I had to be somehow, tenderly, carefully, lovingly, but relentlessly *dealt with* before they could pass me by and get on with their lives together.

Georgie at last had steadily turned to look up at me and our eyes met. Hers were big, intense, troubled, yet full of a vitality which might at any moment shamelessly declare itself as happiness. God knows what she saw in mine. In that interchange she could not help, very briefly, now that she had a hold upon her emotions, exhibiting, almost flaunting before me, her new sense of her freedom. She had said that without freedom she would not exist. No wonder I had lost her. I went to fetch the champagne.

As I returned with bottles and glasses I became aware that Antonia was quietly descending the stairs. She had changed her dress and put on a good deal of make-up. She had evidently decided not to go out. When she saw me she paused a moment, gave me a sombre hostile look, and then proceeded slowly to the drawing-room door. I opened it for her and followed her in. The other two, who were sitting together on the sofa and ostentatiously not talking to each other, rose.

I caught a glimpse over her shoulder of Alexander's face.

His features were drawn together as if focusing to a point. The moment passed.

"Well, what a lovely surprise!" said Antonia, her voice a little higher than usual. She was the least under control of the four of us.

"I hope we have your blessing," said Alexander in a low submissive voice. He stooped towards her.

"My most hearty blessing!" said Antonia. "Can blessings be hearty? My blessing anyway. Let me kiss the child." She kissed Georgie, who stared and gripped Antonia's arm as the kiss descended on her cheek. I poured out the champagne.

Alexander and Georgie were exchanging looks. We raised our glasses and I said, "Let me be the one to say, a happy ending to a strange tale! From Antonia and Martin, to Georgie and Alexander, love and good wishes and con-gratulations!" Rather awkwardly we clicked the glasses and drank.

I poured out some more. Everybody was needing the stuff and we drank it like addicts. During this ritual there was a curious silence, all of us staring about at each other. I looked at Alexander. His face, seeming a little harder and absurdly young, had the crazy dazed look which is born of reckless behaviour or happiness. He had turned now to look at Antonia and I saw his features focus once again, drawn out to a fine point of provocative appeal. Georgie, not looking at him, was leaning very slightly in his direction as if responding to a magnetic pull. Their bodies were already acquainted. Georgie was gazing up at me now with a fugitive distressed smile well under control, keeping her glass steady at her lips. Drink always restored her. Antonia, holding her glass away from her in one hand in an Egyptian attitude, was staring at Alexander. Her mouth drooped. I noticed the rouge on her cheeks and how elderly she had become. But after all I had become elderly myself. I reflected that we were like two aged parents wishing the young people well.

To end the silence which had gone on too long I said to Georgie, "How smart you're looking! Quite the up-to-date girl."

Georgie smiled, Antonia sighed, we all fidgeted a little, and Alexander murmured, "There was a young man of Pitlochry, Kissed an up-to-date girl in a rockery . . ."

Still desperately kicking the conversation along I said, "And talking of Pitlochry, where are you off to for your honeymoon?"

Alexander hesitated. He said, "New York, actually," and looked at Georgie. I looked at her too. She looked down into her glass.

We were all silenced again. That had been an unlucky move and I could see Georgie's averted face stiffen and grow burning red.

I said hastily, "How nice. And where will you live? Mainly at Rembers? Or up in town?"

"Both, I expect," said Alexander. "But we certainly intend to inhabit Rembers properly, not just at week-ends." He answered vaguely, conscious of Georgie's mounting distress.

"That will be good for Rembers," I said. "It's a house that loves people. It will be good for it to have a real family in it, to have children there again."

As I said this and promptly wished it unsaid, I heard Georgie draw a sharp breath. She closed her eyes and two tears rolled suddenly down her cheeks.

Antonia heard the indrawn breath and turned her head. She saw Georgie's face. Then she said *Oh*, her mouth worked, her brow reddened, and her own eyes, like two great wells, were instantly overflowing. She bowed her head over the glass which she was holding stiffly in front of her and her tears fell into the champagne. Georgie had covered her face with her handkerchief. I looked at Alexander and Alexander looked at me. After all, for better and worse we had known each other a long time.

* Chapter Twenty-four *

EXTREME love is fed by everything. So it was that the shock of Georgie's decision, once the immediate pain had been suffered, opened as it were a channel down which my desires with an increased violence ran in the direction of Honor. The thing seemed intended; and in that perspective Georgie's action, though hideously upsetting and painful, counted chiefly as a clearing of the decks. I was, it seemed, to be deprived of consolation. I was to be stripped, shaved and prepared as a destined victim; and I awaited Honor as one awaits, without hope, the searing presence of a god. There was nothing which I could reasonably, even, expect: yet all was in the waiting. It was not until I was positively pushing open the door at Pelham Crescent that it occurred to me that I might not, in the course of my embassy, set eyes on Honor at all: so closely did I think of the brother and sister as being connected.

I closed the front door behind me and hung up my dripping raincoat. I had of course set out far too early from Hereford Square and had spent some time walking about in the rain trying to become calm and rational. All the same, my heart nearly choked me, so high did it leap, as I knocked on the door of Palmer's study and went in to the lamplight and the quiet interior, warm and dry and close-fitting as the inside of a nut. Palmer was alone.

He lay outstretched on the divan. He was in pyjamas, with the purple dressing-gown and thick red slippers. Although he had his back to the light I saw at once the greenish shadow on his cheek, the remains of the black eye. I saw it with surprise, having forgotten that I struck him, or having not quite in retrospect believed that his flesh was vulnerable. He was fumbling when I came in with a large box of paper handkerchiefs. A wastepaper basket full of crumpled paper was beside him and his first words were, "My dear fellow, don't come near me, I've got the most devilish cold!"

I sat down on a chair against the wall, as if I were in a waiting-room. I looked at Palmer wearily, passively. Perhaps after all I had only come to be judged and punished. I waited for him to act.

He sneezed violently several times, said, "Oh dear, Oh dear!", and then "Do have some whisky. There's some on the side, and ice in that barrel thing. A cold always goes straight to my liver so I'll stick to barley water."

I helped myself and lit a cigarette and waited. It now seemed clear to me, desolately, that I was not going to see Honor; and if this, inconclusively, was the end it was a terrible one.

"How is Antonia?" said Palmer.

"Very well," I said.

"I doubt that," said Palmer, "but she will recover. Falling out of love is chiefly a matter of *forgetting* how charming someone is. She will forget soon."

"You demon," I said. "You speak as if you were not, yourself, in the least involved." I spoke dully, however.

"No, no," said Palmer. "Don't misunderstand me. I was very carried away by your wife, very carried away indeed." He sneezed again and said "Damn!"

"Have you succeeded in forgetting how charming *she* is?" I asked.

"Do you want me to?" said Palmer.

"Leave me out," I said.

Dear boy, how can I?" said Palmer.

"That's the trouble," I said. "No one can leave me out. Yet I don't fit in either. Never mind."

"Why did you come?" said Palmer.

"Just so as to close the matter. Antonia likes things neat."

"By 'neat' do you mean tidy or pure?"

"Tidy. You flatter yourself, by the way. *Elle ne vous aime plus*. But your co-operation is needed to make an end. How exactly you do it I leave to you. These subtleties are in any case your province."

"Does Antonia want to see me?" said Palmer.

I looked at him closely. His clever eyes were upon me. His hand moved slowly to jettison a handkerchief. The darkly shadowed cheek seemed to suit him, suggestive of some half-remembered picture of Dionysus. I thought, he is sure I have told her. I said, "No."

Palmer watched me a while and then sighed and said, "It is better so." He added, "How are you, Martin?"

"Dead," I said. "Otherwise fine."

"Come," said Palmer, "tell me, tell me." His voice was caressing and persuasive.

I was surprised to find myself braced as for a resistance. I said, "Nothing, nothing."

"What do you mean, nothing?"

"I mean, no loose ends."

"You are a liar, aren't you," said Palmer.

I stared at him. It seemed impossible that he should not know all that was in my mind. I wondered what Honor had told him. I said, "Palmer, I came here to take leave of you, on behalf of Antonia, and to arrange to remove the things which she left here. May we keep our attention on those two matters?"

"I've had her things packed," said Palmer. "That will be dealt with. But do you seriously intend to stay with Antonia after all this?"

"Yes."

"You are most unwise," he said. "You should take this opportunity to part. It will be far better for both of you—and harder later. I speak quite disinterestedly, of course."

"Clinically," I said. Some deep attentive thing within me responded to his words as to a longed-for summons. But I continued, "We are not going to part. And anyway it's our business."

"Your marriage is over, Martin," said Palmer. "Why not recognise it? Wouldn't you like to talk it over with me? Indeed if you like 'clinically'. I don't mean necessarily now this minute, but soon. I feel sure I could help you."

I laughed. "For the first time since I met you I find you capable of stupidity."

Palmer looked at me with the deliberate gentleness of the professional doctor. I noticed that behind his head the row of Japanese prints had been replaced. He said, "What seems to you my stupidity is simply my need. We don't want to lose you."

" 'We'," I said, "for heaven's sake?"

"Honor and I," said Palmer.

I tried very hard, deepening my frown, to let my face reveal nothing. "What would not losing me consist in?"

"I don't know," he said. "Why should we be able to define it beforehand? Let me be simple. I think it is important for you both that you should leave Antonia. You *want* to leave Antonia; and this is not a moment for placating your very abstract sense of duty. On the whole, 'do what you want' costs others less than 'do what you ought'. You will destroy

Antonia slowly if you stay with her. Be resolute. And don't be ashamed to accept help. The psyche abhors a vacuum. Honor and I are going away soon to travel, far away, and for a long time. Nothing real detains you. Come with us."

I looked at the ground. Palmer had a talent for making me feel that I was going mad. I had never heard speak more clearly the voice that says 'all is permitted'. And with that 'all is permitted' came also 'all is possible', and a vision of Honor, somehow, somewhere, after all, existing in my future. I looked up again and saw that, coming from the door behind Palmer, she had entered the room.

I rose, and for a second I wondered if I should faint. But then, holding the back of my chair, I saw myself confronting them as a prisoner confronts his judges. This made me harden and I breathed and sat down again, staring.

Honor was dressed in a high-necked black garment of which I could not remember afterwards whether it was a silk dress or an overall. Her arms were bare from the elbow. She stood behind Palmer, whose relaxed body seemed to glow with awareness of her, and they both observed me, Honor with her head lowered and her shining band of hair falling forward to frame her eyes. She stood behind Palmer like a captor, and the voluptuous curve of his relaxed body spoke the word 'victim'. I felt I ought to turn away.

"I've asked Martin to join us," said Palmer. He was watching me with a broad half-smiling face, as one might watch a struggling fish or a fly.

"Are you mocking me, Palmer?" I said. I could not look at Honor.

"Don't fall below your destiny, Martin," said Palmer. "As a psycho-analyst, I don't of course imagine that freedom is to be won by convulsive movements of the will. All the same, there are times of decision. You are not a man to be bound by ordinary rules. Only let your imagination encompass what your heart privately desires. Tell yourself: nothing is impossible."

I laughed and rose to my feet again. "You are mad," I said. "Do you really imagine that I could live, for however short a while, with you two, that I can even go on knowing you two? Am I to take this seriously?" At this my eyes met Honor's over Palmer's head.

In that instant a communication passed between us, and even as it did so I reflected that it was perhaps the final one. I did not imagine it; she gave me a very slight shake of the head and a curtain came down over her eyes. It was a decisive and authoritative farewell: in the pain of which, as I received it, I also knew for certain that she had not talked about me to her brother. It was our first and last moment of intimacy, vivid, but concentrated to a solitary point. I looked back instantly to Palmer.

I said, "We have finished with each other."

"In that case," said Palmer, "since we are going away for good, I doubt if we shall meet again."

"Then good-bye," I said.

"As *you* choose, Martin," said Palmer, "as *you* choose."

✳ *Chapter Twenty-five* ✳

"HE was terribly depressed and disappointed," I said "but as you can imagine, very clear-headed. He told me to say you're not to worry about him and that he'll recover in time. He said how grateful he was to you, how he hoped he hadn't hurt you, how he wished it had all been possible. He was brave though. He said he had to accept your decision and that it wouldn't really have worked. But he said it was a marvellous attempt and he wouldn't wish it undone."

We had been over this a number of times. "I wonder how I know that you're lying?" said Antonia.

It was breakfast-time, a late breakfast-time, on the next day. Antonia and I, still in dressing-gowns, were sitting on over the cold toast and coffee. It seemed that neither of us could move. She was pale, listless and irritable. I was exhausted.

"I'm not lying," I said. "If you won't believe what I say, why do you keep asking me?"

Now that the taboo had been broken Antonia could talk of nothing but Palmer, endlessly remaking her relationship with him retrospectively.

"Whatever he said he didn't say *that*," said Antonia.

I had not the heart to tell her that she had scarcely been mentioned. "Alexander's right," I said. "He's not quite human."

"When did he say that?" said Antonia.

"When he heard about you and Palmer."

Antonia frowned down at the cold cloudy liquid in her cup. She pushed back on to her shoulder the half-undone bundle of her weighty hair. She said "Ach—", and then "Nor is she."

"Nor is she," I agreed, and sighed. We both sighed.

"I hope they go to America or Japan and stay there," said Antonia. "I don't want to hear of them again, I don't want to know that they exist."

"That's what will happen, my darling," I said. "Falling out of love is a matter of forgetting how charming someone is. You'll be surprised how soon you forget." We sighed again.

"Forget! Forget!" said Antonia. "We both seem to be half dead." She lifted her eyes to mine, sombre, restless, cross.

I wondered whether I did indeed want to leave her. Yes, I supposed I did. Not that it mattered. I wondered what, at that moment, she was thinking about me. With curiosity and hostility we examined each other.

"You do love me, don't you, Martin?" said Antonia. She asked it, not tenderly, but with a sort of brisk anxiety.

I said, "Of course I do, of course."

It sounded flimsy enough, and we went on looking at each other morosely, our eyes dark with private grief. It would have needed a great effort to take her hand and I did not make the effort. And as I stared and stared at last Antonia became invisible and all I could see was Honor, her dark assassin's head bowed a little towards me, the curtain falling upon the light of her eyes.

"There's a parcel for you, by the way."

I returned with a start. I broke up some cold rubbery toast in my hand. I wondered if I had the energy to make us some more hot coffee. "Oh, where?"

"In the hall," said Antonia. "Don't move, I'll get it. And I'll put on the kettle for more coffee."

She came back in a moment carrying a long narrow box

covered in brown paper which she put down beside me with the words "Orchids from some admirer!" and then went away into the kitchen.

I looked at the box and picked at my lower lip. My lips were dry and cracked with too much smoking. I lit another cigarette and wondered distantly how I would get through the day. It was a problem demanding some ingenuity. I glanced at the window and saw that it was still raining. I cut the string of the parcel with the bread knife.

I had no fight in me, that was the truth. I did not want to receive any more lashes. Palmer had too much confused me. If he had deliberately intended to place a barrier across the path of my desires he could not have done better; and this made me half believe that, after all, he knew. But with this, and with far more authority, there came the image of Honor shaking her head: Honor utterly secret but lost. I began to pull the paper off the box.

Palmer did not know, but it didn't matter now whether he knew or not. They would go, the infernal pair, to Los Angeles, to San Francisco, to Tokyo, and Antonia and I would forget; and I would do, and she would do, what defeated desire, together with a bored and dim conscience, suggested as remaining for us to do. I opened the box.

There was a lot of dark stuff inside. I stared at it with a sort of puzzled revulsion, wondering what it was. I stood up and moved the box to the light to see it better. I felt I did not want to touch it. At last I did very gingerly touch it, and as I did so I realised that it was human hair. It took me another moment to recognise the long thick tress which filled the box as Georgie's hair, Georgie's whole beautiful dark chestnut-tinted head of hair. I cannoned violently into Antonia in the doorway.

"Georgie", I called, "Georgie," and banged again upon the locked door of her room. There was silence within.

As I got the car out I had exclaimed to Antonia that of course Georgie must be all right since she would be with Alexander, and Antonia had told me that Alexander had rung up from Rembers last night when I was out and had mentioned that Georgie was still in London. All the same, Antonia thought my anxiety was completely irrational. I knocked again.

I listened to the silence. Of course it was ridiculous to be so afraid. The arrival of the hair had had the heavy significance of a token in a dream; but there was no need to apply nightmare logic to it. Georgie's present was doubtless a jest, though a rather bitter and macabre one. She herself was probably at this moment in some nearby library, and I stood outside an empty room. Yet I could not quite convince myself of this and I knew that I could not go away. I wondered if I should make some more telephone calls; but I had already rung all the numbers where she might be found. Almost by now I simply wanted to get into the room as if this in itself would avert disaster. The locked door had become magnetic. Still I waited, until, prompted suddenly by something I thought I heard, I leaned down and put my ear to the keyhole, holding my breath. After a moment I heard a sound and then the same sound repeated. It seemed to be a low regular sigh of heavy breathing coming from just inside the door. I straightened up and stood there for a moment chilled and paralysed. What I had heard terrified me.

Georgie's windows were inaccessible. There was no way in but through the door. I threw myself against it once or twice in a futile manner. Then I remembered the decorator's tools which were still lying about downstairs. I rushed down and began to turn them over. The street door was open as usual and outside on the bright rainy pavements people were going to and fro. I selected a heavy flat-ended cementing trowel and a hammer and raced back upstairs. I dug the edge of the trowel as deeply as possible into the crack of the door beside the lock and drove it farther in with blows of the hammer. Then I used the trowel as a lever. Something cracked inside. A moment later the handle of the trowel broke off. I pushed the door but it was still firm. I took the hammer and struck the door with all my strength in the region of the lock. There was more cracking and then I could see a crevice growing wide. I gave it my shoulder and the door came open.

I went in and pushed it to behind me. There was a heavy silence within. The room was dark, as the curtains were still drawn. The place was airless and smelt vilely of alcohol and stale tobacco smoke whose fumes seemed to linger visibly in the air as I pulled the curtains apart. Or perhaps I only imagined that there was a grey haze. Someone was lying on the floor. It took me a moment to be certain that it was Georgie. It was not just that her shorn head made her hard to recognise; her face too, in a deep slumber of unconsciousness, had quite lost the semblance of her usual self, had become as it were anonymous. It seemed as if she had almost, already, gone.

I leaned over her and spoke her name and shook her by the shoulder. She was completely inert and I realised that she had passed beyond any such immediate recall. Her face was puffed and blueish, and she was breathing raucously through her mouth. I did not hesitate for long. I found the telephone book and dialled the number of Charing Cross Hospital and explained that someone had accidentally taken an overdose of sleeping pills. They promised an ambulance at once. In that area it was a daily occurrence.

I knelt down on the floor beside Georgie. I wondered if I ought to go on trying to wake her, but decided not to. I felt obscurely that I might do her harm by touching her; her condition imposed a taboo and indeed the limp half-inhabited body filled me with a sort of revulsion. She looked like a drowned girl. At first I kept looking at her face whose strangeness fascinated me. It was indeed as if she had become a different person, as if an alien being had taken her body. I could have been persuaded that this was merely a rough semblance of Georgie; and as she lay there completely limp with her mouth open, the lifeless air and the deep regular breathing made her seem like a waxwork. She was lying on her side with one hand extended above her head. She was wearing a blue shirt and black trousers. These I recognised. Her feet were bare. I contemplated her feet. These I recognised too. I touched them. They felt cold and waxen and I covered them with a cushion. I looked at her long trousered legs and at the curve of her thigh. The shirt was unbuttoned and I could see the rise of a breast within. I looked at her neck and at one ear now more fully revealed by the shorn hair. I looked at her extended familiar hand, the palm uppermost and open as in a gesture of appeal or release. All these I had possessed. But now it was as if all had disintegrated into pieces, the pieces of Georgie, the person lost.

I was scarcely at that moment capable of memories or speculations. But I seemed again to hear her voice saying, "Martin, you don't know how near the edge I am." Indeed, there was so much I did not know, had not cared to know. Georgie's stoicism had helped to make me a brute. She had so cunningly spared me her sufferings. I had enjoyed but never had to pay. But someone had paid. As I looked down at her slim inert body I recalled the nightmare of her pregnancy which had ended in relieved embraces and champagne. If she died, I had killed her. I thought this, but stupidly and without feeling. There was no whole presence in the flesh before me and I still could not bring myself to touch her. It would have been like fingering parts of a corpse. Yet with a sense of abasement in which there was an element of desire I lay down full length on the floor beside her with my face close to hers. I could feel her breath.

Some moments passed. I heard a sound at the door and began to rise. Reclining on one elbow I saw a figure enter. The door closed again. Honor Klein was looking down at me.

I got as far as a sitting position and said, "The ambulance is coming."

Honor said, "I was afraid of this. She sent me a very strange letter."

I said, "She sent me her hair."

Honor stared at me. Her face was closed and stiff. Then she looked at Georgie and said, "I see. That's it. I thought she looked rather odd." She spoke with detachment and precision.

I thought, she is pitiless. Then I thought, so am I.

Honor was wearing a shabby unbelted mackintosh. She was hatless, her black hair a little sleeked by the rain. As she stood there, hands in pockets, surveying the room she had a sharp business-like air. She might have been a detective. I rose to my feet.

She said, "As she let us both know let us hope that she has not made a serious attempt. Have you found the tablets?"

I had not thought of that. We began to hunt, shifting books and papers, upsetting loaded ash-trays and piles of under-clothes, and tipping the contents of drawers on to the floor, stepping to and fro over Georgie's inert legs. I undid the dishevelled bed and looked under the pillow. Turning back to see Georgie still lying there amid the disordered sea of her belongings and glimpsing for a second the intent face of Honor as she rifled another cupboard I wondered into what half ludicrous nightmare I had strayed. At last we found something, an empty bottle which had contained a well-known brand of sleeping drug, and we left off our search.

I looked at my watch. It was hard to believe that it was less than ten minutes since I had telephoned the hospital. The ambulance must arrive soon. Suddenly still, Honor and I looked at each other across the recumbent Georgie. It occurred to me that this was the first time that I had been alone with Honor since the night in Cambridge. Only I was not alone with her. We had a terrible chaperone. She was present to me, but only as a torment, as an apparition; and I knew that I was looking at her as I had never looked at any human being but as one might look at a demon. And she looked back out of her sallow Jewish mask, the line of her mouth dead straight between the curving lips, the narrow eyes one black. Then we both looked down at Georgie.

Honor knelt down beside her and began to clear away from round about her the various papers, garments and other oddments which had a little snowed upon her during our rifling of the room. I saw with a curious surprise that Georgie was lying in exactly the same drowned attitude as when I had arrived. When Honor had cleared a space about her she put her hand on the girl's shoulder and turned her onto her back, moving her outflung arm down to her breast. Then she put a cushion under her head. I shivered. As I knelt down on the other side the two women composed for me for an instant into an eerie *pietà*, Honor with bowed head, suddenly gentle with concern, and Georgie slain, alienated, sleeping.

Honor was still touching Georgie's shoulder. As if this contact lent an articulate presence to the sleeping girl, I now felt able to touch her too and I drew my finger down her thigh. I could feel the soft warm leg through the material. But what I felt more, as in an electrical circuit, was the shiver of connection between Honor's hand and mine; and I remembered our two hands almost touching on the blade of the Samurai sword. I covered my face. The ambulance came.

* Chapter Twenty-six *

THE scene round Georgie's bed was animated by a fever-ish gaiety. We were all there, like a family reunited at the bedside of a sick child. Brightly coloured wrapping-paper, chocolate boxes, toy animals, Penguin books and exotic cigarettes strewed the counterpane, and the rows of flower vases on the dressing table and the window ledge made the little white hospital room look like a florist's shop. There was something of the atmosphere of Christmas Day in the nursery.

Georgie, lying back, propped up with pillows, seemed indeed like an over-excited little girl. Her face was rather red and retained a new look of plumpness. Her hair, which she had shorn roughly at the nape of the neck, had been a little trimmed up by the Sister, but was still jagged and stuck out awkwardly on either side of her head, making her look very juvenile. She nervously caressed a white fluffy toy dog which Antonia had brought her, and looked at each of us in turn with a bright diffident imploring smile. We leaned bene-volently over her.

It was now the third day since Georgie's exploit. She had been in a coma for more than twelve hours, but was now out of danger and very considerably recovered. Palmer was sitting close to her at the head of the bed and I was sitting opposite him. Antonia was perched on the bed, her legs curled under her, and Alexander was leaning on the iron rail at the foot. Honor Klein leaned against the window ledge behind Palmer.

"Oh dear, I've caused you all so much trouble!" said Georgie. "I do feel bad."

"All's well that ends well!" said Antonia, her hand impulsively meeting Georgie's in the soft fur of the toy dog. Antonia had been positively rejuvenated by the news of Georgie's attempt. On hearing of it she had completely cast aside her listless and defeated air. After three days of exhilaration and excitement she looked distinctly handsomer and like her old self. Yesterday she had bought three hats.

"And so you should feel bad!" said Palmer. "Strictly speaking, we should have given you a good thrashing, instead of spoiling you like this!" He passed his hand affectionately over her dark cropped head, turning it slightly towards him.

I could feel Honor Klein's eyes upon me, but I did not look at her. She leaned there with a bland cat-like expression which was almost a smile, and did not join in the chatter. Alexander too was subdued, brooding on Georgie with a sad gentle stare, immersed in the enjoyment of his private emotions. I envied his evident ability to feel. I was hollow.

"I felt such a sham when I came round," said Georgie, "and I thought to myself, all the other women on this corridor are here with real illnesses, and I am just a troublemaker. But do you know, they're all in for the same thing as me! The woman in the end room is quite proud because she took the largest dose!"

We laughed. Alexander murmured, "'To sleep! Perchance to dream . . .'" half audibly and then would not repeat what he had said.

I looked at Georgie's nervously twisting hands. I felt compassion for those hands as they jumpily fondled the toy dog. But I could no longer apprehend Georgie as a whole. She had never, after that strange scattering of her, come together again. I felt no grain of passionate interest in the once familiar body which lay extended so close to me. Something, even, in her still changed and alien face repelled me. It was as if she had died indeed. I wanted, when I thought of this, to kneel by her bed and bury my face and groan as a sort of desperate act of mourning. But I went on sitting there with a fixed half-smile. I wondered if, supposing I were to reach out and pat her hands, the gesture would look intolerably artificial. I could still feel Honor's eyes upon me like a cold sun.

"Well, it all makes employment for members of my profession," said Palmer. "Though I must admit it doesn't usually bring me in such delightful patients!"

Georgie, as was usual in such cases, had been asked to undergo some psychiatric treatment, and Palmer had undertaken to satisfy the requirements by enrolling her as a patient. She was soon to travel to Cambridge for a short stay.

"It's absurd, of course," said Georgie. "I'm perfectly sane, in fact—far saner than most psycho-analysts!"

"Thank you, my dear!", said Palmer. "I'm sure you are. But a little sorting out will do us no harm."

I thought, soon Georgie will be telling Palmer all about her sex life. I reached out and patted one of Georgie's fidgeting hands. She shuddered.

Antonia said, "Well, my child, I mustn't spend all day on your bed! I've got a hairdressing appointment. I must dart off." She pulled herself off the bed without looking at me and smoothed down her smart spring suit. She looked radiant.

Alexander said, "I'll drive you. I've got to fix up about that exhibition." He gave Georgie his deep sad look, pressed his two hands over her feet through the bed-clothes, and left the room in the wake of Antonia.

The sun was shining, the bright cool late-January sun, with misleading hints of springtime, and the white room was gay with it. I wondered if I had better go too and leave Honor and Palmer with Georgie. I ought to have been tasting hock that afternoon. There was still time to get along. Only it seemed to have become extremely difficult to move or speak, as if I were being subjected to some paralysing ray. Palmer was holding Georgie's hand. He too looked exceptionally well, with his hard clean look, the skin brown and unwrinkled, his crop of light grey hair as smooth and dry as an animal's fur. When I saw him too so positively glowing it passed through my mind that he might conceivably have re-established some relation with Antonia. But that was impossible. I looked at Honor Klein over Palmer's head. She was still smiling like an archaic statue.

"Suppose you kids run along," said Palmer. "I want to talk seriously to my patient!"

I got up and said, "Well, good-bye," and kissed Georgie on the brow. She murmured something and smiled after me, her feverishly brilliant eyes wrinkled up with anxiety. I went out and down the stairs. I could hear footsteps behind me.

✳ *Chapter Twenty-seven* ✳

HONOR KLEIN caught up with me at the door of the hospital and I said without looking at her, "May I give you a lift?"

She said "Yes" and I led the way in silence to the car.

I retain little memory of the drive to Pelham Crescent. Oddly, in retrospect that journey is jumbled in my mind with my first journey with Honor from Liverpool Street station. I recall only a blaze of exhilaration which came with the certainty of what I was about to do. Through the rush-hour traffic the god that protects drunken men protected me.

When we arrived I got out of the car and followed her to the house, which seemed not to surprise her. She opened the door, held it for me, and then went into the drawing-room. The bright sun made the sombre room seem bleak and soulless, taking the warmth out of its dark rich colours. It looked dusty. I came in and shut the door behind me. We faced each other down the length of the room.

It was now indeed that I felt that I might faint, and I remember grinding my wrists against the panel of the door so that the pain might steady me. She was watching, still with a trace of the archaic smile, and I felt the power in her. I controlled my breathing.

With an evident and relentless attention Honor waited for me to speak.

I said at last, "I suppose you realise that I am in love with you."

She considered this, with head slightly on one side as if listening, and said, "Yes."

I said, "I doubt if you realise how much."

She turned away, giving me her shoulder, and said, "It doesn't matter." She spoke quietly but without weariness.

"That I love you, or how much?"

"The latter. I'm touched that you love me. That's all."

"It's not all," I said. "Honor, I want you savagely and I shall fight for you savagely."

She shook her head and turned back now to meet my eyes. She said, "There is no place for such a love." Her 'no place' seemed to search the universe and fold it into a box.

I would not take this. I said, "When did you know I loved you?" It was a lover's question.

"When you attacked me in the cellar."

"So you knew what it meant when I appeared in Cambridge?"

"Yes."

"But you did not tell Palmer."

She simply stared at me and I saw the old snake in her looking coldly out through her eyes; and I saw again in a vision the darkness of her breasts and how I had found her with her brother, and I shuddered not so much at what I had seen as at the fact that I had seen it. She could never forgive me.

"You wrote me a lying letter," she said. She stood looking at me, her head thrust forward, the collar of her overcoat turned up behind her black wig of hair, her hands in her pockets.

"I wrote you a foolish letter," I said. "I didn't know at the time it was lying."

There was a slight pause and I was afraid she would dismiss me. I flattened my hands against the door behind me and almost prayed. I divined distantly within her some obscure hesitation. If I could only find the right words I could keep her talking, I could in this brief and vital moment for a little longer hold her; but for a single blunder I would be sent away.

I said, picking my words carefully, "I am glad that you are not sceptical about my being in love. If anything is evident at least this must be. And you must also see my difficulties, since you and circumstances have not allowed me much opportunity for self-expression. It would profit me little now if I were to tear your clothes off. But I would walk through sea and fire if you called me." I spoke this in a low reasonable voice; and as I spoke I thought of Palmer's return and of the perilously limited time that remained to me.

She listened as if attentively to this, her dark eyes pondering me, and said, "You do not know what you are asking. Do you want my love?"

This startled me and I said, "I don't know, I don't even know if I think you capable of love. I want you."

After a moment she laughed, and then said, "Martin, you are talking nonsense." She turned away and pulled off her overcoat with a sudden gesture and went to the side table where the drinks and the glasses stood. She poured out two glasses of sherry. I noticed with ecstasy that her hand was trembling.

I did not leave my post. She placed one of the glasses on a little table half-way down the room and retired to the fire-place. I came and fetched it and returned to the door. I felt that if I came too near her I might tear her in pieces; and I felt a quivering joy in my blood which was my sense of her re-alising this too. Then with a delayed reaction I apprehended her having used my first name, and I had to make an effort not to cover my face.

"Nonsense about doubting your capacity to love, or nonsense about simply wanting you?" I said. I was terrified of putting a foot wrong.

"You don't know me," she said.

"Let me know you. I have an apprehension of you which is deeper than ordinary knowledge. You realise this also or you would not be talking to me now. You are not a woman who wastes her time." I trembled too, yet irrationally and almost with exasperation I felt that only some thin brittle barrier divided us from a torrent of mutual surrender. If I could only see what act of mine would break it.

"Return to reality," she said. "Return to your wife, return to Antonia. I have nothing for you."

"My marriage to Antonia is over," I said. "Palmer is right. It is dead."

"Palmer spoke out of his own conventions. You are not a fool. You know that there are many ways in which your marriage is alive. In any case, do not think that *this* is more than a dream." And she repeated, "Return to reality." Yet still she did not dismiss me.

"I love you," I said, "and I desire you and my whole being is prostrate before you. This is reality. Let us indeed not be blinded by any convention about where it is to be found."

"Convention!" she said, and laughed again. I laughed too, and then we were both tense and solemn once more. I was stiff with concentrating and with bending my eyes and my will upon her. She stood there in her ancient dark green suit, feet apart and hands behind her back, staring at me.

She said, "Your love for me does not inhabit the real world. Yes, it is love, I do not deny it. But not every love has a course to run, smooth or otherwise, and this love has no course at all. Because of what I am and because of what you saw I am a terrible object of fascination for you. I am a severed head such as primitive tribes and old alchemists used to use, anointing it with oil and putting a morsel of gold upon its tongue to make it utter prophecies. And who knows but that long acquaintance with a severed head might not lead to strange knowledge. For such knowledge one would have paid enough. But that is remote from love and remote from ordinary life. As real people we do not exist for each other."

"I have at least with you," I said, "paid all the time. This precisely *does* make you real for me. You give me hope."

"I do not intend to. Be clear about that."

"What anyway does a love do which has no course?"

"It is changed into something else, something heavy or sharp that you carry within and bind around with your substance until it ceases to hurt. But that is your affair."

I felt that I had displayed weakness and that this perhaps was fatal. She moved and her shadow moved upon the floor in the cold sunshine. As she fumbled for cigarettes in the pocket of her overcoat I felt sure that in a moment now she would send me away.

I began to advance down the room and as I did so she froze for a moment; and then with deliberation went on lighting her cigarette. She finished and looked at me, her hands hanging loosely at her sides, one holding the smouldering cigarette. Her solemn face of a Hebrew angel regarded me, ready, stripped of expression. But I could no more have touched her than if she had been the Ark of the Covenant.

When I was near to her I fell on my knees and prostrated myself full length with my head on the floor. It happened as spontaneously as if I had been knocked to the ground. It was strange, but I could have lain there for a long time.

After a moment or two she said, "Get up," in a steady voice, very deep.

I began to rise. She had moved back and was leaning against the mantelpiece. I could not prevent myself from supplicating. On my knees I said, "Honor, let us not fight like this. Only see me a little. I ask only that. I know nothing of how you are situated yourself or what you want. But I feel certain that this thing which has been shivering and trembling between us in this half-hour is a real thing. Do not kill it. That is all I ask."

She jerked her head, frowning in an exasperated way, and I realised that I had broken whatever precarious spell it was by which I had in these decisive minutes held her. I got up.

She said, "We are not *fighting*. Please do not deceive yourself. You are living on dreams. You had better go now. Palmer will be here soon, and I had rather you went first."

"But you will see me again?"

"There would be absolutely no point in my doing so. Palmer and I are going away almost at once."

"Do not speak so," I said. "I want you abjectly."

"Dear me," she said mockingly, "and whatever would you do with me if you had me?"

These words, conveying to me the simple truth that she could not regard me as an equal, stopped my mouth at last.

As I got into my car I saw Palmer getting out of a taxi near by. We waved to each other.

✳ *Chapter Twenty-eight* ✳

IT was nearly lunch-time on the following day and I was getting very worried about Antonia. She had not returned home on the previous evening or all night. Fairly late in the evening I had telephoned her mother and one or two friends, but could pick up no trace of her. I rang Rosemary's flat, but there was no reply. I sat up with a bottle of whisky expecting her to come, and had fallen into a deep sleep lying on the sofa. I woke stiff and desolate in the early hours of the morning. At seven I rang Rosemary again, and Rembers on the off chance, but could get no answer. At nine o'clock I telephoned the hairdresser and was told that Mrs Lynch-Gibbon had had no appointment with them recently. I concluded that Antonia must have changed her hairdresser; or else she had been lying. I could not bring myself to ring Palmer.

At about ten o'clock the bell rang, but it was only the removal men with the rest of the furniture from Lowndes Square. They carried it in, and managed to knock a chip off the Carlton House writing table while bringing it through the door. After they had gone I stood sadly beside the thing, licking my finger and dabbing it on the scar to darken the wood. Then I got some polish and rubbed it all over, but without persuading it to settle down. It retained a derelict temporary air as if it thought it was already at Sotheby's. The room had never recovered.

I did some more telephoning, including calls to local police stations to enquire about accidents, and still to no avail. Just after eleven the telephone rang, but that was Mytten ringing up about the hock. I was, to an extreme and irrational degree, upset and worried. It was not like Antonia to disappear without warning, and I could not help imagining her lying unconscious in a hospital bed or floating face downward in the Thames. The quality of the anxiety brought back to me my frantic distresses as a child about any prolonged absence of my mother; and as then, I tried to comfort myself by saying: in an hour, in two hours, she will have returned, everything will be explained, everything will be as usual. But meanwhile the minutes ticked silently past without bringing any news.

Of course it was true, and this was the proof of it, that my marriage was still in many ways very much alive. It may sound abject, but I came home from Honor wanting to be comforted by Antonia. I had made her Martini as usual, expecting her soon after six o'clock. There is no substitute for the comfort supplied by the utterly taken-for-granted relationship; and after all, in spite of all that had happened, Antonia and no one else was my wife. It did not occur to me to reflect that there was anything illogical in this; and indeed there was nothing illogical.

When I left Honor I was in extreme pain, a pain produced by our last exchanges. However, as I sat waiting for Antonia and before I began to be anxious, I had been invaded rather by a profound exhilaration. Considering the extreme difficulties and dangers of the enterprise the interview had not gone too badly. I was impressed by the fact that Honor had been willing to talk at all. I was pretty certain that she had even now not told Palmer of my condition. I recalled with delight her trembling hand. She had told me that she intended to give me no hope. But she had, effectively, given me hope; and she was no fool. Of course I knew soberly that it was a small, a very small hope. But when one is in love a little light shines a long way. What I most needed was a sense of reprieve. I could not believe that Honor and Palmer were really going away, far away or for long; and I was certain that I should see her again. Of the claims of my wife and of her brother I made, by a double method of thought, nothing; either I would lose Honor, in which case all would be as before, or else, *per impossibile*, I would gain her, and this would create a new heaven and a new earth and the utter sweeping away of all former things. I would be a new person; and if she were relentlessly to draw me I would come to her even if I had to wade through blood.

To this soliloquy my worries about Antonia broke in; and it was not until nearly noon on the following day, when sheer exhaustion brought about a pause, that my thoughts returned fully to Honor, and I thought of her words about the severed head. I had been glad on the previous day to reflect that I had not sent her my original letter in which my behaviour had been, in such dreary terms, explained. I did not love her as a substitute for Palmer, whom I loved because he had seduced my wife: I was certain of that; and I had as little sympathy for her own method of explanation. I did not love her because incest inspired irrational horror; although, as I thought, I knew that the scene in Cambridge was something still active and scarcely touchable in my imagination, something un-assimilated and dangerous. I closed my eyes and saw again what I had seen then.

There was a flurry at the door and Antonia came running into the room. I leapt up, both relieved and oddly frightened to see her. I ran to her and shook her by the shoulders. She laughed as I did so, and then took off her hat and coat and threw them on a chair. She looked elated, almost drunk. I stared at her in amazement.

I said, "Damn you, I've been nearly off my head. Where were you?"

"Darling," said Antonia, "we're going to have a drink now, a nice big one. Just be patient. I'll tell you everything. I'm sorry I couldn't let you know. But you'll see. Sit down and I'll get the glasses."

I sat down on the sofa. Now that she had come back I felt only weariness and irritation. I decided I had better go off to bed. Last night's comatose sleep had done me no good.

Antonia sat beside me, put the drinks on the table, and then turned my head gently with one hand so that I faced her. Then she poured most of her drink out of her glass into mine. There was something vaguely reminiscent about the gesture. She returned to looking at me with her bright moist tawny eyes. Her hair shone like pale copper, and I could not think how I had seen her as growing old. Her reddened mouth worked with inarticulate tenderness.

"All right, all right," I said, "I'm glad to see you!" I took her hand.

"Darling," said Antonia, "I don't know how to say this, because I don't know how much you know."

"Know about what?"

"About me and Alexander."

"You and *Alexander*?" I said. "Are you sure you've got the name right?"

"Oh, darling," said Antonia, "I'm afraid it's serious. But surely you knew? You must have known for ages."

"Known *what*?"

"Well, that I and Alexander—well, to put it quite bluntly, that Alexander has been my lover."

"Oh, Christ," I said. I got up. Antonia tried to retain my hand, but I pulled it away.

"You mean you didn't know at all?" said Antonia. "Surely you must have guessed. I was sure you knew. Alexander wasn't so certain."

"What a fool you must both think me," I said. "No, I didn't know. Of course I realised you were very fond of each other. But I didn't know *this*. Do you imagine I would have tolerated it? How little you know me."

"Well, you tolerated Anderson so well," said Antonia. "That was one thing that made me feel you must have known, you must have *understood*, about Alexander. Besides it was so obvious."

"You are stupid," I said. "Palmer was different."

"I don't see why," said Antonia. "And what do you mean by saying you wouldn't have tolerated it? I loved you both, you loved both of us, Alexander loved—"

"You make me feel ill," I said.

"You knew I had to have both of you," said Antonia.

"Well, from now on you're only having one of us."

"Don't say that, darling," said Antonia with urgency. She got up and tried again to take my hand. I put it in my pocket. "It's true that we both love you and we can't do without you and we won't do without you. You were so splendid about Anderson. Don't spoil things now."

"I've spent all my splendour."

"Be rational, my dearest Martin, my child," said Antonia. "And, oh darling, don't look like *that*. After all, this situation has existed for a long time. It isn't as if I'd only just thought of it."

"Well, I haven't known about it for a long time," I said. "How long in fact has it existed?"

"Oh, always," said Antonia. "I don't mean that we always met very often. That varied. But the situation existed."

"Always? You mean ever since we got married?"

"Really since before we got married. I fell in love with Alexander practically as soon as I met him. Only I didn't start to believe in my love until it was too late. You remember you wouldn't let me meet Alexander until after our engagement was announced. You said he always took your girls away. And then everything was so public. I hadn't enough nerve."

"You mean our marriage never really existed at all?"

"Of course it existed, darling. I loved you both. I love you both."

"I don't think you understand that word," I said.

"You hurt me terribly," said Antonia. We looked at each other. Her face had a hard dignity and she withstood my gaze. She had certainly, since the last occasion, travelled. She still looked like an actress. But a great actress.

I walked away to the window and looked out at the magnolia tree. The weak sun revealed the moss upon its old trunk. It looked dead.

"Why didn't you tell me?" I said.

"As I say, I thought you knew. I thought you preferred it all being gentle and inexplicit."

"Well, why are you making it all nasty and explicit now?"

"Anderson woke me up," said Antonia. "He made me in some way more absolute. After *that* it was impossible to go on in quite *this* way. I *was* in love with Anderson, I was terribly carried away by him. I couldn't help myself. It was both wonderful and terrible. I'd never felt the earth give way under me quite like that. Of course it nearly killed Alexander. He saw it coming from miles off—and I was practically afraid for his reason. He suffered far more than you did."

"Did he know before I knew?"

"Yes. I couldn't deceive him. And anyway he guessed."

"But you could deceive me."

"You deceived me," said Antonia.

"That was different," I said.

"You keep saying things are different that aren't," said Antonia. "Of course our marriage could never have been *quite* right. You realised it, after all. You had to have someone else too. I would have forgiven you."

"No marriage is ever quite right," I said. "But I believed in ours. Now you tell me it never was. I haven't even got the past left."

"You are such a dreamer, Martin," said Antonia. "You like to dream along without facing things. Well, you must face things now. And do stop being so sorry for yourself."

"Don't be brutal to me, Antonia. I just want to understand. You say that Palmer woke you up?"

"Yes, he made me honest. Made me braver, perhaps. It is better to be explicit and to try to hold things all the same. It was wonderful how I managed it with you, over Anderson. And somehow I held on to Alexander as well. However much he suffered, we never lost touch. That was wonderful."

"Wonderful. I see. So you're trying it out on me again?"

"Dearest," said Antonia, "I knew you'd come round!" She came up behind me and I could feel her gentle touch on my shoulder. I still stood looking out at the magnolia, my hands behind my back.

"What makes you think I'm coming round?" I said.

"You must, you must!" she said with tender urgency, and began to undo my hands and take them in hers. Without turning I let her hold them.

"But what about Georgie?"

"Oh, that was sheer despair," said Antonia. "Alexander

had been so dreadfully hurt by the Anderson business. While it was going on he was in too much pain to be angry. He kept his anger until after it was over. Then he wanted to punish me."

"You mean he never really intended to marry Georgie at all?"

"Well, he *thought* he did," said Antonia, "but he deceived himself, poor dear. We were estranged from each other for a short time, and it was hell for both of us. Surely you must have seen me suffering. He imagined he wanted something new, and he started it off with Georgie just as a distraction. He was half mad. But then of course he realised that it was no good. That was why Georgie tried to kill herself, when she found out that Alexander really loved me." Her voice droned on quietly over my shoulder.

"Is that right?" I said. I was becoming dazed and stupid. I felt like an empty vessel that is struck again and again. Even Georgie's love was being taken away from me. It would take little now to make me believe that Georgie had loved Alexander all along. At any rate she had been *waiting* for Alexander all along. Yet she had sent me her dear hair.

I turned round and faced Antonia and we stood together in the window. She caressed my arms, leaning her head forward with the old look of possessive tenderness.

"Poor Georgie," said Antonia. "But she's young, she'll soon find someone else."

"You must be pleased with yourself," I said. "It turns out everyone loves you in the end."

Antonia smiled her triumphant smile. "I'm good at it!" she said. Then she touched my cheek. "Don't resist my love, Martin. I must keep you in my loving net. We'll hold you, you know, we'll never let you go! After all, you were unconsciously living it before. Perhaps we were all a little in a dream. Now it has come fully to consciousness, and things will be put right, as they would have been at the start if I had had more courage. And if we are brave and good it will all be better now that we are truthful, oh better, far better!" She spoke softly, rubbing my cheek as if she were rubbing into it some spell-binding ointment.

I removed her hand and scratched the place where it had been. "Well," I said, "it's nice that you won't have to change your name. It will be so much less confusing for the trades-people. I'm glad we're keeping you in the family."

Antonia laughed tenderly. "Oh darling," she said, "I know you so well, you dear ironical creature! You move me so much when you try to conceal your goodness in that flippant way."

"So I've got the same old part, have I? I can't seem to stop being the angel of light and mercy."

"Your goodness is too much for you, Martin," said Antonia. "You couldn't be harsh if you tried. You have a far better character than your brother! Oh, I *do* love you!" She embraced me in a flapperish manner, lifting one high-heeled foot impetuously behind her. I suffered her embrace.

"What did Palmer think of your capers with Alexander," I said over her shoulder. I wanted to draw some blood.

She drew back from me and her face, touched by a real pain, looked less histrionic. She hesitated, and then said, "I never told him."

"Why not?"

"Because Alexander meant too much to me. I couldn't bring myself to. It was *our* secret. And Alexander didn't want me to. I suppose I would have told him in the end, but I kept putting it off. And then he found out."

"Did he? How? When?"

"How, I don't know," said Antonia. She was turned a little away from me, her mouth agitated, twisting her hands. "I half thought for a while that you'd told him, but of course that was impossible, and anyway you wouldn't have. When, was that week-end when I went to Mother's. He must have found out then. Perhaps he found a letter or something. And he was too terribly hurt to go on."

"I see," I said, "I see. Poor Palmer. But it was all for the best in the end, wasn't it?"

"Oh yes!" Her face softened and the moist radiance returned. "Oh *yes*! I am so terribly relieved that I shall not lose Alexander after all. Somehow this test with Anderson has shown it to be so utterly the real thing. That's why I've got to have it in the open now and have my life properly in order. I'm very grateful to Anderson, really."

"You won't lose Alexander," I said, "and you weren't going to lose me anyway. So aren't you a lucky girl?"

"*Aren't* I a lucky girl!" she echoed gaily, standing back and taking my hands.

Someone knocked at the door of the drawing-room. We moved apart like surprised lovers and I called "Come in." It was Rosemary. She was neat, in a new little black hat, carrying an umbrella as thin as a pencil. "Oh, hello," she said primly. "I've just got back and I thought I'd call in for a moment." She advanced and put a bag down on the writing-table. "I've brought you some avocado pears," she said. "I saw them in Harrods, and I thought I'd better buy them while I could, they don't always have them, you know. They aren't *quite* ripe, but the man said they should be all right to eat in a day or two if you keep them in a warm room."

I turned to Rosemary. "Great news for you, sister," I said.

"My wife is going to marry my brother. Isn't that splendid?"

"Darling!" said Antonia.

"It only remains," I said, "for me to fall madly in love with Rosemary and then we can all go and live happily together at Rembers!" I began to laugh.

"Martin!" said Rosemary. She held out something to me. "This letter was on the mat. It must have been delivered by hand."

I took the letter and stopped laughing. It bore a Teutonic hand-writing which I had not seen before. But I knew where it came from.

I said, "You girls entertain each other while I go and get some champagne. I want to toast my wife's engagement." I left the room banging the door behind me.

I went into the dining-room and closed myself in and began to fumble with the letter. I could hardly get it open. When I had ripped the envelope across I recognised Palmer's writing on the inside, and I felt cold. I pulled out his letter which I had crumpled and torn. There was no other communication. His letter read:

Martin, we are flying to America on the eleventh, and we intend to stay there. I shall probably be practising on the west coast, and Honor will be with me at a university job. There is no reason why our paths should cross again; and you will understand me when I say that it will be better for all of us if they do not cross. On reflection I feel sure that in returning to Antonia and mending your marriage you have done the right thing. You have, after all, a talent for a gentler world. I mean of course the right thing for your happiness and for the ultimate needs of your soul. I will not insult you with hollow words about morality. Your freedom from *those* bonds was what first made me take you as a companion. On what has passed you will not require, or receive, any commentary from me or from any other. Let the dignity of silence cover like the sea an enterprise which partook of madness to an extent which I think even you never realised. I wish you and Antonia well and will never forget that I loved you once. Do not reply to this letter which constitutes, from both of us, a final and authoritative farewell.

P.

I thrust the letter into my pocket and stood quite still for a minute or two. Then I opened the sideboard and fumbled for glasses. I went to the cellar for champagne. I only realised after I had got the bottle that I had somehow found it in the dark. I returned to the drawing-room.

The two women broke off their talk abruptly and looked at me nervously to see what I would do or say. I put down the glasses and began to open the champagne in silence.

"Martin," said Rosemary, "you're not being angry, are you?" She spoke as to a sulky child.

"Of course I'm not being angry," I said. "Why ever should I be angry?"

I could see the two women exchanging glances. I realised then that Rosemary must have known all along about Antonia's relations with Alexander, since doubtless it was at her flat that they met. The champagne cork hit the ceiling.

"Dear heart," said Antonia, "don't fret, be still, be still. We all love you, we do." She came up to pluck again at my sleeve and I gave her a glass. I gave one to Rosemary.

I said, "I shall give you the Audubon prints as a wedding present." I drank and began to laugh again. They watched me with disapproving puzzlement.

❋ *Chapter Twenty-nine* ❋

MY child, I feel as if we two are like survivors of a wreck, who have suffered so much together that they can hardly, thereafter, bear to see each other. It is indeed for some such reason that I have avoided you, and I have felt that on your side the same reluctance must exist to renew a relation which has occasioned so much torment. What has happened to us, my darling Georgie, since that day before Christmas when we lay together in front of your fire like two children in a wood? How much innocence we must have *had* then, as we have *lost* so much since! You may say that it is about time for the robins to come and cover us with leaves. Indeed I can hardly guess at your sufferings, considering how little I understand my own: nor can I guess at your bitterness against me, nor do I know whether anything remains between us which can be mended. I write this almost without hope of salvage, and yet I have to write; for I feel as if we had been actors in a play, and there must be some exchange between us for the drama to be complete. This seems a cold way to greet you, but I must be honest and confess to you how stunned and how half alive I at this moment feel. I must see you, do you understand, even if it is only to find out certain things uncertainty about which torments me; and yet with the hope, when we look on each other again in the solitude which this carnage has created, of more than that. Will you at least try, my Georgie, my old friend? If I don't hear anything from you to the contrary I will ring you up next week. We did really love each other, Georgie, didn't we? Didn't we? In the name of that reality—

                                                  M.

I completed the letter and looked at my watch. It was nearly eight o'clock. I decided I had better move to the departure lounge so as to be well installed in some

unobtrusive position before they arrived. I wanted to see
the last of them.

It was the evening of the eleventh, and I had been at
London Airport all day. It had not been difficult to discover
when Honor and Palmer were going. They were on an evening flight. And having decided on this course of action some
time ago, when the day came I was unable to stay at home.
I had sat in various bars and eaten various sandwiches. At last
in a desperate effort to distract my mind I had started writing
to Georgie; I was not sure if the letter would do, I was not
sure if it said what I felt, I was not sure what I did feel. Only
in the most abstract possible way was I able to attend to
Georgie. I was really conscious of nothing except that soon I
should see Honor and it would be for the last time.

I had not replied to Palmer's letter. Of course I had
started on half a dozen replies, but in the end it seemed
slightly less painful to accept the blow in silence as, what it
clearly was, final. I read his letter again and again trying to
see just what insight into my condition lay behind it, what
possible discussion between the pair of them about how best
to finish me off. One might as well have guessed at a conversation of gods. But it was certain that now Palmer knew.

Antonia and Alexander had gone to Rome. I was profoundly relieved when they went. I had moved back with all
my belonging to Lowndes Square. The removal men seemed
to have got quite used to moving the things to and fro. I did
not know whether I would stay there, but I had had to get
out of Hereford Square, and had indeed got out on the very
evening of Antonia's second revelation. I had of course
proved a disappointment to Antonia. I did not know quite
how keenly she felt it and I did not at all enquire. I treated her
with a mocking friendliness which kept her puzzled, and met

her continual affection with continual irony. I could not forgive her and I wanted her out of my sight. I too had become harder and more absolute, and a constant and unmixed sense of my loss kept me so. The talent for a gentler world which Palmer had remarked upon was precisely what had now died in me. It had been at best no very saintly talent; merely a quieter mode of selfishness. Yet I did not once break out, and neither Antonia nor Alexander knew exactly what I was thinking. It gave me a little satisfaction to keep them in the dark.

That the gentle Alexander had so long ago put horns on my head I could not forgive either. This particular treachery had a quality so pure that it seemed almost independent of Antonia. It was as if Alexander had done something to the whole of my past, to years which stretched far back, beyond my marriage, into the nursery, into the womb. That he in whom, more than in any other, my mother lived again should so quietly and so relentlessly have defrauded me cast a shadow that was like a scar upon an innocence of the past which I had believed to be impregnable. It was not that I judged him morally. It was not that I believed he could not to some extent 'explain'; and indeed he wanted to. He suffered more than Antonia from my misleading levity. He wanted, I knew, to tell me of his doubts, his scruples, how he had been led imperceptibly from this position to that; in short how it had all happened. I even occasionally sensed in him a desire for confidences which would have excluded Antonia; and I wondered with a little sympathy and curiosity how much of his own will had gone into the making of the present situation. I had no doubt that the story would be a good one. After all, I knew from my own case how gentle, how far from cold-blooded, can seem to the deceiver the deliberate deception of a beloved person. But my reaction to Alexander was something much more automatic than a judgment, and much more relentless. It was odd that the pain of it felt so like loneliness. Through him so much of my past had been peopled, which was now a stricken solitude.

I settled myself in the departure lounge in the far corner and spread out a large newspaper in front of me. I thought it very unlikely that they would see me. In any case I was ready to take the risk. Outside the enormous window lighted aircraft passed by slowly on their way to the runway. In the warm lounge half-audible voices gave sing-song instructions through loudspeakers to tense people who seemed to understand them. It was like a waiting-room for the Last Judgment. I drank some whisky, keeping the paper well up, and round the edge of it I kept a watch on the head of the escalator. There was still nearly an hour to wait before their plane was due to leave, but I was too sick by now to do anything but watch. I felt as if I were about to be present at a murder, though as the victim or as the assassin was not quite clear.

Extreme love has a voracious appetite. It is also true that, by some metamorphosis brought about by its own violence, it can live on almost anything. I had lived through this interval of time upon the thought that I should see Honor again; and it was as if at that moment I would die. I saw nothing beyond and was concerned with nothing beyond. To see her actually going, to see her leaving my life forever through a certain door, was like an act of self-destruction which held its own dark satisfaction. Yet even this idea was, when the day came, obscured, and in my reeling consciousness there was nothing left but the notion of actually seeing her. This, it seemed, was miracle enough, was painful joy enough, even if it only lasted for a moment.

I looked at my watch and wondered if I dared to go to the bar again for some more whisky. I decided to stay where I was. I subsided behind the paper. One arm was beginning to ache. A kind of blank exhaustion came over me. The end-of-the-world atmosphere was beginning to be oppressive, and I could not determine whether a distant roaring noise was made by aeroplanes or by my own blood. The whole day had been a vigil. Perhaps I was now falling asleep. I found my head nodding as if it would fall off. In a few seconds I was adrift in a dream which I had had several times lately, a dream concerning a sword and a severed head; and then I saw Palmer and Honor naked in each other's arms, enlaced, closer and closer, until they seemed to have become one person.

I jerked my head upright and secured the paper which had wavered a little. I had nodded only for a moment. I confirmed this by looking at my watch; and I peered again round the edge of the paper. Then like demons rising I saw them come. They were gliding up from below side by side, first their two heads and then their shoulders as the escalator bore them up towards the level. I moved the paper back into position and blotted them out and closed my eyes. I wondered now if I could sustain the scene at all.

It took me several minutes to collect myself. When I ventured to look again they had gone over to the bar and now had their backs to me. Palmer was ordering drinks. He ordered three drinks. Then I saw that they had a girl with them, a smart pale girl with neatly cropped hair wearing a new Burberry overcoat. They sat down all three together still with their backs to me. Something in the way the girl handled her drink was suddenly familiar to me. She turned her head, stroking down her nose with a forefinger. It was Georgie.

I lowered the paper a little farther and became absorbed in staring at them. I could not quite believe that I was seeing them, so little did my eyes feed the voracity of my mind. Honor and Palmer showed me each a turned shoulder and part of a cheek. Georgie sat with her back to me directly, revealing her uptilted profile as she turned from time to time, now towards Palmer, now towards Honor. These two seemed to have their attention centred on their young companion. They leaned forward solicitously, making a trio of heads, and now one hand and now another reached out to pat their charge upon the shoulder. It might have been two parents with their child. Georgie herself seemed over-excited and dazed. I observed her plump face and her uncertain movements. Something was dulled in her. Perhaps it was that glow of independence which I had so much loved, which had made her, for my particular depraved purposes, possible. For all her protestations, I had never enslaved Georgie. She was, I conjectured, enslaved now. She kept fumbling in her bag, and at last in response to some laughing enquiry of Palmer's brought out her passport and a long coloured ticket which she laid on the table. It was only then that I realised that she was travelling too.

As they sat there talking and laughing, bathed in an almost unbearable glow of significance, they seemed like actors, and I half expected everyone else to fall silent so that their words might become suddenly audible. I had prevented myself so far from looking especially at Honor. I looked at her now. Her lips moved and smiled but her brow was gathered. Her face was strained and sallow and I recalled how she had looked when I first saw her in the fog at Liverpool Street station with the drops of water upon her hair. She looked to my eyes of farewell touchingly mortal, as she had looked then, her demon splendour quenched. Only now I could see, in her ugliness, her beauty. It was almost too much. She was hatless, and kept passing her hand through her hair to smooth it back behind her ears. The oily black strands kept falling forward again; and from time to time I saw her full profile as she spoke to Georgie or Palmer. Her curving Jewish mouth, with its natural red against the yellow tinge of the skin, was fixed in a stiff smile, while the hand moved and moved. She looked very tired.

"WILL PASSENGERS FOR FLIGHT D 167 TO NEW YORK PLEASE COME FORWARD TO THE EMBARKATION DOOR," said a superhuman voice. "HAVE YOUR TICKETS AND PASSPORTS READY PLEASE."

Everyone sprang up, and in the shock of the moment I rose too. I had not noticed the time. It was too cruel. There was a little flurry as Georgie dropped her handbag and Honor picked it up for her. Then the trio moved forward together. Palmer in his soft tweed travelling-coat looked clean and bland like a big bird. He looked, it came to me, a man in triumph. I could hear his youthful laughter; and as if picked out by a spotlight I could see his hand slip through under Honor's arm. The grip closed affectionately as he drew her along beside him.

I had thought, once, that I might have to run forward to her. But they were already as remote from me as persons seen in a film. I saw them take their places in the queue. All I could see now was Honor's dark head, and her shoulder pressed against Palmer's. I knew that I could not wait to see them go through the door. It was like witnessing an execution. I turned away from them and walked toward the escalator.

✳ *Chapter Thirty* ✳

I TURNED all the lights on. I was back at Lowndes Square and it was even now only a quarter to ten. The scene was as I had left it in the morning, my camp bed unmade, a few rugs askew on the floor, cigarettes and water and aspirins beside the bed, an overflowing ash tray and yesterday's evening paper. I stared at these relics. I went over to the window. Down below I could see the lights of the cars as they passed in endless procession and wheeled round into Knightsbridge. The street lamps lit up the stripped trunks of the trees. The pavements were damp and reflected the yellow light. It must have rained today. I could not remember.

I pulled the curtains, using the cord at the side in the way Rosemary had insisted I must. The problem of the pelmets was still unsolved. I turned on the electric fire. The central heating was not quite sufficient. I examined the Carlton House writing-table and noticed another scratch which had appeared during the latest move. I licked my finger and dabbed it. I went out into the kitchen and looked vaguely around for something to eat. There was a tin of Bath Oliver biscuits somewhere which Rosemary had brought. I took off my overcoat and felt in the pocket of my jacket for some matches. I found my letter to Georgie which I read again and then tore up. I found the matches and lit a cigarette. It appeared that I had run out of whisky again. But perhaps in any case I had had enough alcohol for one day. I took a milk bottle from the fridge and poured some milk into a glass. The Bath Olivers were on the shelf where one would expect them to be. Rosemary had evidently laid in a store of expensive-looking tins. That was kind of her. I put the biscuits and the milk on to a tray. I took off my jacket and returned to the sitting-room in my shirt sleeves. Perhaps it was rather hot after all. I sat down on one of the Chinese Chippendale chairs with the tray at my feet.

After a discussion with Antonia in which she had been tearful but vigorous and I had been flippant but listless, we had agreed to divide the set of Audubon prints between us. A terrible energy pervaded Antonia at this time and it tired me extremely to be with her. In a frank unassisted attempt to select the prints which I liked least she had taken what seemed to her the dullest ones which were the ones which in fact I liked best: the nightjars, the puffins and the great crested owls. The gold-winged woodpeckers, the Carolina parrots, and the scarlet tanagers now stood in a dusty row against the wall and I tried to wonder where I would put them. They seemed meaningless without the others. I looked about the room and saw that Rosemary had put the Meissen cockatoos one at each end of the writing table and I got up to put them together. They were better so. Then I decided I would like to drink some wine and I went back to the kitchen. An emergency rack had been fitted into one of the cupboards. The rest of my wine was still at Hereford Square. That was another problem. I pulled out a bottle at random. It weighed pleasantly in my hand like a familiar tool or a weapon. I saw that it was Château Lauriol de Barny. That seemed suitable for a libation of farewell. I opened the bottle and returned to the sitting-room where the lights were painfully bright. Rosemary had not yet had time to get me any lamps.

Of course I was still in a shocked state. I noticed my trembling hand, a tendency to shiver, a chattering of the teeth. I poured out some of the wine. Having been in the warm kitchen it was not in too bad heart. I recalled in my mind the red stain spreading on Palmer's carpet. But the wine itself was innocent, empty of memories. This was as it should be. It was after all the first moments of some entirely new era. I supposed I would survive, I would find some new interests and revive old ones. I would get back to Wallenstein and Gustavus Adolphus. I tried to think these thoughts but they remained intolerably abstract, while a pain in my body told me what was real. I pictured myself indeed as a survivor. There had been a drama, there had been some characters, but now everyone else was dead and only in me a memory remained of what had been; and perhaps mercifully that memory too would fade, as in some crazed old prisoner who cannot recall his sufferings and does not even know that he has been released. I attempted, as the pain increased, to cover it with a haze of consciousness, making myself, through some general chatter about my condition, anonymous and so not really suffering. But the sharp truth would not be denied and I became silent in the end and became myself in the knowledge of my unique loss. I covered my face and if I could have found tears I would have wept.

I sat thus for a long time surrendered to grief and to the physical pain which is the mark of a true emotion. Then suddenly I heard, as if inside my head, a strange sound. I looked up sharply. The second time the sound came I recognised the front door bell. It resounded oddly in the empty rooms. I half decided not to answer it. I could not see other human beings at present. Rosemary was at Rembers, and there was no one else in London whom I could endure. I sat stiffly waiting for the next ring. It came, repeated three times, clamorous and urgent. The sound was so alarming that it forced me to my feet and I went softly out into the hall. I could not stand the intervening silence and rather than let it ring again I opened the door. Honor Klein was standing in the semi-darkness outside.

We looked at each other in silence, I rigid with my hand on the door, she with her head drooping, looking at me from under her eyebrows. On the curving reddish lips the faint stiff smile was still there.

I turned back and let her follow me in towards the light. I went into the sitting-room and crossed over to the window so that the camp bed was between us. As I turned she closed the door behind her. We still looked at each other silently.

She said at last, and her smile deepened a little, narrowing her eyes, "You left the airport so quickly, I was not able to catch you up."

I was not sure whether I could speak, but when I tried the words seemed to come out all right. I said, "I thought you were going."

"As you see—"

"Did the other two go?"

"Yes."

"When are you going?" I said.

"I'm not going."

I sat down on the chair by the window and said, "I see," although I saw nothing. She sat down opposite to me on the other chair. I shook my head several times. I did not dare to feel anything but dismay and fear. This was perhaps some ultimate torture. I held bitterly on to my dignity.

"Well," I said, "what are you doing here?" I spoke very evenly.

I let myself really see her now, and as she gave back the intelligence of my look I could not but experience her consciousness of me as a kind of ecstasy.

"I came to see you," she said, her level narrow smile holding me like a beam of light.

"Why?"

"Because you wanted me to."

"I didn't *ask* you to," I said. "I thought I'd got rid of you," I kept my face stony and intent.

She pursed her lips, altering her smile into a look of amused acuteness. She still looked tired and some characters of recent suffering were written on her face. But the demon was awake again. She looked round the room a little, pushed her overcoat off on to the back of her chair, dug her hands deep into the pockets of her green suit, crossed her legs and returned to watching me.

I said, "Have some wine. Take my glass." I pointed to the tray. She held my look a moment and then poured out a little of the wine. As she did this I felt deep in my consciousness the little germ of some great joy, tiny still as the image of the whale far beneath the ship. But I kept my bitter front and rose, putting one foot on my chair. I leaned on my knee and looked down at her. It was easier so.

I said, "You're not going at all?"

"Not at all."

"How long is Palmer going for?"

"For good, as far as he knows."

"So you've left Palmer?" I said. "You've parted? It's finished?" I wanted things to be clear. I wanted to be told very simply that what I so unutterably desired was true.

She braced herself against the back of her chair. Her face was very still now. "Yes."

"I see," I said. "And Georgie?"

"Palmer and Georgie became very fond of each other,"

said Honor. "I don't know what they'll make of it. But Palmer wanted to get away, he was frantic to get away."

"Away from you?"

She gave me her still look. "Yes."

"And you yourself—?"

I had had her for just a moment, during those unavoidable questions, at my disposition. But now, her body relaxing, she simply smiled back at me, turning the wine a little in her glass before drinking it. I adored her insolence.

"Well, may I ask again why you're here," I said. I came to lean against the writing-table, still looking down at her. "If you've come merely to torment me or to amuse yourself you'd better go at once." An intoxicating sense possessed me that at last we were treating on equal terms. I kept my face stern, but there was so much light within, it must have showed a little.

"I haven't come *to* torment you," said Honor. She was serious, but there was an ironical lightness in her gaze.

"Of course, I understand it may happen inadvertently," I said. "I know you have the temperament of an assassin." I was taken with a trembling and to control it I had to move. I walked to the window and back and as I faced her once more I could not help smiling. She smiled too. Then, as if startled, we both became serious again.

"But why, Honor," I said, "why here, why me?"

She kept me in suspense. Then, "Have you ever read Herodotos?"

I was surprised. "Yes, a long time ago."

"Do you recall the story of Gyges and Candaules?"

I thought a moment and said, "Yes, I think so. Candaules was proud of the beauty of his wife and he wanted his friend Gyges to see her naked. He concealed Gyges in the bedroom

—but Candaules' wife realised that he was there. Then later, because he had seen her, she approached him and forced him to kill Candaules and become king himself."

"Well," said Honor. She was watching me closely.

After a moment or two I said, "I see." I added, "You once accused me of talking nonsense. If I'm only privileged because I saw you embracing your brother—"

She was quiet, smiling again. I tried not to smile back. I said, "You told me you were a severed head. Can one have human relations with a severed head?"

She was silent still, compelling me with her smile. I said, "As you yourself pointed out, I hardly know you!" I could not now stop myself from smiling.

She continued silent, leaning back, her smile now glowing with all its insolence.

I said, "We have lived together in a dream up to now. When we awake will we find each other still?"

I came round the bed and stood near to her. I worshipped her closeness. I said, "Well, we must hold hands tightly and hope that we can keep hold of each other through the dream and out into the waking world."

As she still would not speak I said, "Could we be happy?"

She said, "This has nothing to do with happiness, nothing whatever."

That was true. I took in the promise of her words. I said, "I wonder if I shall survive it."

She said, smiling splendidly, "You must take your chance!"

I gave her back the bright light of the smile, now softening at last out of irony. "So must you, my dear!"

THE END